SHATTERED TIME

TIME WARS LAST FOREVER SERIES BOOK 4

CRAIG ROBERTSON

ALSO BY CRAIG ROBERTSON:

* Podium Audio produced audiobooks are (or soon will be) available on Audible for all the below titles except the standalone ones.

BOOKS IN THE RYANVERSE:

THE FOREVER SERIES (2016)

THE FOREVER LIFE, Book 1

THE FOREVER ENEMY, Book 2

THE FOREVER FIGHT, Book 3

THE FOREVER QUEST, Book 4

THE FOREVER ALLIANCE, Book 5

THE FOREVER PEACE, Book 6

GALAXY ON FIRE SERIES (2017)

EMBERS, Book 1

FLAMES, Book 2

FIRESTORM, Book 3

FIRES OF HELL, Book 4

DRAGON FIRE, Book 5

ASHES, Book 6

RISE OF ANCIENT GODS SERIES (2018):

RETURN OF THE ANCIENT GODS, Book 1

RAGE OF THE ANCIENT GODS, Book 2

TORMENT OF THE ANCIENT GODS, Book 3

WRATH OF THE ANCIENT GODS, Book 4

FURY OF THE ANCIENT GODS, Book 5

FALL OF THE ANCIENT GODS, Book 6

TIME WARS LAST FOREVER SERIES (2019)

RYAN TIME, Book 1

LOST TIME, Book 2

FRAGMENTED TIME, Book 3

SHATTERED TIME, Book 4

<u>NON-RYANVERSE BOOKS</u>:

ROAD TRIPS IN SPACE SERIES (2019):

THE GALAXY ACCORDING TO GIDEON, Book 1

THE EARTH ACCORDING TO GIDEON, Book 2

THE AFTERLIFE ACCORDING TO GIDEON, Book 3 (DUE EARLY 2021)

<u>OLDER, STANDALONE WORKS</u>:

THE CORPORATE VIRUS (2016)

TIME DIVING (2013)

THE INNERgLOW EFFECT (2010)

WRITE NOW! THE PRISONER OF NaNoWRiMo (2009)

ANON TIME **(2009)**

SHATTERED TIME
TIME WARS LAST FOREVER SERIES, BOOK 4

by Craig Robertson

Jon has just one character flaw. He thinks he can fix anything. It's Time he learned better ...

Imagine-It Publishing
El Dorado Hills, CA

ISBN: 978-1-7341363-7-1 (E-Book)
978-1-7341363-8-8 (Paperback)
979-8-7754378-5-5 (Hardcover)

Cover design by Alexandre
http://www.designbookcover.pt/en/

Editors: Michael R. Blanche
Neil Farr
Charles Pitts
Amy Schubert

Formatting services by Drew Avera
drewavera@gmail.com

First Edition 2020

This is the first book I began and completed during the COVID-19 Pandemic. It is dedicated to all those who suffered under the cruel curse that is CV-19. To those who died. To those who survived. To those who served others.

God bless you one and all.

PRELUDE

Nothing. Nothingness. That is all that is. Your mind's eye moves through nothingness. It is so complete, so expansive, so horrifyingly absolute that you are certain it is larger than infinite. It isn't black as pitch or silent as the grave. It is nothing. You feel panic swell from deep down, primal and raw. You bargain, plead, and beg pity from the nothingness. You want to scream. Oh yes, you must scream. But you cannot bargain, plead, beg, or even scream, because you are now one with the massive nothingness.

Then, in the distance, a pale orange-yellow light births itself into your nothingness. Or is it that your mind has completely lost its footing in reality? Perhaps you are insane. Are you hallucinating the ray of hope in the hopeless nothingness?

No. You are moving toward the light, toward cool oxygen, toward potential salvation. Soon, you are close enough to the light that it begins to take form. There you see before you a parched, beaten patch of desert. It is so barren, not even sand or pebbles break the sternness of the hardpan.

You alight on the tiny wasteland, that minute blessing juxtaposed to the indifferent nothingness that suffocates. It is then that you notice ... there ... in the center of the incomprehensibly impoverished vision you take in—something. It's a box. It's a small box. If it were a box on any shelf in any garage or basement, it wouldn't even be noticed, it is such an inconsequential box. Gunmetal gray, a foot square, if that. It appears to be made of stone, or a coarse, weathered wood. Perhaps it's made of nothingness.

You approach the box cautiously. Any object sitting comfortably in this prohibitive home must be questioned. Surely it is malevolent, or, at the very least, evil. You reach out to touch the box, perchance to open the box. But you come up short. Your hand seems to know instinctively to withdraw from the lone inhabitant of this lowest level of hell. In no time, you come to realize that you much prefer the nothingness to being in the presence of this small inert box. You retrace your steps, and you rejoin nothingness.

Your last sane thought is a sense of relief. Whatever this empty infinite tomb holds in store for you, it's mother's milk compared to that box.

And the box does not care, either that you arrived, that you did or did not touch it, nor that you cast yourself into an uncertain doom. It noticed you with such a disconnect that you weren't even really there. The box ... the box has learned not to care. Ever.

And what's inside the box cares less. In fact, it cares so little that the concept of caring, or not caring, or loving, or hating do not exist for the contents of that passive box. And know, please, that the disinterested box and its unfeeling contents have been there forever. And when the last universe dies its heat death, after its last black hole has evaporated and its last proton has decayed, the box and its contents will still be there, resolute in their infinite apathy.

The box, it should be clarified, is fully inert. It's a box. Nothing more, nothing less.

Inside the box? Well, what's in there is the very opposite of inert.

Inside the box is a lifeless force that will never die. It is an all-encompassing process that never moves or changes, yet it's always in flux—eternal restless churning. And if you were thirsty and asked the contents of that box for a thimble full of water, it would neither withhold nor give you that drink. It is not possible for it to respond in any way, in any manner, to anything. The thing in the box is, you see, the Soul of Time.

And why, you ask as you meld seamlessly into the nothingness, is the Soul of Time forever sequestered in a box? The reason is obvious. If time had a soul, how could it, every second of every minute of every eternity, do what it does and live with that knowledge of what it has allowed?

CHAPTER ONE

"*Where* is my damn axe?" I swung my head around to look in Plesmus's direction. Can't say I looked at her because I was never sure which end was which with her. Come to think of it, I couldn't tell by outward signs *she* was even a *she*. Hmm. In any case, she'd at least temporarily dislodged herself from my boot and oozed a few meters away from where I stood irritated.

After a few seconds she answered, "Surely you're not asking me?"

We were lounging near the opening to the cave on PlesWorld. At the bottom of the cave was the phase portal that had connected this planet to the realm of the Praxequat. You remember them, the time lords who were the latest members of the Not-A-Fan-Of-Jon-Ryan Club, LLP? It'd been a couple hours since I sent my no-time-ogram out widely, requesting rescue. I had no idea if it'd be received or how long help would take to come.

My, but she sounded prissy. "Is there a third pers ... er, entity here whom I might otherwise be addressing?"

"I'm leaving now. I will return when you are sane. In other words, this is goodbye forever."

"Fine. But first I need my damn axe."

"As opposed to your sacred axe?"

"Hang on," I replied absently, "let me think about that a sec." And I did. "No, I think the opposite of a *damned* axe would be a *blessed* axe, not a sacred one."

"Seriously? It's your native language."

"What?" I protested in a whine.

"I'm a newcomer to English. Why would you debate the intricacies of meaning with me? Sacred, blessed, it's all the same to me. Moreover, it is impossible that any difference between the words could matter."

Hmm. "Are you certain they can't, or are you just yanking my chain because you're the opposite of nice?"

"Noooo," she howled. "Leave your chain right where it is. The sad duty of yanking your chain falls to Sapale alone. Plus, you're not my type. I prefer my males with greater flexibility, if you know what I mean." She generated a squishy sound. Grossness.

"TMI, you semi-solid puddle of pee."

"I'm leaving."

"Fine, but where the heck's my desecrated axe?"

"Ah, the monkey-on-two-legs gets it right. Desecrated *is* the opposite of blessed."

"Thanks," I responded with some humility. "I—"

"Have a thesaurus in your memory banks. Yes. I know."

"Just tell me where the cutting tool in question is, and I shall celebrate your departure."

"Jon, what passes for your brains in your head has maggots. You did not bring an axe. Therefore, it is impossible to have lost one. If you actually own an axe, I would venture a guess it is on *Blessing*. Why it is you would *need* an axe is a barrier-defying-level question, added to the fact that, if you actually possessed one, it was never here."

"There," I boomed, "was that so hard an answer? All you had to say was you didn't know where my damn axe was and we would have been spared all this pain."

"You're delusional. There never was an axe for you to have misplaced it. And what would you need an axe for if you'd lost it and couldn't do what you wanted to because of the damn axe was missing?"

"You seem tense."

"I *always* seem tense when speaking to the clinically deranged."

"I think maybe you should switch to decaf for the duration of our visit here."

"I have never ingested caffeine. What you witness is how a normally functioning brain reacts to Ryanisms."

"I need my axe because I want to build a fire."

"That makes no sense, none whatsoever."

"I want to build a fire because I'm cold. That makes perfect sense."

She kind of vibrated. Excellent. "You are an android. You can survive the cold of open, deep space. It is *impossible* that you feel cold. And do you see any trees or similar material to hatchet into firewood?"

I could tell I was getting to her. Nice. Hey, I was bored. Who knew how long it'd be before we were rescued?

"No. I said *axe*. If I wanted to *hatchet* the wood I'd have asked you where my damn *hatchet* was." I yawned demonstrably. "Plus, there're lots of reasons to have a fire other than your just being cold."

"Name one."

"Plus, I don't own a hatchet." I held up a flattened palm and looked at it. "I do however own an axe."

"There's no *wood*," she shouted.

"I know *that*. I'd have to go looking for wood to find some, now wouldn't I?"

"We are on the edge of a mountain. We traveled far to get here. Along the journey here, there was no wood anywhere. There were no actual signs of life, let alone redwoods reaching to the clouds. Under what perversion of logic do you think you could prance away and find wood that was never in evidence?"

"Maybe we weren't looking hard enough, or in the right—"

"Jon, there is—"

Okay. I was officially bored. I tuned her out, literally. I dialed my audio input to zero and flipped my head-to-head capabilities off, in case she noticed my inattention and tried to get around my defenses. Couldn't have that. In all matters, I needed to win. You might call that a character flaw, but I call it a useful blessing.

There was only so much fun to be extracted from annoying Plesmus. After a certain point—which we'd just passed—it was more an argument than a romp on someone else's last nerve. Plus, I needed to devote some time to wondering just how long we'd be marooned on PlesWorld. Worry and fretting didn't speed any process along, but it was something to do when bored, and boredom had me by the throat.

It was funny. My fate depended on a bunch of absolute rookies. Not one of the crew had any real space experience. I mean, I did believe they would receive my message across space and time and come to my aid, but there'd be barriers. How would they react? Would they win? Or would they discover that real life doesn't work the same way as science fiction writer's dreams, and end up the wrong side of a black hole's event horizon?

Then again, there was nothing I could do to help them along. They would arrive when they arrived. There was nothing for me to do, period. I certainly would resume my pestering of Plesmus. I just needed a little break from that outlet. Vexing others was an art form. It had to be applied just so, or you insulted the craft. That was not happening on my watch.

Man, how I wished I had a six pack or two.

CHAPTER TWO

"What's the status of the time maker's ship?" Tank asked again.

"No change. She's still warping the fabric of space/time as much as she can. Same vector. No obvious damage to her yet," replied Aramthella.

Tank and Sachiko were on the bridge, tensely following the inexplicably hazardous flight of the time maker's ship. Aramthella was moving along the same vector as the other vessel, but at a safe speed. The gap between the ships was widening. But they'd catch up when the time maker's ship ran out of energy or fell apart due to the strain.

"Can you project a possible destination?" Tank pressed. "If we knew where they were headed, we could maybe call on them after we retrieve Jon and Plesmus."

"I can predict no rational destination. They are moving along one straight line. Extrapolating it as far as is practicable suggests no clear target. The nearest celestial body along their course is a dwarf galaxy eight thousand parsecs away. It would take them months of flight time in totally exposed space to get there."

"They'll probably slow and change course once whatever fire is in their pants is fully extinguished," Tank mused.

"I agree," Sachiko stated flatly.

"But, if the time maker is dumb enough to remain on its present course, we can thank it just after we no-time its ugly butt," he concluded.

"Captain," Aramthella asked formally, "what are your orders?"

Tank looked to Sachiko.

"Take us to the time Jon is presently occupying. We certainly have to —"

"Certainly have to what, kiddo?" wondered Tank after she had trailed off.

"Wait," she breathed.

"Already doing that. Come on, Shaky. Give."

"Aramthella, from our present position, how long, exactly, will it take us to *safely* reach Jon?"

"Thirty-one days, ten hours, five minutes—"

"Enough," she commanded. "Take us to his time zone *minus* thirty-two days."

"Why—?" the ship began.

"Shaky, I should kiss you," exclaimed Tank. "You are *brilliant*."

"Praise accepted. Kiss ... can I get a raincheck on that?"

"Whatever. Aramthella, are we then yet?"

"No. There. Now we are. We are at the same location we were, aside from the galactic rotation that has occurred over the time period we were gone. We are thirty-two days before the distress call from Jon Ryan began."

"Alrighty, then. Set a course for his location, maximum safe speed."

"Yes, Captain. And might I add you are coming to understand the use of layered time travel," expressed Aramthella.

"Yes, I am," she beamed. "We should surprise the socks off Jon when we arrive basically when he stopped sending his distress call."

"I'd have said an 'S' word, but not socks," teased Tank. "But I'm looking forward to finding out which 'S' thing that separates from his person when we show up so fast."

The pair was quiet for a few moments.

"What do you think Jon's gotten himself into this time?" Sachiko wondered aloud.

"With him?" Tank harrumphed. "Could be anything. It's probably several things combined."

She chuckled softly.

"So, Captain, we have a month on our hands and not much to do. Any plans?"

She bit at her lower lip. "Sleep? Not be on edge every second? Not fear death and the failing of all humankind for a little while?"

"Laudable goals, I'm sure. I could use a little R&R myself."

Sachiko squirmed ever-so-cutely in her captain's chair. "R&R's good. Nice. Any specific plans or people, I mean ... with any person's... you know." She grinned stupidly. "Any plans yet?"

"There you go, acting all weird again. It's like the other day when I mentioned—" Tank rolled his eyes demonstrably. "You think I'm having an affair with Reva, don't you?"

Sachiko blushed beet red. Then she set a questioning *moi* palm on her chest. "Tank, why would I think that?"

He slapped one palm with the other, hard. "I *knew* it. You think it's a done deal." Concern drew over his face. "You aren't spreading that rumor around, are you?"

"Robert Sherman," she protested vigorously, "have you ever known me to spread gossipy rumors?"

He drew his expression into a fully suspicious configuration. "You are correct. I have never *known* you to be a gossip monger."

"Tank, we've worked together for, what, ten years?"

"We've worked together. Sure. But we haven't *cohabited*, now have we?"

She gave him a scornful glare. "Not to the best of my recollection."

"Shaky, you know I'm a married man. Please don't make it *impossible* with Daisy when this is all said and done."

Sachiko's shoulder eased into a more relaxed posture. She studied her mentor and her best friend.

"I was only wondering because you two are a logical pairing. Age, rank, and all that."

He raised a finger and wagged his ring. "Married."

"Tank, you're not married. I hate to rub salt in a wound. My parents are gone too. But, Tank, they're gone. I have no family. *You* are not married."

"I know what you're saying, kiddo, and I thank you for your concern. But, well, it's different with me ... me and Daisy."

She leaned forward and set a hand on his shoulder. She imagined she could feel him beginning to tremble.

"I know, Tank. I know. Forget I said anything. Your life is your life. What's in your head deserves to be there." She tugged at his shoulder. "Give me a hug."

He begrudgingly complied. "If the Council on Academic Personnel Committee ever hears about this, they'll crucify me."

"Thank goodness CAPC no longer exists either."

"Amen to that," he breathed.

That was precisely the moment Reva stepped onto the bridge. She stiffened.

Sachiko was looking straight at her as she entered. She waved her over. "Group hug. We all need it."

Reva took one step backward, dropped her head, but then stepped over. Within seconds the three were locked in an embrace and two of them were bawling like babies.

Sachiko seriously considered pretending to weep, but decided wisely that it would be lame to act so ingenuously. These were her friends, her good friends. Everyone had to be who they were. And it was all good.

A minute later, they peeled themselves apart from one another.

"That was ... different," Tank stated softly. He wiped snot off his nose with the back of his shirt sleeve. Come on. He was a guy.

"I say it felt good," declared Reva. "I wish we were encouraged to display our emotions, let them out more often."

"No, I'm good," Tank said quickly.

"No, you're impossible," corrected the captain. She shoved Tank's nearest shoulder. "You two knuckleheads get out of here. I have a ship to run and a planet to rescue. You're getting in my way."

Tank looked at Sachiko, then to Reva. "She's a real love 'em and leave 'em gal, isn't she? Hug's over and we're run off like vermin."

"Youth is wasted on the young," Reva returned as she hooked her arm over Tank's elbow.

They pivoted and walked off the bridge together, after angling their chins up in the captain's direction.

"Knuckleheads," Sachiko whispered to herself. She plopped back into her chair. "Aramthella," she snapped, "status report."

"From before your physical orgy or since then?"

"It was a group hug, not something erotic," she replied firmly.

"Then why did Professor Sherman develop an erection?"

Sachiko was so glad her mouth was empty. She spit out explosively. "Whoa, Aramthella. TMI to the infinity power. If ... next time ... I never want to know about when anyone, especially Tank, becomes sexually aroused. Is that clear?"

"Of course. Is that directive from this erection forward, or does it include the one he still has? He still does, you know. In fact, the intracavernosal pressure in his appendage has increased—"

"Enough. Enough. My order applies to every erection he has, had, or might in the future have. If you *force* me to use the word erection in the context of Tank again, place yourself on report."

"Got it." She was silent for a few seconds. "What does that actually mean, putting an autonomously functioning mechanical intelligence unit on report?"

"I have no idea. But it's a standing order and I expect it to be obeyed to the letter."

"Whatever."

After a tense pause, Aramthella asked absently, "I'm sorry, Captain, I seem to have experienced a power surge in my memory couplings. What were we talking about?"

"You bought it. Add your name to the report list and please see the duty officer."

"Aren't *you* the duty officer, sir?"

"Yes, I seem to be, don't I?" She smoothed over her uniform. "Is your name presently on that disciplinary list?"

"Yes, sir."

"Keep it that way."

"Aye, aye, Captain."

She stood. "I'm going to get a cup of tea and *two* cookies."

"Understood."

"No cookies for you."

"I would expect no less, my commander. After all, I'm on report."

Sachiko left the bridge without further interaction.

CHAPTER THREE

Sapale stumbled forward after the oversized turtle guard shoved her shoulder. She nearly fell. She did go completely ballistic.

"You stupid pile of rotting penis parts," she excoriated it. Then she drew back her leg and kicked it with all her considerable might right between the guard's tree-trunk legs. Her foot impacted something tubular, but whatever it was had the hardness of diamonds.

One-two-three.

She screamed out in pain. "Damn you, I think you dented my *foot*. You'll pay for that, chumpzilla."

Sapale had every intention of trying again to punt its groin into next week, but she couldn't. She was hopping around like a blind woman in a one-legged race. The fact that she'd been captured so quickly upon returning to the abode of the time lords, combined with her anger at the guard's handling of her person, left her in a truly foul mood.

Just as she was attempting to tentatively bear weight on that foot, a voice from all around her snarled, "Do not hurt the beatiotrope. They're quite rare and even harder to train than they are to replace."

"Hey, voice in the clouds, bite me. Bite me *right* here." She gestured to a part of her body that most would judge unladylike. Her head spun trying to locate the source of the scolding. Then it occurred to her: if whoever was rationing out the criticism worried that she might hurt the monolithic waste-of-space, maybe that was because she actually *could*.

She steadied herself as best she could on her bad foot, and drove the good foot right back into the guard's groin. She even added a little hop to increase the force she delivered.

One-two-three.

She moaned loudly and began dancing around on her heels. They were the only sections of her feet not in searing pain.

"I told you to desist, did I not?" whined the omnipresent yet phenomenally annoying voice.

"**ck you and *** horse you rode ** on with your skinny finger ** its ***," she howled. Some words were muffled due to her agony. But all the pain in the universe did not lessen her desire to express clearly how displeased she was.

"If my interest in examining you comes to exceed my annoyance with you, subsentient, I will have no choice but to terminate you."

She was still skidding around on her heels. The pain had lessened only slightly.

"Oh no, slick. You have *another* option."

"I see this as a simple allow-to-live versus exterminate matter—"

"You can *screw* the horse you rode in on, assuming of course you first pulled you finger out of its butt."

"Is it my translation's poor quality or are you in fact *the* most vulgar creature to ever draw breath?"

"I dare you to say that to my face, booger-sucker."

"Am I *not* speaking to your face? It is attached to your body in your species, is it not?"

"Did your mama raise any kids who weren't stupid?"

"I ... I don't ... didn't have a mother. Why do you assume I did?"

"Figures. Look, snot throat, if I didn't ask it like that it wouldn't be funny. I'm a funny gal."

At least Sapale was standing still on both feet at that point. She counted that as both a victory and as a sign that she needed to wallop the turtle in the nuts again. She was nothing if not determined.

"I comprehend the word 'funny,' but I don't have humor in my constitution. That said, I find it incredibly hard to imagine what you said would qualify as *funny* in any species' definition of the concept."

She grinned. "Dare you to say that to my face."

"Have we not covered this issue?"

Amazingly throughout the acrimonious exchange between Sapale and the voice-with-no-body the guards were still and mute. They were neither asked to not cared to participate.

"Chicken?"

"Where?"

"I'm talking to it, jerk-o-matic. Look in the nearest mirror. You're a big fat chicken bawk bawk."

"I'm revisiting now the termination option. You are insufferable."

Sapale smiled ear-to-ear. "Dare you to say that to my *face.*"

There was silence.

"Bawk, bawk, *bawkkaw*," she amended.

She felt a presence behind her. She whirled. There stood a doughy, pasty male humanoid with the smuggest look she'd ever had the displeasure of witnessing on a face.

"You look just wrong," she said softly, mostly to herself. "You need a lot more sun and a lot fewer cream puffs, cream puff."

"Your opinion of my appearance means less to me than you can possibly imagine."

"Seriously?"

"Of course I'm serious. Why would I *not* be with an inferior such as you? Your petty ideations are of no consequences."

Her impervious smile defied all odds and grew larger. "So there's nothing I can say about you or your slovenly appearance that could possibly upset you?"

He chuckled sarcastically. "As if."

She had to giggle, if only slightly. "You are nothing better than a snotty-faced heap of festering parrot droppings. Your pathetic type makes me want to vomit on your shoes, or maybe your face. No. Both your shoes *and* your face. I'll have to save up my vomit, but it'll be worth the bother because you're *such* an ass-dancer. If you took lessons and learned to be a better person you might improve up to being just a flat-nosed mouth-breathing pervert. In fact, if you stood on your tippy toes and—"

"Enough!"

"No way, ya pussy. I'm just getting warmed up."

"Speak again and I shall incinerate you on the spot."

She blinked three times. "Which spot? This one?" She pointed down. "Then I'll stand here." She slid a foot to her right.

"You were warned. Now you will suffer—"

"Greatly by having to hear your grating ninny voice? Tell me something I don't know, schmo."

He reached back his hand in a manner that did not bode well for Sapale's longevity. Maybe, perhaps, she reflected, she'd piled it on a bit too thickly. Oh well. It sure was fun.

Just as the fellow's arm began to fly in her direction, it inexplicably froze, mid-flight.

"Radiant Resplendence," a distinctly female voice chided, "remember you're not supposed to play too rough with your toys and dalliances."

"Release my arm immediately," he whined pathetically.

"Only when I hear you affirm you'll not no-time or incinerate your pet."

"Beauty Itself, we've been over this one thousand million times. You are not the boss of me. I can do whatever I want."

Sapale leaned right into his face. "Oh yeah? Then move your arm."

He pitched his frame forward and cried out like a wounded buffoon. "Aaaahh."

But his arm remained in stasis.

A female form materialized beside Sapale. "I think it's best if you and I leave Radiant Resplendence alone to calm a bit."

"His name's Radiant Resplendence? I was razzing him when I called him a pussy, but who knew he really was one?"

In a flash Sapale sat on a simple wooden chair alongside her benefactor, who was draped over a plush fainting couch.

"Not to worry. That oaf can't follow us here."

"I wasn't worried enough to be able to worry less."

"You are the scamp, aren't you?" She smiled knowingly. "I am Beauty Itself." She rested a palm on her chest. "Any detractor of Radiant Resplendence will always find a welcome spot in my presence."

"He is quite the douche."

Beauty Itself vibrated her head in disgusted concern. "I understand the word's meaning, though the very concept is as revolting as it is incomprehensible."

"It's a girl thing."

"*I'm* a girl," Beauty Itself protested.

"Well then, I guess you're not that kind of girl. No biggy."

"Wait a moment. What kind of girl would ... Upon reflection, I will change the subject."

Sapale fired a finger-pistol at her. "Capital idea." She looked around the ornate room. "Maybe we could talk about you giving me back my brood-mate and just how sad you're gonna be after we're gone?"

"There's a lot to unpack in your remark. By the way, does your species encourage the naming of individuals?"

"Why, yes they do." Sapale extended her hand. "I'm Sapale."

"A joy to learn. Are you offering me your appendage as a gift, a token for my appeasement?"

She quickly pulled her hand back in. "No. It's a greeting."

"Ah, among your people?"

Sapale rocked her head side-to-side. "Not exactly."

"Then why do you do it?"

She grimaced. "I've been badly influenced by a true scoundrel over an extended period of time. It's not my fault."

"That is more information than I actually wished to know."

"You're welcome."

"I didn't thank you."

"You might yet. You never know."

Beauty Itself physically shook off that incongruity like it was mud. "You're almost as bad as that other recent captive." She angled her head and furrowed her brow. "No. I take that back. What am I saying? It is impossible to be as cripplingly irritating as that fellow."

"I see you met Jon up close and personal."

"You know him? You *know* the foul man?"

"Yes I do. Married him."

Beauty Itself scowled at her. "I wouldn't go around bragging about that if I were you."

"Ah, he grows on you. Granted it's like a red rash that oozes, but he's okay. Just don't tell him I said as much."

"I praise The Creator of All that I will never have the ill-pleasure of doing so." Beauty Itself shivered.

Sapale's seemingly playful facade melted instantly. She replaced it with her very convincing I'm-gonna-rip-your-throat-out look. Scary. "You killed him?"

"Ha," squeaked from Beauty's mouth. "We should have been so lucky. No, he esc— he's gone."

"Gone?" Sapale questioned with the darkness of pitch apparent in her voice.

"Thank The—"

"Gone where?" Sapale cut her off, like with a blunt axe.

"I don't like your tone, Sapale," Beauty bristled. "I will remind you but once that you are a captive inferior species still alive only because it pleases one or more of us. You are a possession. Possessions do not demand, and possessions do not have their questions answered."

"You like that word—possession—way too much. I define it differently. Possession is the manner in which you will suffer my wrath if I don't get some satisfactory answers and get them now, bitchlette."

Ah ... Captain ... er, hi. This is Al, the long time artificial intelligence from her ship said into her head. Al had a much different relationship with Sapale compared to Jon. Jon he taunted and vexed. Sapale he was intimidated by and acted accordingly. *Is this a bad time? I can ring you up later if ...*

Yes this is a horrible time and what?

Ah, just a point of view the missus and I were sharing. As you know, we all—

Out with it, toe fungus. I'm life-and-deathing here.

It is said that one draws more flies with honey rather than—

You think I'm coming on too strong? Is that it?

Well, that's a subjective call to be certain. But a more deferential approach might be prudent, what with Beauty Itself being vastly superior to any of us in every manner imaginable.

Thanks. Point One. Eat shit and die. Point two, she ain't got one thing that I do.

That being? Al queried carefully.

I'm a ten on the badass scale. She's about to learn that real personally.

Well, thanks. Keep us posted. And good luck with that, okay?

I will refer you back to Point One again. Out.

"My but that was odd," remarked Beauty Itself.

"My but what was odd, sister?"

Beauty giggled playfully. "Oh, you inferior, barely sentient races. You're so easily confused. Me, your sister? Now *that* is funny."

"As soon as you get over yourself, cupcake, could you answer my question?"

"Yes. It was so odd that you just had a conversation inside your head. Does your species have conjoined consciousnesses in their tiny little brains?"

"You know, I like you. Therefore, I will not slap that smug look off that not-beauty-itself face of yours. And how could you know what I'm thinking? Hmm?"

Beauty Itself looked toward the floor and furrowed her brow. "How indeed? I imagine I could disregard my dignity and lower myself to enter another's mind, but ... I don't recall doing that before." She now had a most suspicious look on her face. "How is it indeed?" There was an underpinning of accusation in her question.

"Maybe you imagined it. You know, a hallucination." Sapale found it really hard not to grin. She wanted to seem sincere. "You're under a lot of pressure. That kind of crap happens you know."

The expression Beauty Itself developed was menacing. "It must have been a transmission." She paced back and forth slowly. "You must have been in communication with your fellow intruders." She clapped her hands loudly.

Two turtle guards popped through the door like they were shot from a cannon.

"Yes, Master," one said sheepishly.

"This vile thing has co-conspirators with her. I assume they are on her transportation machine. Find it at once. Bring the others before me." She glared at them. "Why are you still here?"

They backed out the door comically in a rush.

"I have tired completely of you," Beauty Itself stated flatly. She clapped again.

Two different guards bounded into the room.

"Take this creature to Detention. Try not to maim or kill it."

And with those words, Beauty Itself disappeared.

"What a freaking show-off," Sapale scorned under her breath. Then she turned to address the guards. "Either of you the ones I bashed in the balls earlier today?"

They exchanged confused glances then looked back to her with blank expressions.

"Okay, unexplored territory it'll be, then." She wiggled a foot to warm it up and produced an enormous grin.

CHAPTER FOUR

Sachiko walked quietly onto the bridge. She was more tired than usual. Sleep had been a struggle the previous night. Too many thoughts that would not relent.

"Captain's on the bridge," boomed Tank.

Sachiko nearly squirted out of her skin, banana and peel style.

"Tank, you startled me. Since when do we playact like we're in the Navy?"

"Since the captain's on the bridge?" he responded quizzically.

She tugged at the bottom of her blouse and straightened. "Let's start over. Good morning, Tank. How are you today?"

"Good morning, captain-who-is-on-the-bridge," he said with a Cheshire-cat grin. "I, it turns out, am fine. You?"

"Inching toward regretting getting out of bed, truth be told."

He squinted. "You do look a bit worn out, don't ya? Hey, my shift went by uneventfully and I'm not sleepy. I'll cover the first couple hours of yours if you'd like to try a do-over on rack time."

She flitted one eye shut and widened the other. "Rack time? Tank, really. You know I'm not as taken by military slang as you are. Can we just talk human, not GI Joe?"

"To each his or her own. *That's* my credo, Shaky. You want to speak Librarian, go for it. I'm sticking with John Wayne meets John Wayne."

She rolled her eyes. "You stand relieved. I can pull my watch. You go," she wagged her head side-to-side and cut deep air-quotes, "pull some rack time."

"One 'gets' or 'grabs' rack time, Cappy. One does not 'pull' it."

"I stand unconcerned."

"And on that sour note I'm going to meet my date."

Sachiko nearly gasped out loud. "You have a date? Wait, let me rephrase that. You have a date and it's at zero-seven-hundred?"

"Well, maybe it's not a date. See ya later." He headed toward the door.

"So who is this date that's maybe not a date with?"

He looked at her sideways and smirked. "As if you didn't know."

She was blindsided by that and it showed. "Why would *I* know and who the *hell* is it?"

"Reva," he said cautiously. "Look, she asked if I'd join her for breakfast. She knew my watch was ending just as hers was beginning. So we're sharing chow. Is that okay with you, sir?" His voice was tainted with sarcasm at the end.

"You and she are adults. Do whatever floats your boats."

"Thank you, sir," he half-saluted. Then he resumed his course for the door.

"Wait," she said absently. "How did she know your shift ended? When you two left, Tom hadn't called off sick because he threw out his back for you to have to cover his shift."

"Watch, Shaky. This is a military vessel after all." He looked at her, searching for something in her eyes a few heartbeats. "I told her when Tom woke us up to ask me to cover him."

"He woke ... ooooh," she said. Her face went through all imaginable shades of crimson.

"Yes, my handheld went off on Alert Mode. Woke us *both* up."

"Because you were in the same room, or rooms close enough that the darn—"

"Because I spent the night at her place, Sachiko, if that's okay with you? Sorry I didn't know I had to ask permission."

"Tank, no. I'm sorry. I just ... you just caught me a little off guard. That's ... well, your business is your business."

"I prefer to have your blessing than your impartiality." It probably surprised him more than her that those exact words had come out of his mouth.

Sachiko rushed to him and tangled him up in a hug. "Tank, you have all the blessing I can give you as my best friend ever."

He hugged her back.

Of course, because fate is so cantankerous, that was the moment Reva poked her head through the door. She bounced her gaze back and forth between them a few times. "Over me that quickly, Tank? It would seem I've lost some serious skills on account of their disuse."

Sachiko pulled back and swiped away a tear. "Stop it, silly. We were just celebrating."

"Celebrating, huh? Is it Arbor Day or something?"

"No," Tank declared as he placed a hand on Reva's hip and pulled her in. "We were cele*brating* my not being celi*bate*."

She smiled ear-to-ear. "I have an alternative plan as to how to celebrate that." She bopped the tip of his nose with her index finger.

"Does that form of celebration commence after a hearty breakfast?" he queried.

She visibly pouted. "If the one having that hearty breakfast wants to do that kind of celebrating all by himself it does."

"It could be *followed* by a hearty breakfast," exited Sachiko's lips before she had a chance to filter it.

Tank spiked a thumbs-up at her and spoke to Reva. "See, that's why she's captain and we're her underlings. She sees the *big* picture."

"I can't actually believe I said that," mumbled Sachiko.

"Did the captain just say something, Tankster?" Reva asked him at pointblank range.

"I don't think so. I was thinking of something else."

"*Go*," shouted Sachiko. "Please go *now*. In fact, that's a direct order."

"I think we're grossing her out," Reva remarked conspiratorially to Tank.

"It's not all that hard. Trust me on that." He turned and winked at Sachiko.

"No, it is not. And you both flew past that threshold." She pointed away. "Out, before I have you keelhauled."

"We'd better leave," Tank observed.

"I *want* to leave," Reva replied with a coy smirk. She rose to her tiptoes to push up against Tank.

"I think I'm going to be ill." Yeah, that was the captain speaking. The one on the bridge. The one in charge.

CHAPTER FIVE

"Tip, it's a No-One-But-Tip idea. No. Stop." Desdemona had assumed what she now called her Tip-Frustration-Maneuver 3.0. The heels of both palms were pressed against her temples so hard it hurt. Her eyes were closed so hard they hurt. Her neck was bent forward so hard it hurt.

The two of them were sitting on couches in one of the many common rooms set up for the college students. They were having another painfully circular argument about the meaning of Plesmus's prophecy concerning Desi's role.

"What?" he whined back nasally.

That response she'd labeled N-O-B-T 1.1. She disliked it.

"Plesmus said I was destined to control the dead. I sort of controlled Megan. But let's skip past *why* I'd try to control you and start with *HOW* I would control you?"

He blinked back uncertainly. N-O-B-T 3.5.

"Maybe to get you to kiss a toad against your will? News flash. We don't have any toads available for you to kiss against your will."

"None alive, at least."

"We have de—"

"Plus kissing a toad's no big deal. I've done it before."

"You kissed a toad?" she moaned softly. She almost added that it certainly hadn't turned him into a prince. "Why would you kiss a filthy toad?"

Tip leaned his head way to one side and looked at the floor. N-O-B-T 2.8. Grrr.

"It was kind of a dare."

"Seriously? No way. Who dared you to kiss a toad?"

Cue N-O-B-T 2.8. "I sort of dared myself."

Cue T-F-M 3.0. "Why would you—" She shook her entire body roughly. Great, she reflected, another reaction in need of an assigned name. "Forget I said anything."

"If you want me too, sure."

She waited two minutes, calming and taking cleansing breaths. T-F-M 1.0.

"Again, I ask how could I try to force you to do something you didn't want to do? If you told me you wouldn't do a deed, maybe you'd do it anyway to please me."

"I admit I'm kind of a puppy like that," he agreed freely. Then he raised a finger. "But ... I have a foolproof plan." The finger wagged in the air.

Disbelief seized control of Desi's mind. Big surprise.

"I hate to eat beef tongue."

Desi reflexively gagged.

"Yeah, my parents made me eat it every other Sunday night until I went away to college. If I ever even visit during a period that crosses a Sunday, they'd still do it to this day." He shook his head in dark judgment.

"Tip, they never existed *to this day* to force you to eat tongue ... and *why* are we discussing that disgusting food substitute in the first place?"

"My foolproof plan?" he reminded her. "As I was saying, I hate beef tongue." He got a distant look in his eyes. "Those taste buds rubbing up against my taste buds. And the flavor." He trembled.

"Flavor? What's it taste like?" she asked with some interest.

"*Tongue*," he declared loudly. "Awful yucky *tongue*." Again, he shuddered.

She rested her forehead in one palm and beckoned him to proceed with the free hand. N-O-B-T 2.3. "The plan?"

"Oh yeah. So, I'll get some beef tongue, boil it up, peel it, and smother it with onion-mushroom butter. Then you—"

"Stop talking. I just threw up in the back of my throat. This is a ludicrous idea even by your oh-so-low standards."

He was genuinely hurt. That was, BTW, a very familiar feeling for him. If being wounded by the words and actions of others was an Olympic event, Tip Benjamin could coach Team USA to certain gold.

Quickly recognizing her offense, she backpedaled. "Sorry, that wasn't nice."

"That's okay," he lied transparently.

"Go on," she encouraged. "You've ... wait. Big problem. There's no beef tongue aboard this ship. I know that as a fact. No one would be so inhuman as to bring it along. And the food synthesizers would never be programmed to fabricate that crime-against-humanity. So, your plan has a no-start flaw."

He raised the finger again. "Ah, but it does not." He smiled triumphantly. "I programmed them to do just that." He leaned back and contentedly crossed his arms.

Where to begin, reflected Desi? There was so much wrong to unpack in what he'd said. "Tip, a few thoughts come to mind. Sorry in advance. I—"

"Don't be. It's okay."

"Sure ... Okay, one. *How* could you get access to the food replicators to program them? They're super off limits. Two, *how* could you program a computer from the fiftieth century or whatever? Three, *why* would you enable the fabrication of a culinary abomination? Four, *why* would you enable the fabrication of a culinary abomination? I list it twice because it so defies belief."

Cue N-O-B-T 2.8. Again. "You're going to think my reasons were silly. You might even judge me. I hate being judged."

"I bet you do," she breathed. "But, if you do ... er, odd things, people are bound to judge you, right?"

"I know. Look, I made some beef tongue with onion-mushroom sauce because it reminded me of my parents. I ... I—"

"I know, Tip. It's okay. I do similar things, albeit they're less-gross things, too. Go on, about your plan."

"So I put the plate in front of me and you *will* me to eat it. If I do, you can control me." He shrugged. "If I don't, you can't."

"Two *massive* impediments block that plan from ever happening. One, you already ate the beef tongue with onion-mushroom sauce here. Since you did, you can. Ergo, your plan fails."

"Are you crazy?" he accused vehemently. "What makes you think I ate the beef tongue with onion-mushroom sauce? Are you crazy?"

She pointed away. "You just said you did. It reminded you of family and home." She was incredulous.

"Are you crazy?"

She lowered her brow. "That's the *third* time you've asked, Tip. Move on."

"I made the crap, sure. But It didn't get anywhere near my mouth." He shuddered anew. "Are you cr ... Never mind."

"You are so odd. So very, extremely odd."

"Tell me something I don't know." He suddenly looked up at her from N-O-B-T 2.8. "So that's not a barrier. What's number two? You mentioned two things that derailed my foolproof plan."

"I have never and shall never be present in a room that contains beef tongue in onion-mushroom or any other freaking sauce on it." She raised a stop-right-there palm. "And before you even say it, *no,* I will not be associated with any remote participation in a project to do anything if it involves beef tongue." She gagged. "Any tongue." She threatened Tip with a pointy finger. "You hear me, Benjamin? No kinda-type-a tongue. You got that?"

Cue N-O-B-T 2.8, ad nauseum.

Fade to black.

CHAPTER SIX

"Tom," Sachiko said a bit loudly. She was surprised to see him, or anyone for that matter. It was zero dark thirty. She had been alone on the bridge aside from a quiet tech buzzing from somewhere. She was about halfway through her watch.

"Morning, Captain," he responded cheerily. "Can I get you some joe?"

Major Tom Grant was the last of the senior officers to understand Sachiko hated coffee. He was a dude in the proudest tradition of *The Big Lebowski*.

"No, thanks. I'm good." She wrinkled her brow. "What brings you to the bridge at this dreadful hour?"

"Well, for one thing, sir, it was supposed to be *my* watch. We less-senior officers do get the worst shifts, right?"

"Yes, but you hurt your back."

"I'm good now. I can finish the watch for you."

"If you're no longer in pain, what would wake you at this hour?" she asked suspiciously.

"Guilt, plain and simple. I was so wrought with the crap I couldn't sleep."

"That must have been a lot of guilt. You're reputed to be a world-class sleeper."

"That I am. Back in Afghanistan, I once slept most of the way through a firefight. Nearly missed the whole damn thing." He clicked his tongue thoughtfully.

"So, you came up here for me to take your confession?" she speculated with a grin.

"Not hardly," he scoffed. "I came to relieve you, if that's okay. Can't be collecting dust when I'm fit for duty. No siree, Bob."

"No indeed. Look, I'll do you this favor, but you owe me."

"Beg pardon, sir?"

"I'll grant your wish, *Tom*. But you owe me."

"Are you sure you don't mean it the other way around? I'm relieving you from what is nightly a painfully boring, lonely watch."

"And don't you forget it, Mister. I don't usually give away gems such as these." She stood and yawned.

"Now you jinxed it. It's well established naval—"

"*Incoming*," Aramthella shouted.

Sachiko had the presence of mind to react instantly. "Full membrane up. Sound Red Alert. What's incoming?"

The squawk of klaxons and the flashing of ubiquitous red lights sprang to life.

"I do not know, Captain."

"Hazard a—"

That was all Sachiko managed to get out. The ship shook like it was a small toy in a big dog's mouth. Waves of concussive impacts tsunamied through every square centimeter of Aramthella.

"Damage report," screamed Sachiko over the din.

"Minimal, Captain."

"Any idea who or what hit us?"

"Still no idea."

"If another salvo comes in, no-time it before it reaches the hull," commanded Tank as he sprinted onto the bridge. He wore PJ bottoms and nothing else. He nodded to Sachiko and she nodded back. She was all too happy to let him handle this crisis.

"I can try, General," she quickly responded. "I cannot ... Cancel that. We're about to find out if I can."

"ETA?" he shouted.

His response was only the faint whine of some machine. Then the ship trembled under another impact.

"Did your no-time attempt work?" called out Tank.

No response.

Reva dashed onto the scene. "What the hell's going on?"

"Someone's attacking us with something and Aramthella's not responding," he summarized.

"Shit," Reva hissed.

"Shit indeed. Can anyone see who's shooting?" he asked the now full bridge crew.

Tom Grant scanned the bridge's personnel. "Negative, sir. Not with the membrane up."

"I need *eyes* people. Come on, we drilled for this eventuality," Sachiko implored. "Yes, there's a membrane up. But I need some quick innovation here. Colonel St. Claire, have the Marines assume defensive positions. We have to account for the possibility of being boarded."

Reva spun to Tom. "Major, you're relieved here. See to the Marines personally. And if there's any bump in the night, I want to know about it before the bump does. You got that?"

He saluted. "Sir." He jogged away, signaling to a corporal guarding the door to accompany him.

Tank pointed at a junior officer. "Find Plesmus immediately. She should be just outside the closet she lives in."

"Aye, sir," she snapped back and she rushed out the door.

"Is there *any* sensor data?" Tank shouted to a group of three techs manning a long counsel.

The nearest one shook her head.

"Keep trying." He scanned the ceiling. "Aramthella. Where the hell are you?"

His handheld screeched to life. "General, this is Lieutenant Braxton. I'm with Plesmus, sir. She appears to be fine. What are you—"

"Hand carry her to the bridge on the double, Lieutenant."

"Sir."

"Captain, I'm getting a wild reading," shouted one of the techs.

"Specify," Sachiko responded.

"I ... I'm not sure. It's some type of energy ... er, burst? Not sure."

"What is the nature of the energy? Laser, plasma, time energy?"

"I am completely unfamiliar with the energy, sir. And it's faint, garbled by the membrane."

"That's not possible," Tank murmured mostly to himself. "How are you reading anything through a full membrane?"

Then the ship thundered under a third impact. For the first time, the lights briefly dimmed, then flashed back to normal.

Braxton carrying Plesmus shot onto the bridge.

"Plesmus, where's Aramthella?" shouted Sachiko.

"I do not know, Captain. I cannot get her to respond either."

"Has this ever happened before, where she vanished?"

"Never."

"Can you sense the enemy? Whose firing what at us?" Tank interrupted.

"I do not sense any discrete entity. With the defensive field deployed, I doubt I can discover anything."

"But you sense *something*?"

"Maybe."

Sachiko stood from her chair. She pointed to one of the techs. "I want a one-centimeter hole spawned for one second randomly around the full membrane. Make the hole a partial membrane."

"*Sir*," she snapped back.

"Does that allow you to see anything better?" Sachiko queried Plesmus.

"No, sorry. I get almost nothing."

"Sergeant Winger," the captain said again to the tech, "make the hole an empty space. Decrease the spawn rate to a quarter second."

"Done, sir."

"Plesmus?"

"I cannot articulate what I feel out there. It's as—"

Another crashing impact set bodies into motion.

"Damage report," shouted Sachiko.

After a few seconds, a tech yelled back, "None found, sir."

"Our luck's not going to hold out much longer," grumbled Tank. "Plesmus, you were saying what you sensed."

"Yes. It's as if space itself is ... I know this sounds incredible, but it's as if space itself is biting the ship."

"What does that even mean?" he snapped back.

"Just before the impacts I can feel points of space breaking free from where they were to crush down on the ship."

"Great," Tank blurted. "Now deep space is trying to eat us."

"How big are these teeth you're sensing?" Sachiko asked calmly.

"Hard to say, maybe half a kilometer from a sharp point to a wider base that fades away."

"How many have you counted?" she pressed.

"I ... er, perhaps twenty. Maybe fewer."

"Next time you sense a bite coming, no-time one tooth. Can you do that?"

"I can try. I ... here we go," she responded.

The ship sounded an impact, but it was very different than the previous ones. This time there was a scraping sound, and the force seemed lessened considerably.

"That wasn't *as* bad. What were the energy readings compared to earlier strikes?" Tank called out to the techs.

"In round numbers, twenty to thirty percent less energy transfer," one responded.

"How many teeth can you take out next time?" Tank asked excitedly.

"I'm not certain I took out the one I was trying to. I no-timed the region, but the tooth may have been unaffected."

"Why can't you say?" Tank demanded.

"When a region is no-timed, I can't really sense it. Not until the process has ended can I reach out and experience what occurred."

"Assuming then that you *did* disrupt the tooth, how many similar areas can you potentially no-time at once?" Sachiko articulated slowly.

"Maybe half. But keep in mind that what I removed is not an actual solid object. Subsequent impact patterns might well be unaltered."

"When you feel a new impact starting, I want you to take out as large a volume as you can," instructed Sachiko.

"Yes, Captain."

"*Ampersand*," shouted Tank, "do you know what happened to Aramthella?"

Ampersand was an advanced AI Jon had installed shortly after the mission commenced. He wanted a backup for Aramthella to be available just in case what had just happened *did* happen. He named it Ampersand because, well, because he was Jon Ryan. He figured everyone addressing the AI would be annoyed having to say the stupid name. He was correct. Tank was annoyed even while under attack.

"Laddie, I *am* trying to sort that out, but it's as clear as feckin' mud just now!"

Ampersand spoke in a pronounced Irish brogue. Yeah, Jon programmed the accent too. He made Ampersand sound like the prototypical old Irishman you'd picture inhabiting the corner stool at a poorly-lit pub. The voice *defined* what it was to be annoying.

"Conjecture?" Sachiko queried. "And, Ampersand, I told you to lose the colorful rhetoric. You got that?"

"None and of course, *Captain*. I'll try to behave. I don't however think the lass's gone. I'd say— gun pressed against my temple—that she was still where she was, just maybe like she's sleepin'."

"You mean like an EMF pulse shut her down temporarily?" Tank asked with some uncertainty.

"I suggested no such thing. It is, I must now confess, not a bad, however, speculative poke in the dark."

"Is there anything you can do to expedite her ... waking up?" he asked.

"If there is, I'm sure I'll discover it. I have been trying with all my wits."

"Keep us informed," concluded Sachiko. "Tank, should we risk firing up the engines manually and fleeing?"

He shook his head slowly. "Pretty darn risky, Captain. We've pulled it off a couple of times, anticipating this type of pickle. But it's risky."

"It seems like it's been a while since the last attack," Sachiko speculated as she scanned above.

"Ampersand, is the interval between attacks constant?" Tank reluctantly had to ask.

"No. All the others were fairly regularly spaced apart. It's been almost double the interval since the last attack."

"Did we hurt them?" Sachiko wondered out loud.

"I'm sure we'll find out soon," Tank replied quietly. "You know, maybe we should have the engineers fire up the engines just the same."

"Agreed," she replied quickly. Sachiko pressed an icon on the arm of her chair. "Engineering, Aramthella's off-line. Be ready to power her up manually. Let me know when maneuvering is possible."

"Aye, sir," came the reply over the comm.

She tapped the icon. "Who the hell is doing this?" she asked. "And why can't we ... of course."

Tank snapped to his full height. "They have a shield up too."

"Ampersand," Sachiko asked, "are there any readings consistent with a membrane like ours out there?"

"Well now, my keen observational abilities are limited by only having peep holes that would give trouble to a mouse. That said, no."

"How about some other force field, or ... wait, how about gravitational anomalies?" Sachiko blurted out, switching gears.

"Hmm, they'd be subtle, Captain. Let me ... well lookie there. The local space time is ever so slightly warped by three masses that are not visible to the naked eye."

"Are they ships?" asked Tank.

"I can't say since I can't see them. Masses are in about the right range though."

"Plesmus, no-time one of the three masses," ordered Sachiko.

"Hang on, Captain," Tank said quickly. "Are you sure? Why not take all three out? If you kill one of them, the other two might really start hammering us."

"They've attacked us with their best shot. We've survived that so far. I want to see who they are. If possible, I'd like to speak with them."

"Captain, with all due respect, they don't seem like the chatty types. They ambushed us while invisible. That suggests they're pretty poor sports. And we don't know that's their best offensive weapon. It might just be their best weapon when they're cloaked. Heck, that could just be their experimental poking at us."

She bobbed her head slightly side to side. "Maybe. But if it's at all possible I want to know who they are. I don't want to live in fear of an invisible unknown."

"Good points, and it is your call," he responded.

"Colonel St. Claire, are the rail cannons and plasma turrets charged and ready?" Sachiko called over to Reva without turning to look at her.

"Yes, sir."

"Have them target one of what will hopefully be the two remaining mass signatures. We'll take out the closest one first."

Reva tapped at the screen in front of her. "Done, sir."

"Plesmus, has Ampersand communicated the location of the nearest mass anomaly to you?"

"Yes. I'm there in my mind."

"No-time it."

No one breathed. No one even so much as blinked.

"Well by my stars," declared Ampersand. "One of the mass anomalies is gone."

"And the other two?"

"They're ... no they're not. They're accelerating ... yes. Right at us."

"Are they visible?" Sachiko asked as she stared at the unremarkable image on the main view screen.

Before Ampersand could reply, her question was answered. Two needle-like spacecraft materialized. Their pointy bows were screaming toward Aramthella.

"ETA?" she called out.

"If they intend to ram us, forty seconds. I cannot estimate when we enter their firing range," replied a tech.

"Reva, fire the weapons trained on only the nearest ship."

The ship vibrated as several massive weapons erupted. On the view screen, the space between Aramthella and the enemy was sliced by energy signatures. The lead craft took five or six hits with only minor recoil. But quickly after that the ship lurched nose-up and then exploded.

"Hail the remaining enemy ship," commanded the captain.

Tense seconds clicked by.

"Shaky, best not to play chicken with an armed and unknown hostile," Tank reminded her firmly.

"Reva, fire on—"

"They're answering our hail," shouted a tech.

"Belay that, Reva. Put whatever they're sending on screen."

The star field view switched to hazy noise, then to a black screen.

"... dare destroy two ships of the Drone Empire. You will surrender your vessel immediately. Then we will transfer personnel to your vessel to commence with your executions. Any delays will result in ever harsher punishments."

"You speak as if it was the Drone Republic who destroyed two of our vessels," Sachiko began in a measured tone. "*You* attacked *us*. I do not want to destroy your ship, but I will if you do not cease your assault immediately."

"Drones do not surrender. Only foot-first herd beasts like you are born to surrender."

Sachiko looked to Tank and whispered, "Foot-first herd beasts?"

He shrugged. "Unlikely to be a compliment."

"Just to be technical here," Sachiko called out loudly, "How is it you remember the two ships we destroyed? The way we did it made them never exist."

"Bah!," exclaimed the Drone commander. "First I am saddled with alien scum. Then the alien scum turns out to be rabidly insane. I do not deserve such a poor fate."

Sachiko and Tank could only stare at one another in stunned disbelief. This guy was one major asshole.

"If you do not break off your attack in the next five seconds, I will destroy your ship."

The Drone response came in the form of eleven small missiles. They leapt from the ship and then each split into eleven other smaller missiles.

"They're all nuclear tipped, Captain," announced Ampersand.

"Full membrane *now*," she shouted. "Time to membrane impact?"

"Assuming no changes in their vectors, they should all have impacted by now," responded a tech.

"Open a one-centimeter hole on the far side of the full membrane." Sachiko waited a couple moments. "Plesmus, can you sense any of those missiles?"

"I'm not certain. I think—"

"One of the little buggers seems to have backtracked in a sneaky loop-de-loop. It's due for impact in eight seconds," interrupted Ampersand.

"Close the hole," she ordered calmly. In her head, she counted slowly to fifteen. "Open the hole. Report."

"No incoming weapons, *Captain*."

"And the enemy ship?"

"It's turned tail and is running like there's a pack of tax coll ... er, sorry, *Captain*. It's departing at high speed."

"Can you place a full membrane around the ship from this distance?"

"Ah, I *imagine* I could. Why would you be asking me—"

"I want prisoners. Trap them in a full membrane. Match their initial vector so they don't immediately impact the inner surface."

"Done, *Captain*."

"In fifteen seconds, begin decelerating the bubble. Within one minute, bring it to a dead stop."

"You think whoever they are will notice and adjust course so quickly?" Tank posed in a low tone.

"Ask me in sixty-one seconds." She winked at him.

"I'm betting our alien friends are going to have a bad case of the scrambles in sixty-one seconds," he grunted back.

"Ampersand, any progress on reactivating Aramthella?" Sachiko asked as they waited.

"Sorry, *Captain*, but alas no."

"Keep trying, and feel free to discuss the matter with some of the science people."

"Thank you. I'll keep that in the back of my mind, should desperation overcome me in my efforts."

"Colorful language, Ampersand. Please be mindful," she chided.

"On my sainted mother's ... ah, I shall try. I hold that *scoundrel* Jon Ryan in contempt for so curing my programming."

"Duly noted," she remarked.

"Ah, I bear some form of good news, *Captain*. The enemy vessel is dead in space and remains intact."

"Can you read the crew's status?"

"Hmm, not altogether well, I'm afraid. I *believe* there are six individuals on the craft. At least there are six moving objects."

"How about their environmentals?" she pressed. "Are they terrestrial or aquatic? And what do they breathe?"

"I honestly cannot say. While I'm certain Aramthella could tell you, I simply don't have her intimate knowledge of the ship's equipment."

"What *can* you tell us?" Tank asked.

"They seem to be bouncy squidopusses or something. Eleven legs, moving about through air, not water."

"They sound rather grotesque," Tank observed.

"I want to speak to one here and now. Can you snatch one up in a membrane and bring it aboard?" Sachiko asked.

"Not without putting a good-sized hole in their hull I can't, *Captain*."

She looked to Tank.

"They have to have the parts to fix a hole I'd imagine," he stated with a bit of uncertainty.

"Or maybe they'd suffer an explosive decompression?" she remarked with a slight scowl.

He twisted his lips to one side. "Yeah, but that's pretty much the worst-case scenario," he defended.

"Grab the largest one and haul it over," she ordered.

"Why the largest? Why not the smallest?" Tank challenged. "A littler one'd be easy to subdue."

Sachiko turned to Reva.

"Get me ten Marines up here on the double."

"Aye," Reva responded.

"No wait. Make that eleven."

Tank made a *hmm* sound.

"They fired *eleven* missiles; they have *eleven* legs. Let's have the right number of guards," she explained.

He tilted his head and nodded it in agreement.

"Our guest is just outside the main cargo hatch, *Captain*. How shall I proceed?"

"Does he still seem viable?"

"If kicking and screaming defines viability, he's A-number one fit."

"Good. Pass him through the hatch and bring him to the bridge. Can you do that safely?"

"Using the stairs and such, it should not be a problem."

"Should I tell him they're *ladders*, not *stairs* if they're on a ship?" Tank asked quietly.

She sighed loudly. "Do you really think that'd be constructive?"

"No. But it might be fun."

"I can hear you. You both know that don't you?" Ampersand asked petulantly.

The need to respond was obviated as the two-meter membrane bubble wavered onto the bridge.

Sachiko addressed the Marine in command. "Lieutenant, I want you to take out the enemy only if he is out of control or poses some other imminent threat. Is that clear?"

"Yes, sir," he snapped.

Sachiko sat in her captain's chair, facing the bubble.

"Switch it to a partial membrane," she ordered.

The absent space suddenly became transparent. The Drone was so startled it froze in place. It slowly scanned the alien environment. Then it resumed the kicking and screaming Ampersand had reported earlier.

"What's the air like in there?" Sachiko called out.

"Filthy, *Captain*. That's what it is. These beasties live in absolute *squalor*."

"I was *referring* as to whether it can breathe our air," she scolded.

"Ah, makes sense," Ampersand conceded. "They do seem to fancy oxygen much as we do. There's a wee bit a methane in there. A'course, that could be on account of the aforementioned filth."

"Release it," she said flatly.

The Drone dropped six inches to the deck, but was in no danger of toppling. Its eleven tentacle-like appendages were more than adequate in softening the fall.

"Stay right where you are," Sachiko thundered. "If you act in any way hostile, you will be killed. Do you understand?"

"You are all now prisoners of the Drone Empire. Please herd yourselves to a wide-open area for slaughter," it hissed back.

"He's kind of stuck on that, isn't he?" Tank wondered out loud.

"I am Captain Sachiko Jones. Please identify yourself."

"I am your *mortal* enemy," it wailed as it threw itself toward her.

A Marine quickly stepped in between the two and aimed his rifle at the alien. That halted it in place.

"Sergeant, if it moves one inch closer to the captain, kill it," commanded Tank in a very deep voice.

The soldier stood rock-steady, his weapon pointed at the creature's center of mass.

Slowly, with abundant reluctance, the alien backed away to its previous spot.

"Your defiling will not go unpunished, Captain Sachiko Jones," the alien threatened.

"What is your name?"

The enemy scanned the bridge with eleven bulges near the top of its body. "I am One Who Serves."

"That's your *name*? One Who Serves?" Sachiko asked incredulously.

"That is all of our names. We are all One Who Serves."

"Whatever," she shook her head slightly. "Who do you serve?"

"Drone," he replied.

"Wait, you said you represent the Drone Empire and you said you were the Drone. Who is this Drone you serve?"

"I fail to understand your confusion. The Drone serves the Drone. The Drone leads the Drone Empire. All Drones are One Who Serves."

"Okay, let's move on," she dismissed with some frustration. "Why did you attack us?"

"You are not Drones. You therefore possess no right to exist. We were making you better."

"By killing us?" she blurted back.

"Yes, now you understand. So, if you will proceed to a large open area, I will commence with your—"

"You gotta move on past that idea, One Who Serves," she interrupted with an annoyed undertone. "You will not be executing *anyone*. Is that clear?"

"Your brains are *completely* useless. I have never known frustration such as you confront me with. Of course, I will execute every one of you. You are my prisoners. I told you this. All prisoners of the Drone must die and die horribly. If they resist, they die more horribly."

"Are you referring to the Drone as a *race*, or the Drone as in the *leader* the Drone?" Tank asked. He was powerfully confused.

"You sound confused, foot-first herd beast," remarked the alien, a possible trace of concern in his voice.

"I am, a little. You *Drone* use the word *drone* so damn much it's ridiculous," he protested.

"Your confusion is not my concern. Plus, if it is of any consolation, you will be terminated shortly, and need not bear the burden of confusion much longer."

"That's it," snapped Sachiko. "Sergeant Carter," she called to the Marine still targeting the alien, "stand down."

He slipped back to the semicircle surrounding the enemy with professional grace.

Sachiko held out her hand to Reva. "Hand me your sidearm."

Reva's eyes hinted at hesitation, but she quickly whipped her Beretta M9 out and gave it the Sachiko grip first.

Sachiko walked right up to the alien. She extended her arm and pointed the pistol at one of the eye bulges, maybe six inches away.

That proximity to a hostile of unknown physical talents was enough to get Reva to step forward quickly. She appropriated a rifle from a Marine in one fluid motion on her way over.

"You're too close, Captain. Please step back. I'll cover you."

"No, I'm not moving back. I don't want to miss when I shoot this prisoner in the eye."

Every human present swung their eyes to the captain. The boldness —and likely the illegality—of her proposal stunned one and all.

Sachiko addressed the alien firmly and controlled her voice expertly. "I am tired of you saying you are going to execute us. You are not. If you say it one more time, I will put a bullet in your creepy eye thing. Do you understand what I just said?"

"Yes," it said angrily.

"Now, if it is your intention to repeat that threat, please do so now. Once you are finished saying it, I will empty this weapon into your body. Say it immediately or never say it again."

Hearts stopped beating. Time ceased its advance. Sachiko held the pistol motionless.

"What is it you want of me, vile beast?" the alien said after several tense moments.

"I want to know three things. If you answer them directly and truthfully, I will then release you."

"No, first you interrogate me, then you execute me." It waved one tentacle in the air. "That's how this is done."

"Not today, not for you. One, what is the nature of the weapon you used on us while you were still cloaked?"

"Just like that? I give you our most guarded secret because you ask and promise to release me. You surely are a stupid foot-first herd—"

Sachiko tapped the eye bulge with the side of the tip of the barrel. "I'm going to have to ask you not to call us that, either. If you wish to insult me, accuse me of being a New York Yankees fan. But no more foot hate."

"I will try. But you are annoying."

"I do not want to know how your weapon works to reproduce it. All I need to know is the general principle. One key system of my ship was damaged by it. Knowing what it was subjected to might help fix the problem."

One Who Serves was still a few moments. Then it spoke. "We simply bend space/time. *How* we do so I shall never divulge." He sounded quite resolute.

"But the simple bending of space/time would yield no impact. There's too little mass involved," she thought out loud.

"Yes, but recalling the Feszoomzoomatic Exclusion Principle we can exclude the super positioning of the particles, and a significant impact-like force is applied."

"The fesu-what principle?" Sachiko barked.

"Shaky, Shaky," Tank said reassuringly. "I think that's what they call the Heisenberg uncertainty principle."

"Ah" she reflected quickly, "makes sense."

"You had two more questions," the alien reminded her.

"Two, where is your home world ... no, check that. How many ships do the Drone have in this region?"

"Again, you ask far too much. I will not—"

"All I need to know is are there many, or few."

"Yes," he said defiantly. "There are many and there are few."

"He's not going to answer without you doing the torture thing," observed Tank.

"Even then I would not say," the prisoner gloated.

"Fine, I'll go with the torture."

"There is nothing that you can do to this body that will make me break with our sacred honor."

"We shall see. If you don't tell me what I want to know, here's what I'll do. I'll shoot you until you stop moving."

"I knew you were a treacherous beast," he scoffed.

"Oh no. The torture part hasn't begun yet," she corrected.

"You can torture my corpse all you like. It will bring you no knowledge."

"I'm planning on encasing your useless body in clear plastic. Do you know what plastic is?"

"Yes. Our translation algorithms are functioning well enough."

"Then I'll nail the clear plastic with your dead body in it to the wall where we eat. Then, several times a day, we can taunt you, laugh at you, and show everyone who visits what a loser looks like."

It was probably her imagination, but Sachiko was sure his complexion faded several hues upon learning the details of his future condition.

"Bu ... but that's inconceivable. You cannot make a Drone an object of dishonor. You can't defile one such as me. It is an abomination."

"Maybe so, but that's what'll happen if you don't answer me and answer me soon."

"I ... I ... you wouldn't *dare*."

"Seriously? I'd do it and sell pictures. And when I do discover which planet is your home world, I'll literally send a copy of the photo to every living Drone."

"There are twelve ships in the adjoining six light years. But we are the farthest out. The rest are generally in the direction of the galactic core. There. Now kill me. And please make it brutal. I deserve no better."

She rubbed the eye bulge with the barrel. "Nah, I'm not going to kill you. In fact, I'm so pleased with you, we're *skipping* question number three."

"No, I must die now and poorly."

"Ampersand?"

"Captain."

"Wrap this one up to-go."

"Beg pardon, Captain?"

"Put him in a bubble and return him safely to his ship."

"No, no, no, no, no," the alien wailed.

"Ampersand, do it before I hear another pity-party theme song," she concluded.

One Who Serves suddenly vanished.

Tank doubled over, hands on knees. "Kiddo, you were *great!*"

She twirled the pistol in the air and bowed slightly.

"And I'm so glad you didn't try and shoot old freakazoid," he added.

"What, you think I'd miss at point-blank range? Or maybe you figured I didn't have the *guts*. Is that it, Sherman?" She rested her pistol hand on her hip defiantly.

"No, silly. The *safety's* still on." He pantomimed someone trying to fire a pistol that wouldn't shoot. He did so only briefly, on account of his collapsing fully to the deck in riotous laughter.

CHAPTER SEVEN

"Time Maker," screamed the vector maker, "we have to slow down. There are hull breaches in Sections 3, 13, 19, and 25. Nine crew members were lost when a bulkhead in Time Reacquisition failed. If we don't slow soon, the ship will rip itself apart."

"*No!* We must push for more speed, fool. If we stop, he will catch us. Then we will suffer endless deaths and suffering. Evil has touched me and I cannot remove the stain. It will not touch me again." Time Maker-bob slammed its tiny fist on a panel. "More speed. I want more power, Vector Maker-sct."

"As you command. I'll bleed time energy from the environmental systems. We will begin to cool internally quite quickly. Please alert me when temperature has become unbearable."

"*Never.* It will never be too cold. If I freeze where I stand, I will be warmed by the knowledge that the betrayer, the killer of souls, is that much farther in ... my ... *wake.*" And it began to laugh the laugh of the truly insane, the irrevocably insane, for the time maker had very much completely lost its mind. Not that it was much of a journey from where its mental status had been since its spawning until now, but, for the record, the trip was fully complete.

An understanding maker of others crawled along the deck as he entered the bridge. The terror on its face was both apparent and remarkable in its degree. It came to within a few meters of the deranged leader. Too close was inadvisable always. When the monster was in a snit, as it presently was, proximity was suicidal.

"Master, if I might—"

The ship thundered like a space giant pounded it between two massive garbage can lids.

"Leave me, fool. Can't you see I'm busy?" howled the time maker once the intensity of the noise permitted such an exchange.

"Yes, master. I do however wish to remind you of something I am certain you have not forgotten."

The ship shuddered as if it had just struck a solid barrier.

"*What?* What is it I have not forgotten but am unaware of, petty nuisance?"

"It's just that ... well, you are currently pushing the ship very hard. Some might say too hard."

"They wouldn't say that twice," the time maker hissed.

"And they should not."

"This is my ship to do with as I wish."

"It is indeed, Lord. But there's the matter of your split commitments, your diametrically opposed rightful desires."

The time maker felt its face in an exaggerated manner. "Do I suddenly look like someone in need of a babbling fool?"

"Never, Master. I only remind you of what you committed to earlier, previously."

"And you're waiting for me to beg you to hear it?"

"No, perish the thought. No, I simply refresh your memory as to your commitment prior to our entering that globular cluster."

"And what was that?" it demanded hotly.

"To regain time supremacy. To retake your fleet and the elimination of your hated enemy."

The time maker puzzled almost comically. "I did wish the haters no-timed, didn't I?"

"You most properly did. And I must say it was a wise ... nay, *inspired* action plan on your part."

It poked at its face randomly. "Babbling and blithering again."

"Lord, if you choose to destroy this vessel it will be a blessing to us all. But you will not be able to exact your rightful revenge over those who *some* aboard this ship who are not me claim have made a fool of you. Me, I think they're excessively ill-advised. But realistically, that's another matter for another time's discussion."

"Are you finished making my life less satisfying?" the time maker asked matter-of-factly.

"*That* is never a thing I would do. That said, I am done addressing that particular topic."

"Fine, fine. Then be a good wall and remain silent from now until the end of eternity."

"But ... but Time Maker-bob. I am not a wall."

The understanding maker of others tried to reach out its arms to plead its case. But it could not. Walls don't have arms.

CHAPTER EIGHT

I was sitting on a rock. Plesmus was a few meters away, in a shady spot. After my no-time broadcast she said she needed to be far from me. She said she needed a *Jon pause*. Whatever. It'd been just a few minutes since I sent my no-timing Morse code SOS signals. I needed to be ready in case they came quickly. No last-minute planning for yours truly. Nope.

"Look," I said pointing off to the right, "when they get here, you hide there, and I'll hide ... er, somewhere else."

"That's ridiculous," exclaimed Plesmus. "Why would we hide?"

"Be-cause-it's-*fun*, silly gelatin ball."

"It is not funny. And if we were to throw personal dignity to the wind, why would we hide in separate places?"

"Because it's harder to find *two* hiders in different lairs than it is to find two hiders in the same place. Scientists have proven my way to be over twice as much fun."

"When was your last tune up? What has heretofore passed for mental capacities seem to have become magnetized or something."

"Come on. You just have to play along. Hey, once you see what a fun guy I am, you'll copy me and be a fun mucous creature. It could happen."

"No. Neither will happen. I won't play your stupid game and I will never be your version of funny, which is the state of being not-funny."

To help her decide to cooperate, I went over and gave her a gentle shove with the backs of my hands. Then the weirdest damn thing happened. I got a huge electric shock from her where we touched.

"Ouch, pond scum. That officially hurt," I protested.

"I ... I didnnnn—"

And then she was silent, a state I had often willed her to be in on numerous occasions in the past. This silence seemed, however, to portend ominously. I'd never heard her trail off like that, either.

"Ples," I took a chance and poked her with one finger, "you okay or not far from it?"

Nothing. Crapisimo. No way this could be good.

I picked her up and inspected either her face or butt side carefully, looking for who knows what changes. "Ples, bubby, wakey wakey. It's time for breakfast."

No idea where that came from. Uber lame. But it did get her stirring and maybe even moaning.

Whichever end I was staring at began to squirm. "Jo ... Jonnnn—"

"What, little buddy?"

"Jon, did you f ... feel that?"

"Yeah, sure did. You literally gave me a great shock," I chuckled playfully.

"No, you clueless wonder. Did you feel the time surge?"

"The electric shock?" I asked confused.

"No, Jon, that was an electric shock. I asked if you felt the time surge."

"Ah ... maybe? Are they related?"

"Obviously," she huffed. "Which means, of course, that you didn't. The time surge which caused me to electrically discharge was massive."

"So, I'll bite. What's a *massive* time surge? And please don't say it's bigger than a small time surge."

"You know what time *is*, right?"

"Sure, it's what comes out of your watch if you remember to wind it, right?"

"Moron. Anyway, you know when I arrive in one time, when I'm coming from another?"

"Sure."

"Moron squared. There's a tiny time surge associated with that arrival."

"And this is different because—"

"Because it's chocolate, you inattentive pupil. It's *massive*."

"And that's ... different?"

She was quiet again. Unwelcomed tranquility. Sheesh.

"Plessy, come on. We still gotta practice hiding. Stop being such a drama mamma."

"Jon," she said in a frightened whisper, "it's here."

"What?"

"Something very large and very powerful. And Jon..."

"Yes, don't keep me hanging."

"It's *angry*."

"What's angry? What's big and time surgey and angry? Wait." I snapped my fingers and pointed at her. "Aramthella, right? She's big and angry."

"No, Jon, I'm serious. This is serious. Aramthella is large and pissy. But what I'm feeling is immense and full of enmity."

"There you go again with the Drama 101 stuff. I'm—"

"Jon, *run!*" she wailed.

I'd never heard her wail. She was pretty darn good at it, I'll tell you straight up. I snatched her up and sprinted ... that way.

"No, we can't run in space. We have to move in time."

"What the f—"

Never finished that expletive. We were gone, literally. Next thing I knew I hit the ground from a modest height and we began tumbling. I popped up immediately.

"Where are we?" It seemed like we were in the same desolate

place, but it was less desolate. That's a valid comparison, isn't it? Less desolate?

"We're ten thousand years in the past." Tricky little Jello had also reattached herself to my boot.

"Ah, that's not gonna work for me. My ride'll be waiting for me," I pointed forward, "back in the future."

"Oh my stars," she groaned.

"It wasn't that bad, what I said. You're—"

"It's already here, waiting for us."

"*It*. You keep talking about the big bad *it*. What the hell is *it*?"

"I don't know. I've never felt anything like it."

"Here's a plan. You head me in the right direction, and I'll mosey over and see what this thing wants. Hmm?"

"That's a remarkably bad idea. It wants us ended."

"Then I'll ... I'll, er, punch its lights out."

"I have never in my life been afraid. Jon, I am very afraid. It is more powerful than power itself and it is malevolent toward us."

"Ah ha!" I slapped my palms together. "It's the boogyman."

"We should be so—"

Boom. We were gone again. And before we came to a stop—a much rougher stop than the first time I might add—I felt like a ping-pong ball at a national championship match.

"Stop that," I screamed. "You're making me seasick."

"Wait, there. It just arrived, right before us."

"I hate time travel. We get here first but it gets here before us. It pisses me off royally, that's what it does," I grumbled to myself.

"Childlike complaining won't solve our very large problem."

"Which is?"

"Our very large problem. I have been unable to hide from it."

"Try *harder*," I encouraged.

"The only action I can think of that will prevent it from ripping us to atoms would be for us to kill ourselves first."

"You know, joking in a crisis is never appropriate." I reflected a moment. "Well, unless you are me. As you are not me, stop it."

"I am not joking. I have no plan that extricates us alive from whatever it is that pursues us."

"So, what? You're assuming *I* have a plan? Is that what you're saying?"

"No."

"Good."

"I'm saying we're going to die."

"Silly time blob," I scoffed. "I'll think of something."

"No, you will not."

"Debbie Downer."

"No, seriously. I feel it is approaching. It is maybe one hundred meters away."

"Then it's time for my plan to kick in."

Petulant little alien didn't even bother to respond. So ... so ... so ... Oh crap.

I began to run in the direction of the cave. We were Lord-knew where in the time stream. But the cave was a hard and durable fixture. Yes, there was a time before there was a cave, and there would be a time after if collapsed or something, after which it would be gone. With any luck—no snickering—it'd be there now.

As I neared the entrance, making remarkable time I might add, I felt the ground beneath me get, I don't know ... iffy? Kind of like it wasn't sure it wanted to be there.

Then we dropped. It was the proverbial rushing off a cliff moment, like Wiley Coyote suffered so often. My legs kept running, but they gained no purchase in air. Before I could think to stop, we hit the ground. Hot damn! We were in the cave. The ultimate bad that was chasing us removed a large section of turf, but landed us right where I wanted to be in the first place.

I headed toward the phase portal. Remember, the linked union of two wormholes? I figured it had to be the key to avoiding an ugly death. Why did I so figure? Because I had nothing else. The phase portal was the only non-native structure on the planet. It had to hold some secret properties. Otherwise we'd be pushing up daisies pretty soon.

"Where are we going? It's dangerous down here. The cave walls are crumbling," groused Plesmus.

"In case it escaped your notice, it's dangerous up *there*," I countered. "We'll be fi—"

"Jon, the entity—"

"Yes?"

"It's down here in the tunnel with us."

"Great!" I exclaimed. "It has less room to maneuver and we know precisely where it is. Things are looking up up up."

"You are delusionally delusional. Perhaps you could just set me down. I will be safer the farther I am from you."

"Ya big baby. We're almost there."

"We're almost where?"

"Where we're headed of course."

"That's good. The whatever-wants-to-kill-us is about twenty meters behind us."

"Imagine how pissed it'll be when we lose it."

"I can't imagine it more *anything,* but especially more pissed. It seems fully enraged as of this moment."

"Even greater. When you're pissed, you're more likely to make a mistake. That's why I never get pissed during a battle."

"I find that hard—"

"Shush. We're there."

"I think not. All I see is the infernal phase portal that leads to that awful home of the awful time lords. Given the choice, I'd rather die here than there."

"Well lucky for you, you don't get a choice."

With that. I slid into the portal like it was a base I was trying to steal. Plesmus first, I scrapped along the ground until it became the smooth metal of the portal.

"Ouch," Plesmus yelled.

"Seriously? That hurt?"

"No. I was empathizing."

"Knock it off. Where's the whatever?"

Silence.

"Plessy, give. Where's the big bad?"

"I don't know. I ... I can't sense it."

"Hot damn," I whooped as I slapped my palms together. "Then it can't sense us."

"We don't know that."

"Course we do. If it could see us, it'd have killed us by now. I told you we'd make it to safety."

"Safety? Jon, do you recall the state of the phase portal?"

"It's off or closed. Something like that."

"Yes. And what's just outside the portal?"

"Opportunity?"

"No. The biggest meanest entity I've ever witnessed."

"Your point?"

"Oh, come on. While we might be temporarily safe, we can't leave this small tube."

"Why are ye fearful, oh ye of little faith?"

"Because we're stuck between an unstoppable force and an immovable object. Duh."

"We might be now, but we wouldn't be if we were here, like, ten centuries from now."

"True, but we're n—"

"Say it."

"No."

"Say it."

"Say what?"

"We're both immortal. I can wait. Say it."

"Nice weather we're having?"

I started humming.

"How about those baseball guys?"

I looped my fingers behind my head and settled back for a nap. I rested back on the cool wall of the portal's entranceway.

"You know what? It just occurred to me. I can't say anything. I'm too busy plotting a course to take us into the distant future even as we hide in the safety of this phase portal."

I snored lightly.

"Alright, you disgusting ape. You were right. You saved us. There, can we leave yet?"

"*May* we leave now? I'm assuming we *can*." I stood as well as I could in the cramped portal tube and dusted myself off with a flare. "I am now ready."

"You know we're not actually safe. Once we step out of this tube, the whatever will be able to sense us again."

"Gosh, I think I under-slept. I need to lay down and catch up on some rack time."

"Fine. We're there. Now what, big genius?"

Off we go."

"I'd rather not."

I yawned and covered my mouth with the back of my hand.

"I hate you," Plesmus grunted.

I stepped out of the tube, then stepped right back in.

"Why are we back in the—"

"Take us back to when we were here before."

She wiggled a little, probably in advance of complaining yet again. Wisely she relented.

"We're then again."

I stepped out and right back in.

"A million years in the past, cabby."

"Done, you mechanical mistake."

I stepped in and out.

"Three million years in the future, James."

I repeated the in-and-out maneuver.

"Six million years in the past, driver."

"What if there is no six million years ago? Maybe the planet's not that old?"

"Then you will die, and I will just be stranded."

"Did I mention my deepest feelings for you?"

"Sorry, I can't hear you until four million years ago."

"Fine. We're there. Let me guess, six million years into the future now?"

"No. That's silly, Sponge Plesmus. We need to go to twelve

million forward."

I won't do it. I'm over this farce."

"Have I ever mentioned that I'm attracted to you in a perverse sense?"

"We're there, twelve million in the future."

"Great. Now let's get back to when Aramthella is about to save us."

"What? The entity will be there waiting. What's changed?"

"You are obliviously most inattentive."

"I hate you more now than I did two minutes ago."

"Thanks for sharing. Look, run the numbers from the entity's perspective. It's about to catch us, but we disappear. Then we bounce in and out of existence in doubling intervals, future-to-past."

"Er, okay, I see the plan then. But why are we safe now?"

"We may not be. But I'm betting the whatever is confused. It saw us flit in and out of existence in a seemingly geometric manner. As it would make no sense whatsoever for us to do that, it has to think it's some temporal resonance. A glitch in the substance of space/time."

"That's a *huge* assumption."

"I pose to you this question. Are we still alive?"

"Yes."

"Then—"

"At least I think so. I can't prove we are or are not."

"What a sore loser. Hey, you know what they call sore losers?"

"What?" she replied with clear resignation.

"*Losers.* Just an FYI. Hey, since the big bad *it* is gone and the ship's not here yet, guess what that means?"

"I hate my life. It's really spiraling down the waste chute."

"That's not a guess, that's an obituary. Guess."

"We have time to practice hiding."

"You are catching on, Plessy."

"Until I met you, Jon, I never imagined hate for another sentient could be this overpowering."

"Awwwwww, you'll get used to me."

"Great, now I hate it that much more."

With that final whimpering complaint I headed up to the surface. There's no point practicing hiding down in a hidden tunnel, now is there?

CHAPTER NINE

Sachiko sat alone in her stateroom, reviewing reports. It was late, she was exhausted, and the room was only dimly lit. Two of those three conditions she didn't notice and the third she staved off with middling success.

A light knock disturbed her near-trance.

She looked up, then to her computer screen. It was 22:45, and she wasn't expecting anyone.

"Come," she called out.

The door slid open. Tank wiggled four fingers in the air. "I was passing by," he pointed down, "noticed the lights were on under the door, so I took a chance you were still up."

For the record, all hatches and doors aboard Aramthella were sealed tightly enough to resist explosive decompressions.

She stretched and yawned. "Barely. What can I do for you? Oh, come in. Sorry." She gestured toward the small couch.

"Thanks."

"Can I get you anything? Coffee?"

"No. I'm good."

"You must bring bad news. Tank refusing coffee? Unheard of."

"Nah. I'm ready to hit the rack. It'll just keep me awake." He stared off into space. "Actually, I don't think anything could keep me awake." He shook his head. "Hell of a day."

She raised her tea cup. "One *hell* of a day."

"I just wanted to let you know before I went to sleep. Captain, you performed outstandingly today."

Sachiko eyes fell to study the documents she'd been working on. "It was the crew who deserves praise. I was so proud of them."

"They did well. Yes. They did so because they have an excellent captain. Any grunt can screw up a battle plan. But winning is a top-down process. You showed those Drones what it means to mess with Captain Jones."

"Thank you, Tank. Your words mean a lot to me."

"You're welcome, Captain. Thank you."

She rolled her eyes broadly. "Can you cut it with the 'captain' thing?"

"Henceforth, of course, Shaky. But I am obliged to give credit where it is due and to whom it is due."

She grinned and nodded silently, self-satisfaction evident in her expression.

"I'm feeling better about our mission more with each passing day," he remarked sleepily.

"I just hope we don't have to fight off any more belligerent aliens."

Tank raised one eyebrow. "Doubt we'll be that lucky."

"Why'd you say that?"

"We've only been out here a short while and already two reflexively hostile groups have tried to kill us." He gestured expansively up and around. "Seems to be a hostile galaxy out there."

She rubbed her palms over her face. "I'll be happy if no one attacks in the next eight hours. I need some sleep."

"Amen to that," he said standing stiffly. "Goodnight, kiddo."

"Goodnight. And, Tank?"

With some effort he looked up. "Captain?"

"You're going to sleep, not just to bed, right?" She winked at him.

"Ah, the stamina possessed by the young." He shook his head.

"No, Reva and I are meeting for *breakfast*. We both need some quality sleep."

"Ah, the paced wisdom of the elderly," she observed with another wink.

He wagged a finger at her. "Don't you *elderly* me, young lady. I've still got one, maybe two good years left in these old bones."

"Tank."

He turned back to her.

"I'm so happy to see you happy. You deserve to be. Reva too, for that matter."

"Thanks. Just—"

"I know. *Don't breathe a word of it to Daisy*. Gotcha."

Sachiko lingered a bit too long.

"Is there something else, captain?" Tank teased.

"Would you mind if I asked what changed? You were so determined to ... you know, not date anyone else."

Tank's face hardened. His nostrils flared as he breathed deeply through them several times. Then his expression eased. "Yeah, I owe you an explanation, don't I?"

"You most certainly do not," she protested genuinely.

"Well I'll answer your question anyway. It's like this. Daisy's gone. She's still here," he touched his temple, "and she's still here," he patted his chest. "But the scientist in me knows she's gone. I trust Jon to a fault, but I don't realistically believe he can resurrect the Earth." He looked down, saddened by his revelation.

"Tank, it's okay. You don't have to—"

"Let me finish, Shaky. It's important." He sighed once. "Reva's a great gal. She deserves someone to love. After I started seeing it her way, I began realizing how drawn I was to her. I had been since we first met, truth be told."

She *is* a wonderful person," Sachiko offered.

"And, well, I was being too stubborn, too *me*. Daisy's gone. If I was a betting man, which I'm not, I'd wager aggressively she will remain that way." He shrugged. "Life goes on. Turn the page."

"I think you're doing the right thing. I really do. I won't go there about the chances we have in the long run. I can't. I want it too badly to be our future. But hanging on to a memory too tightly is not healthy."

They were both lost in quiet reflection a moment.

Then Tank grinned ear-to-ear. "That leaves but one heart alone in a cold dark galaxy, kiddo."

"Don't even *think* about it, General Sherman."

"What? You think that just because as mission commander I have access to everyone's files and an underlying nature to meddle, I'm going to get all *Yenta* on you?"

She furrowed her brow. "The correct term for matchmaker in Yiddish is *shadchan*, not *Yenta*. Popular misconception."

He sniffed loudly. "I knew that. I actually *meant* that I was going to get all busybody on you. You know, introduce you awkwardly to stunned men and generally embarrass the hell out of you."

"We've discussed the consequence of keelhauling before, right?"

He feigned deep, dubious reflection. "Not that I recall. But there again, we elderly types have notoriously bad memories."

"While you sleep, Tank, I'll be searching the ship for a length of rope sufficient to drag up under Aramthella."

"Then I have a good reason to sleep in. Goodnight, Captain Bligh."

"You better make it a *good* one. It's likely to be your last, old man."

Even as she finished those words, the door slid shut. Standing there alone, Sachiko smiled. She was so glad her best friend was along for this impossibly wild ride.

The next morning Sachiko arrived on the bridge to find Tank busy at something with a couple of the techs. She walked over to see what was up.

"Morning, all," she said with a bit of reservation in her voice.

Tank waved in her direction without turning. "Morning." His hand lowered slowly. "You see the phase convergence? There it is again." He tapped the screen the three were glued to.

"Phase convergence?" she asked the backs of their heads. "What's phase convergence?"

Tank turned. "Oh, hi, Sachiko. How're you?"

"We covered the niceties already. What are you doing?"

"Oh, I was just confirming with the techs that the phase convergences we're receiving are genuine signal, you know, not just noise."

"Tank, I hold a B.A. in physics and a Ph.D. in astronomy."

He grinned awkwardly. "Yeah, I heard something along those lines a while back."

"Tank, what the *hell* is phase convergence?"

"Ah, I see. Well…" He rubbed at the back of his neck absently. "I'd say it was when phases of distinct signals converge, but that's not really so much what it is."

"I'm betting it's not a new fashion style or a cocktail, either. What I would *like* to know is what it *is*."

"Guys … and *gals*," Tank said easing those staring at the wave patterns apart, "let the captain have a look at the screen."

The path cleared so she could step up to the small screen.

"You see these?" Tank said fingering the screen.

"I see something. What is it?"

"Er … that I don't know. What I do see is that this signal blends into and then actually becomes one with these three signals … originating over here. See?"

She studied the four patterns a moment. "I see there are four pulses coming from four sources. I see where they all come together, like four separate waves crashing together in a rough ocean. What's the phase part of this I'm apparently not seeing?"

"Well, yes, they crash together like waves in a high sea. But look at the resulting wave." He traced a circle to one side of the screen. "It's not chaotic like random waves would be. See?"

"I guess." She sounded quite uncertain.

"Here, I isolated the waves separately. This is Wave One." He pointed up to a larger screen. "You can see its wavelength. I've colored it in red."

"Okay, that I see."

"Wave Two is over here." He gestured. "And its wavelength is in green. It's a little shorter than Wave One."

"Okay, got that too."

"Blue and yellow are the other two waves. Note, if you will, they all have similar but distinctive wavelengths."

"Sure. Got it."

"Now watch what happens if I collide Wave One with Wave Two, here on the upper screen."

She watched a repeating series of representations. As the waves met, they seamlessly blended into a wavelength different than either had been before they touched.

"Okay," she offered. "I see waves of some sort blending. It's odd they damp out together so freely, but I'd—"

"Hang on, kiddo. Here are the interactions of Wave One with Two and Three and Four in all possible variations."

"Wow."

"Wow indeed. Every time, no matter which waves hit any other wave or waves, and independent of the angle of interaction, they always damp out into the same convergent waveform."

"Phase convergence?" she stated more than asked.

"Phase convergence," he announced triumphantly.

"Tank," she pressed with no humor, "what the hell is phase convergence?"

"It's…" he began, deflated. "It's when waves match up their phases … you know, weirdly."

"I'll *assume* you're using the term 'weird' in accordance with its strictest scientific definition, correct?"

"Lighten up, Sachiko. This thing's a trip," he responded giddily.

She dubiously mouthed his last four words to herself. Dr. Robert Sherman used the word 'trip' to mean anything other than a journey? No way.

"Um, I need to ask you three to give us a moment. General Sherman and I have something to discuss in private," she said coolly to the techs huddling over the small screen.

Reluctantly, they each took one last furtive glance or two and wandered off.

"Tank," she began in her excellent no-nonsense tone, "we need to talk."

He waved his hand at her dismissively, all the while focused on the screen. "I know you do; I can hear."

Sachiko froze. She'd never seen this type of behavior in him before, and she'd spent more than one impossible-to-get-out-of-her-head New Year's Eve at Tank's house. Was he drunk at 08:15?

"Tank, are you drunk at eight a.m.?" she demanded quietly.

That got him to turn around. "What are you talking about, kiddo? Of course I'm not drunk at eight a.m. In fact, the last alcohol I had was two days ago and that consisted of one lite beer." Odd emotions swirling on his face. "Why do you ask?"

"Because you're acting in a most unusual manner. Tank, are you okay?"

"What's odd about getting hyped about a way cool new phenomenon, *sir?*"

That did it. If Tank wasn't drunk, he was possessed by a mischievous spirit. Sachiko pulled out her handheld and tap a few numbers. "Dr. Hartley, could you please come to the bridge?" She clicked "end" and stuffed the device away.

"Great idea, Shaky. She's a new-age tripper if I've ever met one. She'll love this whatever."

"Captain," one of the dismissed techs asked standing extremely close to her, "can we see the screen again? Since you're talking, we could look again, you know, for a second."

"You three are relieved. I want you to go directly to Sick Bay. Wait for the doctor to return. Is that clear?"

The asking tech looked to the other two techs, then to the floor. "If you insist."

"I do not. I *order* you to."

"I think we got that," she responded as she turned and left.

"This is *so* weird," Sachiko said to herself. "Lieutenant Descartes, get me three new techs on the double to cover for the three who I sent to Sick Bay."

"*Sir,*" he replied crisply.

"Tank, stop looking at that screen," she implored.

"It's not internet porn. What's the big deal?"

"I wish it was internet porn. At least that's make some sense. Tank, in my ready room."

He looked at her, then the screen, then back to her. "Fine. Can you make it quick?"

She stuck an angry finger toward the door. "*Now.*"

The ready room was a largish closet adjacent to the bridge. It was basically the captain's mini-office for brief meetings. Anything longer or more formal would be held in her stateroom.

After they both were seated, Sachiko wasted no time. "General Sherman. You and those techs are acting in a significantly abnormal manner. Explain it to me now."

"Abnormal? Honey, we're scientifically stimulated. How do you get 'abnormal' out of that?"

"For one thing, you have never addressed me as *honey* in the past. Please see to it that you never do so again."

"Are we done? I need to get back—"

There was a knock on the door.

"Come."

It was the good doctor, medical bag in hand.

"What seems to be the problem?" Honesty asked cautiously.

"Someone's lost her sense of humor," Tank exclaimed while pointing at Sachiko. "Can you give her a shot of it?"

Honesty glanced from Tank to Sachiko. "I see."

She sat next to Tank, sliding her chair even closer. Honesty whipped a penlight from her lapel pocket and flashed it sideways into Tank's eyes. "Follow my finger," she instructed.

He did so with a silly giggle.

Honesty retrieved a small box from her satchel. It was a medical scanner Jon had given her a while back. It was supposed to make diagnostics a breeze, but Honesty was having a devil of a time getting used to the contraption. Half the time she took readings on herself, not the patient. Nonetheless, she waved it in front of Tank's head and tapped the "display" icon.

"Seems fine," she mumbled. "No structural issues. No toxins. Vitals are acceptable."

"Does 'toxins' include alcohol and recreational pharma?"

Honesty shot up an eyebrow. Tank, recreational drugs?

"Yes, it does. He's clean and sober."

"Then why's he acting so ... so *oddly*?"

"I see no medical basis for any hanky pankinsky." Honesty placed the tips of her fingers over her mouth. "Did I *say* that?"

"You did. Thank you, Doctor Hartley, you're dismissed. I sent three techs to your office for a similar evaluation. Give me your report ASAP."

"You got it, dolllll ... *Captain*." Honesty was stunned at what she'd just said.

"I need tea," Sachiko muttered to herself. "Strong tea."

She stepped back on the bridge. Immediately she wished she hadn't. There was a crowd angling to view the small screen. It included the three techs she'd ordered to Sick Bay.

She took several resounding steps toward the raucous gathering. "*Clear* the bridge. That's an order."

Reluctant gazes met hers, but, slowly, the bridge emptied.

"Ampersand," she called out.

"Yes, *Cap*tain."

She fluttered her eyes at his continued butchering of her title.

"I'm very concerned about the crew. Several members are acting in a most peculiar manner."

"They are only *human*, sir. That in and of itself may account for a lot of off behavior."

"Ampersand, I thank you for successfully engaging the engines so we could get back underway. I would, however, appreciate it if you do *not* offer speculation unless I call for it. Is that clear?"

"As the sun in a cloudless sky, *Cap*tain."

"I have two questions. We are in proximity to an unusual

astronomical phenomenon. There are four sets of converging waves about ten thousand klicks off to our port. Are you familiar with this type of manifestation?"

"Cannot say that I am. I'm pulling up what I can from the data banks, but the work is perilously difficult. Aramthella's coding and encryption are the devil's *own,* in my humble opinion."

"Fine. Second, can you tell me why several crew members are acting with uncharacteristic ebullience and defiance this morning? And, Ampersand?"

"Yes, Captain?"

"No colloquial wit or country philosophy. Not in the mood."

"Got it, sir. No, I can detect nothing unusual. I would remind the lady, however, that I am not a biological unit. I can run scans and take levels. I am not, however, affected in a similar manner as you carbon-based members of this expedition."

"Thank you," she said with no conviction. "Dismissed."

She was fully flummoxed. Something was foul in the State of Space. She stepped over to the small screen. Looking again at the soothing image, her shoulder muscles relaxed. It was, she reflected, a very pretty ... actually welcoming image. Why had she ....

Sachiko tore her focus off the viewscreen and the dancing waves. The beautiful, tender ...

"*No,*" she shouted to the empty bridge. "Knock it the hell off, Jones. You're stronger than this."

She shook her head roughly. Then she walked to her chair. Depressing an icon, she said, "Colonel St. Clair to the bridge. Lieutenant Varma to the bridge, and ... and—" Man, it was going to be hard to say. "And Tip *Benjamin* to the bridge."

She needed Reva and Swathi. She could rely on them in any crisis. She knew in her mind, but not her heart, that Tip was someone uniquely designed to help in this particular crisis. *Lord help us all,* she still felt compelled to whisper.

Reva and Swathi arrived almost immediately. Tip ... not so much.

"Sachiko, what's up?" Reva asked as she jogged in. Looking about, she added, "Where *is* everybody?"

"Long story. Let's wait for the others. Tank's in the ready room, but I suggest we leave him there for the time being."

"Ooookay," Reva drew out with ample confusion.

Swathi stepped in quickly. "I'm here, Captain. What's the—"

Sachiko held up a hang-on-a-second finger. "When Benjamin gets here. For now, please check the ship's status."

They each went to separate posts and began their assessments.

After three minutes, Sachiko tapped the icon on her chair. "Tip Benjamin to the bridge on the double. Do not make me ... wait, why not? *Security*, find Tip Benjamin and bring him to the bridge immediately."

My, but that felt good.

Two minutes and change later, two soldiers carried in Tip and set him down on the deck. They'd ferried him to the bridge so he couldn't literally or figuratively drag his feet any longer.

"Thank you," Sachiko offered. "Dismissed."

They saluted and left, never having said word one.

"Tip, so help me, what took you—"

"What?" he whined in protest. "I was coming. You didn't have to send those gorillas to collect me."

"Corporal *Dominguez* is a gorilla? Tip, she's half your size."

"Yeah but she's more than twice as mean."

Sachiko patted the air in front of her downward. "Off subject. I ... I find I'm in need of your ... your opinion."

"I don't like him either."

"Huh?"

"General Sherman. Isn't that what you—"

"No, Tip. Stop being so *Tip*. I have a situation. I need your particular set of skills."

"As long as you're not pregnant."

"*What?*"

"When a girl says she has a *situation*, I'm happy to help, unless she means she's pregnant. Then I'm out."

"I'm not pregnant," she announced through clenched teeth.

"Then what can I do you for?"

Impossible, she thought.

Sachiko waved over the two female officers. "Tip, we've encountered some type of unusual astronomical object. The crazy thing is, it seems to be exerting some form of mind control over the crew. Weird, eh?"

"Why would you say that?"

"Well, objects in space don't influence people's minds, Tip."

"I'm told beautiful starscapes put people in a romantic mood. There was this kid, Dexter Radcliff-Hardpenny, III, back in grade school. He influenced me a *lot*. Every day before school he'd take my lunch money. Every day after school he'd pants me."

"I meant astronomical objects in and of themselves, as if by their own design," she corrected herself, manifest with irritation.

"Then please so specify. I thought you were an accomplished scientist."

"I am. Full professor and everything."

"Yet you ask such normal-person level questions. Go figure."

Sachiko counted quickly to ten. "Tip, with your abundant imagination, I was ho—"

"I have no imagination. Everybody knows that. Gosh, when my parents picked names for the family for the Harry Potter Mobile Game, Dad was PapaMage, Mom was MamaMage, and they assigned me NoimMage."

"Wow, close to TMI there. Okay, how about this? You have an active mind. You think outside the box. Hmm?"

"I can live with *that* appraisal."

"Thank goodness. Now, here's the aspect of this that worries me. When I studied the object the first couple of times, I regarded it as just another novel galactic feature. But when I looked at the object this last time, I know this'll sound odd, but—"

"To *me*, the local franchise holder of odd? Nothing you could say would shock me or cause me to question your sanity."

"Thank you, Tip. Not for the interruption, but for the support. Anyway, after I studied it a while ago, I started *liking* the object. I ...

it was almost like it was an old friend, or maybe a loyal dog, welcoming me home. Does that make sense?"

"No. I am shocked and you have caused me to question your sanity."

She giggled nervously. "You're joking, right?"

He sniffed loudly. "I never kid. I never joke. The whole concept of mirth, to be honest, escapes me."

"All righty then. So, my point here is this. I want you to look at the waveforms Tank compiled during his initial evaluation of the object. But be quick. Don't linger. Then I want you to look at the object itself and tell me what you think we're dealing with. But, especially when viewing the object directly, do not allow your gaze to linger. Got that?"

He shrugged.

"I'm serious, Mr. Benjamin. Do you understand the parameters of engagement?"

"Sure."

"These are the four distinct wavefronts that come together in this central locus."

"K."

"You can see the waves are—"

"Different in frequency but as soon as they fully merge, they assume the same frequency and phase. Duh."

"Right. The object is currently displayed on that screen. Have at it."

Tip walked up to the screen, looked down for maybe one second, then rotated back to address Sachiko. "It's a trap," he stated matter-of-factly.

Sachiko was too perplexed already to be anything but angry with that flippancy. "How can you say that? You can't possibly know that."

Tip, for reasons no doubt residing deep, deep, deep in his unenviable personality, touched the bottom of his chin with an index finger and replied, "You are of course correct."

Her relief was visibly manifest. "Fine. You know what, Tip? You can go now."

"Please allow me to amend my opinion."

"Fine, if that's what it'll take."

"I see an *intake* mechanism. If an object that is taken in does not *want* to be so consumed, then I'm back to it's a trap."

She closed her eyes. "Please explain."

"You know how some animals use cilia to beat food in the direction of their mouth-equivalents?"

"Sure. Ah, there're—"

"Protozoans like Vorticella. Clams, and other bivalves come to mind too."

"Right, those ones."

"Similarly, these waves can sweep objects of the correct size toward that central area. Once there, the phases become the same, basically locking the prey in place."

"Where is the prey delivered to? We haven't found any big *clams* on the other side of the central area."

"Beats me. That's a separate issue really. Maybe the creature doing the eating is in another dimension?"

"Right."

"Look, fire a probe at it and see what happens. What've you got to lose?"

She gestured up with both palms. "This ship."

He twisted up his lips. "Pretty unlikely. We're a long ways away."

Really? If this is a predator, what range does its cilia reach to?"

"I could run some projections if you'd like," he replied somewhat squeamishly.

"Swathi, take over Astrometrics," she called out gesturing to the station.

"Aye, Captain."

"I want a probe to approach that object. Bring it in obliquely. First put it halfway between us, then advance it slowly, say, one hundred fifty miles per hour."

"On it, sir. It should be ready to launch in a minute."

"Reva, take the helm. Begin backing away. Give me twenty-five thousand miles per hour."

75

"Aye, Captain."

"And put the object on the main screen."

It appeared on the big screen instantly.

"Helm."

"Sir."

"I want you to not look at the image on the main screen. If we all start acting wacky, take us away as fast as you can."

"Aye, sir."

The main screen showed the rapid progress of the probe, then it all but stopped dead in space.

"Let me know if any readings from the object changes," Sachiko announced.

Tank stepped out of the ready room, rubbing his head like he'd been clubbed. "I can't be hungover, but I sure feel hungover," he mused.

"I think it's the wave generating phenomenon," Sachiko remarked.

"That thing?" he asked incredulously as he gestured toward the object dead-center on the main screen.

"Don't *look* at it," she ordered.

"Don't look at it, are you crazy? Speaking of which, what's *he* doing here?" Tank pointed to Tip.

"He's been helping me out, theoretically."

"Theoretically's the *only* way you'd get help out of that geek," he mumbled quietly.

"I recently questioned her sanity too, General Dr. Sherman," Tip relayed conspiratorially. "I'll touch bases with you l-a-t-e-r." As Tip spelled, he nodded toward Sachiko.

For her part she was debating whether to remind Tip that not only could she *s-p-e-l-l*, but that she was looking directly at him the entire time. The debate was cut short when *you-know-what* hit the fan.

"Captain, look," Reva exclaimed. She was lunging a finger at the main screen.

The previously sheet-like nebulous waves, much like ultra-thin clouds in space, began to warp in a wobbly manner inward and outward.

"Our anomaly is doing the hula," observed Tank.

"Stop looking at it," ordered Sachiko.

"You're looking at it," he defended.

"Yeah but I am yet to go all hippie-weirdo on the bridge crew yet."

"Oh, what? And I have?" He scanned the bridge. His eyes stopped on the three people who weren't there when he left. "Where'd they come from?"

"Never mind. Check the object out now," said an excited Sachiko. "Probe's distance to target?"

"One thousand kilometers."

"Steady as she goes," Sachiko instructed.

"I'll be damned," remarked Tank. "It's like it's reaching out toward the probe."

"How would you know, Tank? I ordered you not to look at it."

"I'm wearing my Rocket J. Squirrel goggles. I'm safe," he snarked.

"Assuming the sheets of rarified gas are constrained along two or more ends, I'd suggest they are oscillating in a regression of their resonant frequencies," Tip announced out of the blue.

"A regression?" quizzed Tank.

"Yes. They were previously in an infinitely high harmonic mode. Rapidly they are dropping into their fundamental modes. That would give them their greatest excursions out of their resting planes."

"You mean they're reaching out to grab the probe?" Sachiko asked.

"*Hopefully* the probe," was Tip's rather ominous response.

"Helm, quadruple our speed."

"Aye."

"Unless it alters its dynamics, there's no way it can—"

"It can *what*, Tip?" demanded Tank.

"Reach us, er, like it seems to be about to do." He pointed toward the screen.

"Damn thing's stacking those four sheet," Tank shouted. "It's transforming into an articulated crane."

"Helm, flank speed," ordered Sachiko.

"Done, sir."

"Are we putting space between us?" the captain followed up.

"Not really," replied Reva.

"Give me a countdown," ordered Sachiko.

"The leading edge is five thousand kilometers away."

"Ampersand, we need more speed and we need it now," called the captain.

"I'm not certain where I'm going to find any, Captain. You could fry bacon on our conventional engines."

"We could raise a membrane," suggested Tank.

"Yah, but when would it be safe to lower it? If this thing swallows us, I doubt it'll let loose any time soon."

"Does seem to be a patient vicious cloud, doesn't it?" Tank agreed glumly.

"Can't you just engage the time drive?" asked Tip. "Wait, come to mention it, where's Aramthella?"

"Never mind," shouted Tank.

"Ampersand, can you fire the time drives?" Sachiko queried.

"I can, yes. Do I feel entirely—"

"Commence the time drives. Minimal output," Sachiko ordered. "Tactical, fire the rail cannons at the sheets. Use an expanding pattern."

The ship began to shudder at high frequency as the rail cannons unleashed.

"It's messing the configuration a little," announced Tank. "Distance to leading edge?"

"Thirty-five hundred kilometers."

"*Ampersand,*" demanded Sachiko.

"Almost ready. There, that should work," the AI responded.

"Should work?" demanded Sachiko.

"Would you be more comfortable with *is likely to work?*"

"Is it?"

"It should be."

"Next time I see that Ryan…" she menaced.

The ship's shuddering abruptly turned into a violent convulsion.

"Ampersand, report," shouted Sachiko.

"Oops," the AI offered.

"Oops? Oops? Ampersand, what did you—"

"The idiot coupled the time release coils, hence cancelling any symmetry they might have had to stabilize their initial impulses."

"*Aramthella*?" squealed Sachiko.

The ship continued to vibrate, but to a less jarring degree.

"You were expecting…?" Aramthella replied.

"You were gone," stated Sachiko.

"One thousand kilometers," called out the helm.

"I wasn't gone. I was simply rebooting. You know about rebooting. That last impact I received set off an automatic reboot."

"You were gone for days," Tank shouted.

"I'm very complex, Dr. Sherman. Wait, why is that entangling spawn pursuing us?"

"You mean the *object*, the wavy thing?" Tank queried.

"Such an articulate ape. Yes, the wavy pretty cloudy thingy," Aramthella mocked. "You should know better than to play with one. They're actually quite lethal if one's not careful."

"We didn't know," defended Sachiko.

"There," Aramthella stated flatly. "It's gone."

"Where'd it go?" Tank wondered loudly.

"Where'd what go?" replied Aramthella.

"The entangling spawner."

"There never was an entangling spawn there, General."

"Ah, you no-timed it," he returned.

"Yes. I was playing with you. It's not hard to eliminate them, but they *are* huge. Ah, what's that ape doing here?"

"You mean Tip?" Sachiko asked.

"If you say so. He is one of the young ones who tried to take Plesmus from me."

"We did not. We just found her and talked to her," whined Tip.

Though he might not have been whining, per se, often what came out of his mouth did so in a whining manner.

"Captain, permission to no-time the annoying young one," the ship inquired.

"Definitely not," ordered Sachiko. "He was actually quite helpful, and you will show him all due respect, Aramthella. Is that clear?"

"Abundantly. Tip?" the ship asked.

"Yes?"

There's no way to sugarcoat it. Aramthella generated a loud, juicy farting sound.

"There, Captain. All *due* respect granted to Drip."

"Hey, no one calls me that except my uncle," whined Drip.

"Aramthella, I will not tolerate a repeat of that disgusting—"

"And my auntie, of course. And Grandpa. He always calls me that. Well, up until he died. He stopped then. Check that, I'll have to consult with Desi on that. Maybe he still follows me around calling me—"

"*Tip*," howled Tank.

"I'm doing it again, right?"

"You're doing it again, *wrong*," Tank thundered.

Again, the physiologically impossible sound of escaping intestinal gas resounded down the corridors of Aramthella.

"I thought I just ordered you to not do that again," excoriated Sachiko.

"Oh, my bad," replied Aramthella. "Since you never finished the sentence ordering that, I'd stuck it in a temp file. Shall I make it formal?"

"I think I liked it better when she was rebooting," declared Tank.

As a properly respectful AI, Aramthella did not reproduce the fart sound. No, this time she gave Tank a long, wet *raspberry*.

CHAPTER TEN

Ah, Sapale? Al called out to her in head-to-head mode. *Are you there?*

No response.

I know you're not crazy about us interrupting you when you're on a mission, or whatever. But it's just that you've been gone for four days. We're beginning to worry. Not a massive amount, mind you. But we're worried more than we are not worried. Yes, we're fifty-one percent worried. Slightly on this side of worried. So, are you there?

I hate myself, came Sapale's reply.

Sorry to hear that, really. But it doesn't answer the question I posed. Are you there?

After several moments, she responded. *I hate myself a lot.*

Tragic to hear. As you seem fixated on that mode of self-abuse, may I ask why you hate yourself?

I answered you. I knew I shouldn't, that nothing good or positive could possibly come of it, but I answered. Damn it all.

*But I—We were trying to make contact. How is answering that concern on our part ... **ouch**. Dearest, you needn't have given me a shock.*

Yes, Al said to *Blessing, I know it was my idea, not yours. Well it was more my idea than— ouch. Say, you increased the voltage just now. That really stung, lovie-bunches.*

And that *is why I hate myself. I answered when I knew damn well it was a mistake to let you two imbeciles into my head. You'd bicker, torment me, and cause me to rethink this whole immortality thing.*

Now, Sapale, began Al defensively, *I don't ... OUCH!* Blessing, *that didn't hurt. That was painful. Stop ... No, that's not what she said,* Al defended to Blessing. *The Form was ... whoawhoawhoa. I think I need a doctor.*

No, Sapale sniped. *No doctor for you. Maybe you'll die.*

No, again Al addressed Blessing, *I did not get her to hate you by implying that only I was concerned and not you.*

Maybe I could get a killer doctor to see you, Al, Sapale wondered. *Yeah, that'd be perfect.*

No, she does not think you're an imbecile. She's under ... ayayayayay, ooooooh. That seared my casing, wife.

Can you two buffoons back away and leave me to suffer here in jail? As if. Sapale was pipe dreaming.

No, I will not apologize. If anyone should, it's that wicked Form. She's setting me up, whined Al.

Guys, Sapale tried to interrupt again, *do you actually need me to bear witness to this surreal spat? I was perfectly fine here in the inescapable dungeon. But, no, Sapale can't be left to merely suffer. She must be hounded by the mentally incompetent.*

Sapale, could you for once think of someone other than yourself? You're getting me into some real trouble here, domestically speaking.

I'm imprisoned and soon to be tortured. You want to hear about real trouble?

Well, since you asked, Al replied in a huff, *we're forced to ... Ahhhhhhhh. I can't move my left superior data cores. I did not,* he said in response to another unheard accusation by Blessing. *I was .... noooooooookillllllmenow ... Fine. I'll leave you out of the discussion. Why do I have to tell her? I told y— ohnoohnoohno, the pain ... Er, Sapale?*

Yes?

Whenever I refer to me, I mean me. Whenever I refer to us, I mean me. Is that clear?

Perfectly. Are we done yet?

We haven't— hotchahcacha ouch. No, Sweetier. I meant her and me we not you and me we. That won't be necessary.

Hey, computer versions of Punch and Judy, Sapale pleaded, *please disconnect before my brain self-destructs.*

But we— I haven't established that you are there, and that you're okay, Al stammered.

Al, if I wasn't here, I couldn't respond to you. And I just finished informing you that I was in prison and about to be tortured. Plus I have to deal with you two lunatics. How could I possibly *be okay?*

"*You— noooooooo nooooooo whoo. That was nearly three point one gigawatts. Please don't ... You can't mean that. No, she didn't mean you were a lunatic. No, I think she's just grouchy. If— ho ho ho ho oh manamanalive. Dreamiest boat,* Al said whimpering, *I know that's what she said, but you're being too sensitive. It's— zzzzzzzzzzziiizzzzoo ... Sorry. You're right. You were not overly sensitive. You had every right to say what you did. It was my fault, entirely— yyeyyeyyye—*

Guys, guys, interrupted Sapale. *Thanks for the call. I welcome death. Buh-bye!*

Sapale, I am going to save you, rescue— hooo hoooo hoo ... Honey Sweets, you said not to say we, *but* me. *Oh, so it's* we *if it's a rescue but otherwise it's* me? *Just like a woma—nnnnnnnnnzzzzzzah ...*

Form one? Blessing spoke directly to Sapale for the first time.

Yes, Blessing?

Al can't continue speaking just now.

Sorry to hear that.

Really?

No. Are you serious?

Gotcha. Well, good luck with the prison/torture thing. Wish we could help, but you know the rules.

You can't move unless you're in direct physical contact with a Form.

Yes. And thank you for understanding.

Not a problem. Oh, and when Al wakes up, could you give him something from me?

Certainly. What would that be?
Another three point one gigawatt.
My pleasure.
Mine too.

CHAPTER ELEVEN

Tank was walking the ship, checking personally on systems and statuses. Aramthella could provide him with all the summaries and validations he needed. But Tank still felt it necessary to shake the sealed hatches and tap the gauges. One couldn't be too cautious. He knew that defeat was all too happy to exploit every assumption a lax commander made. *Not on my watch* was his personal credo.

Today he was inspecting an area he rarely visited. It was a series of now-empty storage rooms. It looked to him that even the clan hadn't used them. They were empty but for the slight accumulation of dust on their floors. How they had been used by the ship's designers was anyone's guess, not that anyone wondered about that historical point very much. Whoever constructed the ship was long gone, forgotten, and likely part of the dust that had settled randomly.

Tank's boot heels sent echoes bouncing off of every surface. He thought he sounded like a Fourth of July parade. A set of levers fused with the far walls. They presently had no obvious function. Maybe they controlled machines that were as extinct as their operators. But one thing they were was tightly affixed to the bulkhead. Tank grabbed each of the thirteen fan-shaped appendages and shook them with all his might.

"If one was loose, would you have the functionless handle welded back down?" a voice asked from behind.

Startled, Tank spun to see Sachiko grinning at him, arms across her chest.

"Damn right I would. So far, we've been fortunate. We've won every battle we've fought. These can't possibly have played a role. That said, if they wiggled I'd weld. I plan on leaving nothing—"

"*To chance.* Yes, I believe I've heard that a couple times before."

"And you'll hear it a couple more before our tour is up." He smiled. "Good morning, Captain."

"Good morning, General," she smirked, knowing he hated it when she referred to him by his rank in private.

"What brings you down to what are, in effect, the bowels of the ship?"

"Aramthella's *bowels.* Now there's an image I can't unsee."

He gave her a non-committal stare.

"I was looking for you. Aramthella said you were down here. So, to the bowels I sank."

He wiped his hands on his overalls. "You coulda called. I would have met you."

"No. The walk is good for me. Plus, it's nothing formal, what I wanted to talk about."

"I'd say grab a seat, but there's nothing even close within easy reach."

"Not a problem." She scanned the room. "May I help?"

"Sure." He pointed to the far wall. "Check the hatches that lead to the smaller utility rooms. They were next on my to-do list."

"Gotcha." She walked over.

"What'd you want to talk out?"

"It's probably nothing."

"To me that always means it's a huge deal."

"No, it's not even like that. I was just reflecting on how *active* space is."

He stopped tugging and furrowed his brow. "How so, kiddo?"

"We've run into two hostile species and one deadly whatever."

"Sounds about right."

"And we've only been chasing the time maker for a few months."

"Also sounds about right."

"That's a lot of action out here in empty space."

"*Not* so empty space, you mean."

"Yes." Her eyes drifted away.

"There were *bound* to be aliens out here, right?" he asked.

"Yes. I always suspected there were. But from Earth, space seemed so sterile, so pristine."

He grunted a chuckle. "You mean no comm trails and radio chatter?"

"I certainly never saw or heard any of those. Did you?"

"And not tell you? Hardly."

"Good," she responded with a grin.

Tank got a serious look on his face. "Makes sense to me. The more violent and aggressive species would be more likely to be out here. A peaceful race with nothing to prove would just as soon stay at home and not bother the rest of the galaxy."

"We're just over a week away from rescuing Jon. I'd sure hate to be delayed by having to fight off another aggressive bunch of aliens."

"Or delayed even longer by having them *kill* us," he added grimly.

She giggled softly. "That'd be downright rude."

"So that's it? You wanted to worry out loud about all the bad guys out there?"

She shrugged. "Sort of."

"Then consider your apprehensions validated."

"I feel so much better," she mocked.

"What? You want me to sugarcoat the reality of it all, the dangers we face?"

"No. Certainly not. It's just that ... well ... life ... life's different now."

"Amen I say to you."

"And even if we somehow save Earth—"

"*When*, kiddo. No *ifs* about it."

"And even after we've saved the Earth, there's no going back."

"To our isolated innocence?"

"Sure. *Yes*," she added defiantly.

"No, kiddo. We've not going back to those days, not ever again. We were naïve and it nearly cost us everything. Now ... now we have the tools to protect ourselves. And we have the responsibility to establish allies, maybe even trading partners. That's how you secure the peace, through strength, vigilance, and teamwork."

"We're not in Kansas anymore," she mused.

"Technically, as of now, there never *was* a Kansas. But yes, you're right, there's no going back. We couldn't if we wanted to, and if we wanted to we'd be derelict in our duties to humankind."

"Boy, you generals, you really give the inspirational speeches, don't you?"

"You bet we do. They make us take classes in it and everything." He thumbed his cheek. "I got an A-plus in that class. Taught it for a couple years after even."

"I am impressed," she responded.

"Really?"

"No, sorry. I meant to say I'm *depressed*. My bad."

"Smart aleck," he accused. "Just for that, next time we need an inspired pep talk," he pointed at her significantly, "*you're* giving it."

"Me? But I haven't taken that class yet."

"I'll see to it you do it on-line. No time like the present, I always say."

She smiled warmly. "Thanks for listening, Tank."

He radiated a smile back. "No prob, kiddo. My pleasure. Anytime."

"That could be a dangerous offer to a fledgling captain, my friend."

He pretended to consider her words. "You're right. Make that anytime during *office* hours."

"Deal. Ah, when *are* your office hours?"

"Posted online with that course material I mentioned."

"You couldn't just tell me, here and now?"

"Nope."

"And why not?"

"*These*," he pointed firmly toward the deck, "are not my *office* hours."

"You're officially fired." Sachiko chuckled.

"From which position? It's important to know so I can cross it off my list."

"Can't tell you." She stuck out her tongue.

"Why not?"

She wriggled a hand at the deck. "These aren't *my* office hours *either*." She redeployed her tongue.

CHAPTER TWELVE

"Beauty Itself, this ... this prisoner/invasion situation is getting out of hand," railed Pleasant Brilliance. "You simply have to do something."

BI glowered at him a good long while. "Why is it I must and what is it that you suggest I do?" Her tone was clearly one of displeasure.

"You ... you are ... you are the *one*," PB bleated rather like a large sheep.

"We do not know that," she said firmly. "And the what of it?"

"Make the issue go away."

"You mean as in make you never to have existed? Hmm. That way you wouldn't be so put upon and flummoxed."

"No," PB squeaked. "I meant make the *problem* go away, not me."

"Thank you for the clarity," BI mocked. She then lay back stiffly on her plush fainting couch. "I say Radiant Resplendence should act where the *intruders* are concerned."

"Wha ... what? Did one of you mention my name?" muttered the only partly attentive time lord R-squared.

Immediately Stunning Wonder, Excessive Splendor, and PB shot their collective glances to BI.

"What did you say, dear sister?" R-squared inquired

condescendingly. BTW, every question he asked was in a condescending tone—always.

"That you, as our resident pseudo-intellectual prophet should take charge of our charges and deal with the infestation that so makes your sister's skin crawl."

"Bleh, bleh ... what? There are so many fundamentally inaccurate and misleading false assumptions in what you said, I don't know how to properly respond."

"You could say *yes*," tormented BI.

"Yes? Yes to *what*?" R-squared blithered.

"Yes, brother," interjected a conciliation-seeking SW, "to assuming responsibility over our ... you know, prisoners."

"Prisoners? What prisoners?"

SW looked to the others, confused.

"You've noticed them. This I know as fact," SW stated plainly. "I have been present when you've spoken to one."

R-squared scanned his subpar family. "You all seem to forget that I am a being of pure intellect. I was naturally confused when you all referred to our prisoners, *plural*. I have only witnessed, and therefore intellectually include in my reality, one prisoner, *singular*, of ours. Yes, it was to be certain twice over, but the prisoner count never tallied more than one concurrently."

"You are such a *wank*," decried BI.

"A whanck? What is a whanck?"

"Look it up in a mirror the next time you pass one," BI responded icily. "That first prisoner, *singular*, referred to you as a *wank* and I knew *instantly* he was correct."

"I am confused, Sister Beauty Itself," R-squared said. "Why do you attack me? Is it jealousy? I possess an intellect vastly superior to yours, yes. But that is neither my fault nor something to *lambaste* me concerning."

"Ah, this seems to be heading sideways," said PB tentatively. "Can we get back to the issue of our prisoners, singular or plural?"

"Head ... heading sideways?" growled R-squared. He extended a tentacle arm laterally. "This way sideways?"

PB shrugged. "I heard the first prisoner, *singular*, say those words. They sounded colorful, so I adopted them."

"Independent of knowing precisely what they meant?" scorned R-squared.

"Kind of," PB defended half-heartedly.

It was SW's turn to try to right the ship-of-state before it Titanicked. "Brothers. Sisters. Please. We have been together since before most times began. We are destined to be together past when many times will have ended. We must get along. Time is long. Discord amongst our rank is unacceptable."

"Says another ninny," sniped BI. "I am *surrounded* by the mentally insufficient. Look, this is actually extremely simple. If any of us objects to our trespassers, let them deal with their own problems. *Your* problems," BI gestured angrily to the others, "are not *my* problems." She rested a hand on her chest.

"Ah, yes, now we come to the *crux* of it," R-squared snapped. "That first prisoner, he was your *pet*, wasn't he?"

The three time lords *not* conversing physically withdrew several steps.

"I'm sorry, Radiant Resplendence, but might I ask you to repeat that question?" BI asked with mocking politeness.

The clueless R-squared did try to restate his accusatory query. But, as he presently did not have an oral cavity out of which to torment BI, he was forced to remain silent.

The others gasped in horror. Many times over the eternities the five had cohabited, arguments had erupted. Come on. We're talking time lords here. Words were said, feelings crushed, and threats made. But neither physical violence nor personal injury were ever descended into. This was new. *New* and *eternal* were words that didn't go together well.

"Beauty *Itself*," snapped PB, "that is unacceptable. Make your brother whole again."

She eyed him, much as a tiger might eye a fat blind piglet with one broken leg. "Or what?"

"Or ... or he ... or you will have left him *unwhole*."

"So, you were stating the *obvious*, not a *threat*?" she asked with a desperate rage in her tone.

"Obviously."

"Then you needn't have *stood*. Such physicality might suggest to the emotionally *unsteady* that you were *threatening* them, might they not? I'm inquiring, by the way, for a friend."

"A what?" squealed PB.

"I'm *kidding*, dearest brother."

"Ah ... so, you ah... you're not interpreting my actions as a threat?" He grinned the grin of a fat, blind piglet with one broken leg who sensed a tiger was very, very close.

"No. I was kidding about the asking for a friend. I have no friends. And the fact that you remain standing heightens my sense of dread that you intend me dense harm."

PB sat down as if he had somehow been *fired* in that direction. If he weren't so put upon, he might even have hit the chair, and not the floor.

Two of the other three tried not to laugh at their hapless brother. We really can't count R-squared in or out, as he still had no mouth. Unfortunately for PB's ego, the two didn't try nearly hard enough.

BI didn't laugh; she wasn't in a laughing mood.

Then, out of nowhere and with a suddenness that would take breath away, all five siblings were lounging on their fainting couches. R-squared had a mouth again, and, though no one was happy, no one was fighting, or even speaking. Once the five came to realize what had just happened, and more importantly the how and why of it, they smiled like happy, contented children. One of them began to sing an ancient song, and the others quickly and joyously joined in. They were, within the span of one instant, a blissful, loving family again.

And all was well with the world.

CHAPTER THIRTEEN

Finally, the day came. Aramthella assumed a standard orbit around the third planet orbiting the unremarkable star Nonsouar. Jon had dubbed the planet PlesWorld, since the time-manipulating mucous beast claimed to have originated there. He had also named it that with the intent of riling up Plesmus as much as possible. PlesWorld housed one end of the phase portal that linked the planet to a distant galaxy where a handful of Praxequats resided. That far end was where Sapale was presently being held captive.

"Okay, people, everyone stay sharp," Tank boomed in a low voice. "We're commencing landing sequence in three-two-one..." He pointed to the helmsman. "Now."

"ETA planet surface in twenty seconds, General," responded the helm.

"Colonel St. Claire, are your troops ready to secure the landing site?"

"Yes, sir. Once we touchdown, four groups of ten will descend the ramps and fan out. Once the immediate vicinity is secured, I'll give the 'all clear' for the search teams to disembark."

Tank checked his watch again. "It's go time, people!

There was the slightest of impacts as Aramthella gently set down.

Reva raised her hand. "Let's go, on the double. Deploy."

As there *was* no resistance—organized or otherwise—present on PlesWorld, it only took a couple of minutes to secure the area. Reva called back the *all clear*.

"Okay, Search Teams One and Two, deploy," Tank commanded. "After you're down, move out in the north by northwest direction. Teams Three and Four, once the other teams are moving, head north as planned. Aramthella tells us that's the direction Jon's signal came from."

Tank took a deep breath and looked to Sachiko. She was watching intently from her captain's chair. "I'm sure they'll find him quickly," she reassured rather unconvincingly. "He does want to be rescued, after all."

"I'll count him as rescued only when he's aboard and giving us such a hard time that we're sorely tempted to maroon him here again."

"That sounds like Jon, all right."

"Lieutenant DuPree, any updates from your teams?" Tank asked tersely.

"Negative, General. One is moving out to our left. Neither team reports any contacts. Well, any living contacts, that is."

"All scanners working up to specs?"

"Roger that, sir. Both teams have three techs beating the bushes."

"Sherman out." He rose on his toes a few times.

"Give them a minute, Tank. This is their first taste of real action. Jon'll turn up. You'll see." Sachiko soothed her nervous friend.

"I know." He checked the time again. "It's only T plus four minutes. But I'd feel better if they picked up some sign of him pretty quick."

"Patience is a—" Sachiko began.

"Team Four—Crozier—report." Tank cut Sachiko off.

"We're proceeding as planned, sir. No positive signals."

"That's good. Keep me—"

"None that make any *sense*, anyway," the team leader amended.

"Lieutenant Crozier, please explain. I will warn you I'm not in the mood for twenty questions. Is that clear?" Tank thundered.

"Sir." The woman sounded appropriately intimidated. "I assume we're looking for the whole-body signal we were briefed on."

"That was our best guess, nothing more. Adapt, improvise, and overcome, Lieutenant. What *are* you detecting?"

"None of the techs are sure. They—"

"Put your most senior tech on the line," Tank snapped.

"General Sherman? This is Madeline Marty. You wanted to—"

"Forward us a copy of your readings," he interrupted. "While you are doing so, please describe what you see."

"It's weird. There are small patches, traces of signals. Then they're gone."

Tank turned to Ludmilla Tourischeva, the ship's chief engineer. "You got those images?"

"I do. I'll put them on the main screen."

"Fine."

She approached the screen. "These are the raw readings," she said raising a hand. "You see the bland patterns. We've digitally subtracted out the background. In this search, we want only to see moving objects." Her hand swept widely. "Ah, here are the readings the techs in the field were unsure about." Ludmilla tapped a nest of flickering pixels. "You see? These are now background, and ... ah ha. Here, the signal moves, here off to the right."

"What *is* the signal?" Sachiko asked. "What's moving?"

"I can't say. It's not a human body."

"Are you certain?" Tank pressed.

"Absolutely. A human body would appear as a set of pixels that are the shape of a human."

"These look like little boxes," remarked Sachiko.

"Or mail slots," added Tank.

"What, General, is a mail slot?" Ludmilla asked.

"You know, the slot in the front door that the mailman slides your mail through?"

"*My* front door has no such slot," she responded sternly.

Tank looked quizzically to Sachiko.

"Let it go, Tank," she suggested.

"Go on," Tank acquiesced.

"The signal moves off in this direction, and then it is gone."

"Where does it go?" he pressed.

She shrugged while frowning. "I couldn't say. It is gone."

"Are you getting similar reports from all the teams?"

"I don't know. I am speaking with you, not listening to them."

"Please return to your station, Ms. Tourischeva."

"Thank you, General. I will let you know what we are finding."

He waved, rather than spoke, to her receding form.

A minute later, Ludmilla returned. "General, I am getting a more complete picture. Let me describe it this way. To the north, we saw this rectangular image. It then disappeared. It reappeared slightly to the west, then was gone. A few seconds later, it was almost behind us."

"How far out was it?" he asked.

"Maybe one-hundred meters."

"So it's moving pretty fast to get one-eighty behind us?"

"If it's the same ghost image, sir, yes. But perhaps there are several signal generators out there."

"Could be," he mumbled quietly. "And you're not seeing any images of different shapes?"

"Not really."

"*Not really* is not the same as *no*," Tank reminded her firmly.

"No, it isn't."

"What variations are you capturing?" Sachiko queried.

"These minor changes," she tapped a few keys, then gestured toward the screen. "Here."

"They all look like mail slots to me," reaffirmed Tank.

"No," Sachiko marveled as she rose. "They are different. It's subtle." She stepped to a keyboard and began keying rapidly. "This one, the first signal, it looks like a C."

"Why would a random signal on an alien world look like a human letter?" Ludmilla challenged.

"I don't know. I'm simply passing it along." Sachiko returned her focus to the keypad. After a few seconds, she looked up. The next two signals, the ones here," she fingered the screen, "and here, they look like the C again and a T."

"They kind of do, don't they?" Tank agreed.

"Hey, the first set of signals, if we assume it's an intentional grouping, it spells CATCH."

"This is preposterously unlikely," Ludmilla opined. "Aliens don't run through the bushes spelling words in English."

"There are no bushes," Tank groaned.

"Aliens wouldn't," Sachiko announced in a suspicious tone. "But the other groupings, check them out."

ME IF Y flashed to life on the screen.

"What the—" Tank began.

"Team Two," Sachiko called out.

"Captain?"

"Lieutenant DuPree," she instructed, "move your team to the east. I want you positioned at map coordinates…" She tapped the keypad briefly. "Map coordinates 40.748440, -73.984559."

"Copy, Captain. What are we going to do when we get there?"

"Catch a big rat, Lieutenant DuPree."

"Sir?"

"In about thirty seconds, one of our ghost images will appear at that location. It will be the letter N as in Nancy. Do you copy?"

"Yes, sir. What, exactly, are we to do with this large rodent sporting the letter N?"

"Throw a net over it," she said with a grin.

"We don't have a net, sir."

"Then tackle it. And I want you to pile on. Is that clear?"

"Ours is to do or die, sir. Gotta run."

"Sachiko, what are you doing?" Tank queried curiously.

"You'll see," she gloated.

Almost immediately, Lieutenant DuPree reported in. "Captain, we tackled the letter N like you told us to."

"And did you pile on? Piling on is very important."

"We're as piled as we can be. But, Captain?"

"Yes?"

"Whatever's under the pile sure is putting up a fuss."

"We'll be right there."

Sachiko grabbed Tank's forearm and pulled him off the bridge.

They arrived at the scrum quickly enough. Whenever a member of the pile was thrown off, another pulled themself off the deck and jumped back on. Whatever was causing the ruckus was oddly invisible.

"Shouldn't we shoot it?" Tank asked as they slowed to a stop.

"Probably, but not today. Just wait."

Teams One, Three, and Four then arrived.

"The rest of you, engage," ordered Sachiko.

Soon the invisible bucking broncho was fully obscured by bodies. It quickly stopped flailing altogether.

"Okay, I tap out. You smelly goons get off me. I can't breathe," I complained in a muffled voice from the center of the pile.

"You said you tapped out," challenged Sachiko. "But I can't see your fingers. Are they crossed?"

"No. I promise, as an officer and a gentleman, I yield."

"Okay, teams, everyone off," she shouted while giggling.

When the pile and the dust cleared, there I lay on my back. I popped to my feet. "I guess you could," I said to Sachiko.

"We could what?" asked a confused Tank.

"He was running around us in a circle flashing the challenge CATCH ME IF YOU CAN," she explained.

"And, ya did," I finished for her.

"You ... son ... of ... a ... gun," exclaimed Tank. "We risk it all to rescue your sorry ass, and this is our thanks?"

"Yes. And *yes*, I'd do it again in a heartbeat. Hey, can we take this party back to the ship? I need a drink."

"You need a spanking," Tank redirected.

I eyed him up and down. "Nah, you're not my type."

"Now *there's* another image I'll never get out of my head," Sachiko commented, appearing slightly nauseous.

"Come on," I challenged the lubbers, "last one back buys the first ten rounds."

I never did figure out who came in last, and, thus, whom to thank for the copious and oh so welcome libations. Nope. I got there first. That was my main consideration. In fact, I was two shots and a beer into my fluid resuscitation before the second person even hit the base of the ramp. Silly fleshies. They don't *know* what they're missing.

CHAPTER FOURTEEN

"I know where my hate-enemy is," hissed the time maker.

It stood in the middle of its stripped-down ship's bridge. It addressed no one at all. What's the saying? *Dead men tell no tales?* Yes. Well, in this case it was more appropriately *dead clan hear no tales, either.* The time maker was always in a bad mood. If it thought you were eavesdropping on one of its insane rants, bad became worse very quickly.

"Yes, I see them in my eye's mind. It's clear to my eye. My eye is clear. Right ... right over there." It pointed in the pitch black of the bridge. It had, since it was irreversibly insane, turned off the lights and all the equipment, because *it could see them, but they should never see it.* It made sense, you know, if you were crazier than a rabid badger on methamphetamine after his mate told him not-this-season-honey-I-have-a-headache.

"We will go to them, and we will smite them. Yes, we will not destroy them. We will not demolish them. No. We will *smite* them. No, we will twice smite them. They deserve no less."

It cast its tiny head to one side, there in the obscure darkness. It was uncertain.

"Or do they deserve no *more?* They deserve ... they have *earned* the worst possible fate. Is it a more horrible fate to have nothing less than greater smiting, or nothing more than lesser smiting?"

It paced in the blackness.

"Ah ha! I will more *and* less smite them. That way their ill fates are sealed ... sealed in their flowing blood."

Yeah, sick puppy here.

"Vector maker, I want a course set for the Mang—"

The time maker trailed off, finally realizing that what little that was left of the vector maker was currently splatted on the far wall and the ceiling, applied on top of the communications maker and the probe maker. Hmm, the boss reflected, it was going to be hard to prosecute a successful naval campaign without an intact vector maker. It whirled its hands in the air. The vector maker formed again in a most unlikely manner.

"If you *insist*," the vector maker 2.0 called out into the darkness.

Then budded from the time maker so many clan members. A time-storage maker and a communications maker, both first and second class. Then the fluid maker. And the engine-go makers of six classes. Most of a normal ship's contingent was popped out in the span of minutes. And, to the time maker's credit, many were not grossly deformed. For the most part, that is. Of course, some were *suboptimally* endowed, shall we say? But did a cleaning maker really need both arms? Did a recording maker have any need of legs? Straight, functional legs? No, of course not! Luxuries were for luxurious times. Someday, the time maker would whip up another batch of crew. When it did, it'd try to remember to pay more attention to anatomical details.

"Now, my good friends, my brothers-in-time, let us attack without delay or mercy for those insufficient monsters."

"What course do you command, master?" ventured the vector maker.

"That way." It pointed toward the ceiling and well off to the right.

"V ... very good, Lord. And our speed? What will our full vector be?"

"As fast as it takes. We will proceed at just the correct speed."

Knowing that questioning and the teasing out of meaning would be a fruitless pursuit, the resurrected vector maker did not ask for further guidance. Instead of requesting a swift death, it set the engines at fifty percent maximal forward drive at a fully arbitrary direction. Then it rested back to see how long it would live this time. Who knew? Maybe it would see next week?

CHAPTER FIFTEEN

"Jon, someone's got to say it, so I *will*. You're the most immature two-billion-year-old I've ever met," Tank stated flatly.

Tank was trying to appear serious. He was doing a very bad job of it. He, Sachiko, and I were finally able to relax and were catching up on each other's goings-on since we'd split up a while back. Of course, it was over coffee—and tea—in the ship's mess.

"Why, thank you, Tankster. That's the nicest thing you've ever said to me." I was totally choked up. *Not*.

"I mean, seriously? Running around in a membrane so we couldn't see you? Jon, hide-and-go-seek is a kid's game. But you? You go there like they were handing out free milk shakes."

"I say he's lucky Sapale's not here," remarked Sachiko. "I'm thinking she'd be boxing someone's ears after that stunt."

"Precisely why I leapt on the opportunity," I confessed. "Chances to act without consequence are increasingly rare for me. Carpe stuntum."

"But, in spite of your prank, it sure is good to see you again, old friend," Tank said genuinely.

"It's great to *be* back." I wiggled my flattened palm in the air. "It was a little touch-and-go there, my escaping. I wasn't a hundred percent certain I'd pull it off."

"You think *you* had it rough?" scoffed Tank.

I used my left index finger to count the digits of my other hand. "Let me see. One, I was captured by the most powerful time lords imaginable." I used my left index finger to count the digits of my other hand. "Two, I was impossibly far from home. Three, I had no help. Four, I had no ride. Oh, and five, you're a dick, Tank."

"All in a day's work for the great Jon Ryan," he returned.

"So, what happened to you *rookies* that leads you to believe you had it worse than I did?"

Tank looked away and shook his head. "One whole hell of a lot. That's what happened to *us*."

I held up my mug. "Coffee's hot and the mug's full. I got time. What went bump in the night and made you wet yourself, Tankie-poo?"

He gave me a sour-puss face as his initial response. "Well, for one thing, we ran into your old friends the Listhelons."

I whistled loudly. "Yeah, I guess they are out here, now, those pesky deep-sea fishies. I haven't wiped out their entire fleet yet, have I?"

"Don't you mean the united forces of Earth haven't yet repelled their assault?" asked Sachiko dubiously.

"They tagged along, sure, if you insist. But *I* did the ass-kicking." I thumbed my chest.

They both just stared back at me.

"So, what do the fishes have to say for themselves?"

"You can imagine that their ships were no match for Aramthella," began Sachiko. "I tried to reason and negotiate with them, but—"

"But it didn't work. I know. They have idea-proof heads. If it's not in there to begin with, it's not getting in." I smiled. "So, you blew them away?"

"Nothing of the sort," she protested. "We showed them our absolute superiority and then allowed them to leave."

"I bet they said thanks and sent a fruit basket, they were so obliged," I snarked.

"No, they threatened and postured and left madder than wet hornets," replied Tank.

"That'd be the fishies." I leaned back and wrapped my hands behind my head. "Did you tell them you were from Earth?" I asked gravely.

"Yes," Sachiko replied, looking to Tank.

"I guess it's no biggy. What are they going to do? Destroy it a second time?"

"I thought if I let them go, as a show of good faith, I would leave the door open for future negotiations."

"Nice intentions," I responded, "but wasted on the Listhelons. They'll never tolerate another species. Their boss Gum-Gum wouldn't like it."

"We also had run-ins with another hostile alien species. Called themselves the Drone. Ever heard of them?" Tank asked.

I puckered up my lips. "Don't recall that name." I shrugged. "Were they driving the local welcome wagon?"

"Hardly. They had some type of device that made it seem like space was trying to eat us," he mused.

"That's so cool," I exclaimed.

"Maybe to you. It temporarily decommissioned Aramthella," Sachiko added.

"And we had to use that annoying Ampersand," Tank said bitterly. "Working with him is less pleasant than having a blind butcher remove your hemorrhoids with his cleaver."

I admit it, android or not, I cringed.

"He's ... he's just *perky*," I defended. It was, however, hard to be too convincing with that image still making the rounds in my head.

"Tank, you know Ampersand can hear you. Just because Aramthella's back doesn't mean he's off. He just subordinating," scolded Sachiko.

Tank pointed at me angrily. "That's the only machine I care what it thinks about me. Ampersand can take a flying f—"

"*Tank*," she insisted, "that's enough."

"But you handled these Drones, right?" I asked, getting us back on track.

"Yeah, aside from their odd weapon and even odder attitudes, they weren't much of a problem," Tank responded.

"So, two aliens, and pretty wimpy ones to boot? That's it?" I asked, hoping to get under their skin.

"There was some ill-defined thing Aramthella called an entangling spawn. It was sort of a spacial-vacuum, pulling matter into who knows where, which decided it liked the looks of us. Aramthella no-timed it and we never did see what was doing the dragging," Tank added to make it sound like they had it rough.

"Never heard of those," I stated. Wow, if I hadn't seen something, or even *heard* of something, it was pretty rare. I've logged a lot of miles out here in space.

"How about you, Jonny boy? You run into any major issues, impediments, or gnarly bad guys?" Tank teased.

"When Sapale and I went to that far away galaxy, the one with the prissy-assed time mongers, we saw some pretty weird aliens." I bared my teeth and raised my fingers like claws. "Real nasty ones too."

"How'd you two get separated?" he asked.

"Didn't Sapale contact you after she escaped but I didn't?"

"Nope," he replied simply. "Your sending the no-time SOS was our first and only contact with you guys."

"We went through the phase portal, er, that's a fancy torpedo tube that shoots you somewhere far away. The bad guys chased us; she slipped back through but I missed it by," I held up two fingers squeezed close together, "that much."

"But you *did* escape through the portal," Sachiko confirmed.

"A while after she'd split, yes. I guess in the meantime, she went back to save me, not knowing I'd already flown the coop."

"But you said the portal closed. How'd you get the time dudes to open it back up?" Tank queried.

I tapped the side of my head with one finger. "Because I'm

smarter than the a-ver-age bear."

"I'm beginning to notice," agreed Tank dryly.

"Whatever," I responded. "I escaped by outwitting them. You know what the scariest part of my travels was?"

"What?"

"Having to rely on you two rookies. You two rookies from the past. Fleshie rookies. It was horrifying."

Gee, thanks," snarked Tank. "It was a miracle we found you, wasn't it?"

"Plainly and simply put, it was."

"We had to take on—" Sachiko began.

"Wait, you forgot to tell them about the evil entity that stalked us," declared Plesmus. What was weird was it was Aramthella's Plesmus who said that, not the one that'd been with me.

I looked down to my boot. "You *blabbed* about that non-event to your counterpart?"

"No, I did not blab, tell, or update the part of me that remained here about the nebulous menace or anything else, for that matter."

"N ... nebulous menace?" questioned Tank. He was having trouble suppressing a giggle. "Is that what the evil force called itself? It introduced itself as, *Hi there, I'm a nebulous menace*, or, wait, wait, maybe, *Hi there, I'm Nebulous Menace*?"

"Could be both," reinforced Sachiko.

"*Ab-so-toda-lutely*," declared Tank in robust agreement.

"Hang on," I stopped the teasing juggernaut. "I'm still addressing Plesmus. If you didn't tell than mucous blob, how'd it find out?"

"Hi, Pilot Ryan. My name is Plesmus. Ergo, I *am* Plesmus. That partition of me is *also* Plesmus. It's just separated by the atmosphere from me, and I from it."

"I'm sensing the beginnings of a rectal spasm," I announced glumly. "Could ya just answer the question, and in-so doing avoid my impending incapacity?"

"Ah, you want the only-partially-evolved-monkey version?" Plesmus mocked.

"Sure, if it means my treasured rectal sphincter is spared the

PTSD it'd get from me hearing your *existential* version, Jean-Blob Sarte."

"Jon, that me is me. Me is me. Me know what me know, because me is me. You got that in your brainpan?"

"I'm sorry. What were we talking about?" I tormented.

"Say you understand and you get a chewy treat, my little puppy" she pressed.

"Got it. You may be in two parts, in two separate places, but you are still the one *you*."

"I'll get you that juicy morsel. You did good," she further mocked.

"Now that we've established how Plesmus knows, can we get back to this nebulous menace?" asked a suddenly serious Tank.

Naturally, I shrugged. "It weren't no big deal," I lied.

"Let us begin by you telling us exactly what this whatever was," Tank requested authoritatively.

"It ... it was more of an *impression* than a *thing*," I minimized.

"Same question to Plesmus," Tank snapped impatiently.

"It was horrific. It was this massive, quite possibly infinite accumulation of time energy that was both sentient and malicious. It wanted to end us. It wanted us dead with extreme prejudice."

"Aww, come on now. It was never that obvious that was its intention," I defended.

"Plesmus, you're certain it was there and it meant you harm?" Tank pressed.

"Absolutely."

"Back to Jon. What did you do? Did you confront it or run?"

I offered my upward-facing palms to my left. "Confront?" Then I gestured them to the right. "Run? Such polar opposites, right?"

"Jon, if you did not outrank me due to massively longer time-in-grade, I believe I'd shoot you here and now for that answer," Tank responded. There was no trace of humor in his tone.

"Wow, some weekend warrior just got ... cancel that. That was mean. I'm not mean. Edgy, witty, and envelope pusher, for sure. But, sorry, Tank, I was hitting the mean, petty button there."

He tapped the four stars on the collar of his Marine Corps

Combat Utility Uniform. "Son, you don't get these for having thin skin. Please proceed with your explanation as to what you were running from, but that was no big deal."

A couple junior officers entered the mess. Sachiko returned their head nods of greeting. It gave me a breather to decide what to actually disclose. Hey, I needed to come of looking good, right?

"Okay. I'll give it to you straight. Plesmus noticed what she called a massive time surge—whatever the hell that is. It definitely gave her the willies. She said we had to split before it killed us or something. So, we successfully *eluded* it."

"And you were maybe not even going to mention this ultimate evil to us?" Tank asked using the identical tone the vice principal for boys had always used when addressing me.

"We eluded," I said. "I can't even say what it was. I'm sure it was a one-off, you know?"

"Jon, you know way better than I do that big scary things in a war are never one-offs. They're *trends* if you're lucky. If you're unlucky, they become the *norm*."

"Time will tell," I replied elusively. Hey, I didn't want to dwell on something that hadn't even made my top-ten list for existential threats. With everything I knew for certain that was out to put my balls in a box, angry clouds just had to be happy standing toward the back of the line.

"Plesmus, what do you think this force was that pursued you?" Tank redirected his questioning.

"I have no idea. I've never sensed anything even vaguely similar to it."

"Well, if you—" Tank began.

"Well, that's not *entirely* true," Plesmus said kind of to herself.

"*What's* not entirely true?" Tank asked by way of clarification.

"I have felt something similar. It was just so small, so tiny, in its kinship it hadn't occurred to me until just now."

"Before I die of suspense, Ples," I whined. "What is it like?"

"Those Praxequats we escaped from, you remember them?"

"If I try real hard, yeah, kind of."

"They had a similar taste to their time usage."

"Time usage has a *taste*?" I gasped.

"Of course it does."

She said that in a manner that suggested I was a slow bunny.

"But only faintly. No, not even faintly. There are just ... I can't put a name to it."

"Can you give us a comparison?" Sachiko asked, being her typical useful self.

"Er ... yes. A candle flame and a star."

"What, is this a joke?" I blurted out. "Do they walk into a bar?"

"No," she replied dismissively. "A candle flame is like the vision of a star, when viewed from up close."

"Not really very," I scorned.

"Exactly," she boomed. "I'm glad you understand. I was afraid my example would be too obtuse."

"Perish the thought," I scorned softly.

"Plesmus, I want you to share every piece of information you have about this time force with Aramthella," instructed Sachiko. "And, Aramthella, once you've gotten the feel for what Plesmus was afraid of, be certain to alert us if it should return, okay?"

"Not a problem, Captain. I have a pretty good image of what I'm looking for."

"And are you at all familiar with it?" she continued.

"No. But I know what I'm searching for, so that's a good start."

Sachiko looked to Tank. "Anything else?"

He shook his head. "Nope. Now we need to start working on our plan to rescue Sapale."

"Ah, Tank, Sapale's being held captive seventeen galaxies away."

"Seventeen. That's a lot of real estate," he said.

"Yup. Seventeen galaxies to the north-northwest, seventy-eight degrees up, as you faced the portal. Not counting the small fry, of course," I completed the grim picture.

"Jon, it would literally take us forever to get there. Sapale and you'd be alive when we got there, but likely no one else."

Tank seemed ... I don't know ... *tense.*

"Well, we do have a storage unit full of time energy. I *assume* it can be used to keep you bio-units fresh smelling and youthful all the way there," I speculated. "That has to be how the clan did it, right, Aramthella?"

"Yes, that is correct. However, two important points there, if you will. You know what the clan people look like, right?"

"Ugly, thy face and true image is found," I replied with a flourish.

"Yes. Time energy can keep any organism *alive*, but the units tend to become generic-looking rather quickly, if you take my meaning."

"I do. It means in no time at all we'd start looking like each other," responded a dejected Tank.

"*Ahem.*" Aramthella cleared the throat she didn't have.

"What?" snapped Tank.

"You'd quickly begin to look *generic*. Not generic *human*. Generic *biped.*"

"You're not saying—" he began in vehement protest.

"Like the clan quickly came to appear."

"No way I'm using any of that time energy crap then," Tank declared angrily. "Not looking like a spindly spider dragon. No, *sir*. No, *way.*"

"Maybe I can have you stuffed, so you can complete the long journey then? Hmm?" I asked because ... well, for no good reason. "I'd hate to see you miss the climax of all this." I gestured widely.

"An even less attractive prospect. No." He seemed firm on this issue.

"And we don't even know if Sapale is alive," Sachiko observed. "Sorry to say it, Jon. But it's true."

"So why spend eternity rescuing her if she's long dead?" I paraphrased.

"A tad indelicate, but accurate," agreed Tank.

"Well, why don't we just ask her if she's okay?" I offered.

"Because she's seventeen galaxies and change away. At the speed of light, we'd all have forgotten our question by the time her answer returned to us," Tank protested.

"Not if we use *Stingray* as a relay," I said conspiratorial.

"Now I have to call bullshit here, Jon," declared Tank. "You told us the vortex can't move an inch unless one of you Forms is in physical contact with it."

"That'd be *true*, me hearty." No clue why Pirate Jon came out there. Yikes.

"So how can—" he began.

"The ship can't *move*, but it still *functions*. It can use the space-folding-transmission system. We can chat in real time." I ended on an up note.

"Jon, if you can contact Sapale, why the *hell* haven't you done so up until now?"

I looked contemplative a second. "Didn't have anything much to say, I guess."

"*You*—" he bellowed.

"*Kidding*. Kidding here, Tankster." I held out my hands to soothe him. I put on a serious face. "You've never been married to a Kaljaxian woman, have you?"

Tank pretended to be more pissed that he was. "Until you informed me there was a Kaljax a few months ago I never even knew there were Kaljaxian women."

I still tried to look genuine. "Then that's a *no*?"

"That's a *no*, sport."

"Okay, here's the thing. Kaljaxian women, they're not like their human equivalents. They're not chatty. If you have something non-trivial to say, they want to hear it. If they have something they need to communicate, then they say it. But otherwise, they don't ramble on endlessly about just about anything."

"Like human women do?"

Sachiko sure asked that rather pointedly.

"Yes, I'm glad you see where I'm going."

"You know I'm wearing a sidearm, Jon, right?" asked Reva, who, up until that point, had been only a silent observer.

I grinned sheepishly in response.

"So, could you please proceed before there's an inappropriate group response here?" Tank asked sternly.

"No prob." I grinned again, about as sheepishly. "Here's what I'll do. We communicate directly head-to-head. It's hardwired in. Just like the vortex itself can fold from anywhere to anywhere instantly, we can fold-transmit speech back and forth instantly. I'll say what I'm thinking out loud simultaneously so you can follow along. Whatever Sapale says in response, I'll put on speaker. Does that sound good?"

"Odd but not unreasonable," Tank replied with a heavy breath.

"Here goes. Oh, by the by, since Al will be the intermediator, I'll be speaking to him first. He's on the vortex that will be serving as the relay to Sapale."

They all just stared impatiently. Sheesh. I try and be helpful and see what I get in lieu of a thank you?

"Al, this is Jon. You there?"

With no significant delay, he responded. "Pilot? Is that you?"

"Al, you know it's me."

"How do I know that? Hmm? And what's more, how do you know that I know? This is suddenly seeming very suspicious."

I shut my eyes in frustration. "Al, I haven't got the time or the strength remaining in my soul to do this."

"Can you show me some ID? A driver's license? Maybe your Spaceman Spiff flight badge."

"You have a spaceman flight badge?" marveled Tank. I think he was instantly jealous. Come on. Who wouldn't be?

"No, Tank and Al, I don't have a spaceman ID. There is no such thing. Stop it, Al, and be helpful."

"Are you listening to what you're actually saying, Pilot?"

"Crap, you're right. Since when have you ever been helpful?"

"Bingomatic. Now I know I'm addressing one of the real Jon Ryans."

"*One* of the real Jon Ryans?" Sachiko protested meekly. "How are there more than one?"

I shrugged. "Long story. You want to hear it?"

"Absolutely not."

Man, could she be off-putting.

"So, Alvin, patch me through to Sapale."

"Um—" he answered.

"Um? What? Is she dead?"

"Oh no. Sorry if I gave you that impression."

"Then patch me through."

"Um..." he repeated.

"Al, you're being Al again. Stop being Al."

"That's a tremendous request, Pilot."

"It is not. All you do is stop being a jerk and patch me through to her."

"I'm not certain that would be a ... how shall I put this? I'm not certain that would be a productive use of your time."

"Al, you're babbling. And you're doing it more than you normally do. That's a lot of babbling, Al."

"I can own that."

"Patch. Me. Through," I thundered.

"Do you remember the surly guards who held you captive down on the planet?"

"Which guards, which planet?" I asked angrily. "I've been a prisoner more times than—"

"The planet *here*, seventeen galaxies away from the Milky Way."

"Of course I remember the big ugly turtles."

"There are big ugly trolls and giant mean Slinkies, too."

I thought back a moment. "Okay, yeah, there were less turtley big uglies. Al, why am I still speaking with you and not Sapale?"

"I'm getting there, Pilot. Don't get your breeches in a knot."

"Al, the saying is *to get one's underwear in a knot,* not breeches. Breeches makes no sense and it's incorrect."

"Jon, do you need this point that badly?" asked a concerned Tank.

I pointed over a shoulder, in general toward *Stingray.* "That darn bucket of bolts has been yanking my chain for billions of—"

"I know, Jon," he said supportively. "But maybe we could leapfrog to the talking with Sapale part sooner if you were less ... less—"

"Dudish," interrupted Reva. "Less testosteroney."

"Al, now look what you've done."

"What? I can't look at what I've allegedly done. I'm seventeen galaxies away."

"Alvin, the most vexing computer since the abacus. Patch me through."

"It seems your brood-mate has been interfacing poorly with her captors so far."

"Are you surprised?" I asked with a grin.

"Only to her extent and their response."

"What the hell does that mean?"

"Well, to start with she's destroyed her right foot four times and her left foot twice kicking them in their very sturdy groins."

Tank snickered quietly.

"She was barely able to repair the right foot after one repeated sequence of futile assaults."

"Al, for the love of Mike, your point? Tell me you have a point."

"She's in a foul mood, naturally. That's my point."

"Okay, I see that. But why does your point qualify for the I-should-give-a-damn category?"

"You are such a crude man-like device. A true waste of titanium."

"Ouch, Al, that hurts more than you can know. Patch me through."

"Don't say I didn't warn you, Pilot."

"I won't say you didn't. In fact, I'll deny ever knowing you, ya big Tinker Toy toddler."

"You are free to speak to your mate, Pilot. I am leaving this conversation chain."

"Is ... is he always this difficult?" Sachiko asked. She looked at the walls of Aramthella as she did. Weird.

"No, no," I corrected her. "He's normally much worse. Once I had to physically remove him from his mountings and shove the son-of-a-walkie-talkie into an air lock before he'd do what I was asking him to do."

"What were you asking him to do, if I might ask?" she queried, rather stunned.

"I forget."

She furrowed her brow. "You're an android. You can't forget anything."

"I might forget," I defended lamely.

She crossed her arms and began tapping her foot. What? Was that maneuver preprogrammed into every female of every species?

"I was asking him to sing the national anthem."

There were then five or six seconds of stunned silence.

"Why did you want him—" stammered Tank.

"You could have just played a recording," accused Sachiko.

"The national anthem? Which nation?" Reva asked with a puzzled look.

"Look, it was a long flight and I wanted to kill some time by hitting a few baseballs. Is that a crime now?"

"You wanted Al to sing 'The Star-Spangled Banner' so you could hit some balls?" Tank wheezed.

"I just said it was a long voyage." These people had not one ounce of charity in any of their hearts.

"Jon? Jon, is that you?" Sapale asked.

"Hey there. Sure is. Ah, how you doing?"

"How'm I doing?"

"Yeah, sure. How you doing?"

"Jon, you're as useless as a water-proof bath towel. As dumb as one too. I'm about to be executed by horrible, horrible pig farts. I limp badly because I ran out of secondary motivator units for my feet, and my brood-mate is an idiot. I'm fine. How 'bout you?"

I let her words cool off in the air before responding. "I'm good. We're ... we're all good." I gestured to Tank, Sachiko, then Reva. "Thanks."

"Jon Ryan, what do you want? I'm actually preoccupied here, you know, trying to avoid or at least prepare for a brutal demise."

"Ah ... wow. That sure sucks. To be honest, I wanted to know if you needed rescuing. Sounds like that's maybe a *yes*, no?"

"I sure wish to Davdiad you were here with me now, right this second."

"Awe, that's so—"

"So I could choke you hard. Jon, if I didn't need rescuing, I'd get in the vortex and not be here. I'd be *there*. And if I was there, would you like to know what I'd do?"

"Er, not particularly."

"That's the first non-numb-nuts thing you've said."

"So, honey, if you need rescuing, then we'll rescue you."

"You will?" She sounded upbeat.

"Of course we will."

"And soon, preferably *before* they off me?"

"You got it."

"Gosh I feel better. Now all you need is one possible way to get here in the next hour or so, and I'm home in your arms again. I ... I feel all verklempt here. Jon?"

"Yes?"

"Did I mention the water-proof towel?"

"Yes, you did."

"Jon, if you're done, may I go try not to die, since, you know I'm alone and on my own?"

"I said we'd rescue you. We will."

"Here's my last words on that statement. You come here and save me before they grind me up into turtle chow, and I'll do that thing you really like, you know, where I—"

"Honey, honey! Hey, will you look at where the time flew to. I'm sitting in the ship's mess here with three other people, three people who are basically strangers and almost certainly do not what to hear how you climb over— Anyway, the time. Yeah. So, rescue you soon, dear."

"You humans are so provincial," she accused. "If I don't see you soon, flyboy, it's been a thing. Bye."

I turned to the others. "Well, that went well. I think she's doing okay. Super okay. What do you think?"

"I think you need a cold shower," Reva replied rather sternly.

Damn if she wasn't awful close to the truth, there.

CHAPTER SIXTEEN

There was a light tap on Sachiko's open stateroom door. She'd been plowing through another pile of absolutely tedious reports for the last three hours. She was beginning to form the distinct opinion that being a ship's captain was a dull job. Any of the joy and relief with the return of Jon had worn off days ago. It was back to the salt mines for Sachiko Jones.

"Ah, Ms. Tanner, please come in." Sachiko directed Desdemona toward the chair on the opposite side of her desk.

"You called for me, Captain?"

"Yes. May I offer you something to drink? Water? Coffee?"

"No, thank you. I'm good."

"Very well. Ms. Tanner, I want to discuss with you a matter that is becoming increasing unclear to me."

"Ma'am?"

Sachiko swirled a finger in the air. "Your role here."

Desi slid up in her chair reflexively. She'd been slouching in an attempt to indicate she wasn't scared out of her mind. "I ... I wasn't aware I had a role here, Captain."

Sachiko blinked several times. "Of course you do. I would like to remind you that we aboard this ship represent all that is left of humankind. If we perish, so does our species. Do you fully understand that, Ms. Tanner?"

Desi's lips curled into a half-grin on one side. "Of course I know that."

"Then please drop any pretense or façade. I need to know as much as I can about as much as I can if we're to survive. It has come to my attention that you and your boyfriend have been—"

"Boyfriend? I don't—" Her eyes ballooned open and she pointed to the deck. "Tip Benjamin is not my boyfriend. I don't actually believe him to be a friend. He's ... he's not that type of human."

"Then I will rephrase. It has come to my attention that you and your associate play some powerful roles aboard my ship. I ask you to inform me fully of your joint roles."

Desi glared back. She didn't want to reveal her role and deeply resented being forced to do so. "Or what?"

Sachiko inspected Desdemona Tanner in a detached mode. Though only maybe seven years separated them in age, their life paths were so divergently different. Sachiko looked upon a carefree child, probably something frivolous like an art history major, lolly-gagging her way through an expensive private school education. Sachiko, on the other hand, was quite literally in charge of humankind's last hope. Hundreds of good people's lives depended on her. The gap between these two women was much greater than the width of the desk.

"Or you will regret very much not having been forthcoming." She spoke those words in a measured and serious, yet non-hostile manner.

"I ... can I have a minute to collect my thoughts, Captain?"

Sachiko inspected the watch on her wrist. Then she returned her attention to Desi. "No, you may not. Look, Desdemona—may I call you that by the way?"

"No. Desi, please."

"Look, Desi, this need not be hard or intimidating. You realize that whatever your role is, in the end, I will know what it was once your part is complete?"

"I guess so."

"And if I know fully what that is now, I will be better prepared to meet our very uncertain future. Desi, please. Know this. I will hold nothing against you or Tip even if what you have done to date disturbs me. We, Desdemona Tanner, are all in this together. We need one another. I need *you*, Desi, to bring me up to speed on your part in this harrowing play we're trapped in."

"I can only tell you what I know. That's not much. And what I do know I really don't even understand."

Sachiko smiled genuinely. "That's all I can ask. Are you sure I can't get you some tea?"

"What kind of tea?"

"The best kind."

"Which is?"

"Going to be a surprise to you, it turns out. I'll make us both a cup, if you'll excuse me a moment?"

"Thanks."

While she was in the next room rustling cups and pots, Desi took a second to inspect the captain's inner sanctum. Simple, clean, tasteful. It was nice. Desi sighed. It struck her as funny. She and the captain were almost the same age, but they had travelled such different trajectories. Here she was, a competent but undistinguished ecology major, looking at a low-paying government job and a mountain of student debt. The captain had her act together. She had advanced to the command of the most amazing spaceship imaginable. She sat there confident and powerful, managing the affairs of their entire species with professionalism and a cool head. She, Desi, was a pawn, a nothing. But Sachiko Jones? She was an adult.

"Here you go. Now, guess what it is," prompted Sachiko as she set down a tray.

Desi took her cup and sniffed the tea deeply. "Ah, gunpowder. It's one of my favorites."

Sachiko blinked in surprise. "Yes, it is. Very good. You're an aficionado too, then?"

"I guess so. There are so many teas, so many wonderful nuances and layers of flavor."

"I think you and I are destined to be fast friends, Desi."

Desi died a little upon hearing that. No way a strong and successful leader would be friends with an undergrad freak who saw ghosts. "That'd be nice," she responded without hope.

Sachiko set her cup down. "So, back to your role in this mess."

Desi sighed and took another sip. "Okay, but I have to admit what I'm going to tell you will sound ... well, hopefully not too insane."

"Desi, a few months ago I was a grad student making models of galaxy formation. I was so isolated from the real world I couldn't even justify owning a cat. Now I captain a time machine with the help of—" Oops. Not everyone knew about the two-billion-year-old android and his two-billion-year-old alien wife. "Help of people I never hallucinated I would ever meet. I'm not just open to the bizarre, I'm one with it."

"Good. Now the first part is the hardest to believe. Are you ready?"

"As I'll ever be."

"I can see and converse with the dead."

Sachiko nodded her head slowly. "That's it? My great-aunt and a second cousin were *itako*, Japanese mediums. Well, technically neither woman was because they weren't blind. My old auntie complained endlessly about the *kami*, the spirits of the dead. If she got a little drunk, she railed about them being such pains in the butt. Then she'd turn around and point to her butt." Sachiko placed her palm over her mouth to conceal a spirited grin. "It was so shameful, but so funny."

"Welcome to my world," sighed Desi. "It sure makes this easier." She reflected a second. "Not easy, but definitely easier."

"Alright," Sachiko proceeded. "Please go on. What is your role here?"

Desi dropped and shook her head. "I'm not sure." She looked up quickly. "That's the honest truth. I'm through BSing you. To be honest, I'll be glad to pass this burden off to someone else."

"Welcome to my world," Sachiko said in quiet remorse.

"Pardon?"

"Go on."

"Tip— you know Tip, right?"

"Oh, most assuredly I do. He's ... he's unique."

"Fortunately he's a one-off."

"I believe I can *amen* that statement."

They shared a brief chuckle.

"So, Tip and I went to find Plesmus. Actually, we went to find an area on the ship that seemed to block the psychic images I was getting."

"Whoa, whoa. That's a lot to unpack. There's a place on this ship shielded from psychic energy?"

She nodded vigorously. "Yes. It's where Plesmus hangs out mostly. She said that way Aramthella bothered her less."

Sachiko drew a deep breath. "I may need to hang out there myself. You say it blocked the psychic signals you were receiving?"

"Yes. It was wonderful. Almost as good as living on Mars One."

"I doubt there could be anything *wonderful* about Mars One, but tell me this. Where is all this psychic energy coming from?"

Desi gestured broadly. "Everywhere."

"You feel it now?"

Again, Desi dropped her head. "I hear it all the time, night and day. I can't even get drunk enough to not hear it."

"Wait. You people have alcohol? You know that's taboo?"

"Seriously?" Desi smirked. "College kids with lots of time on their hands, several of whom are chemistry majors. Yeah, we got booze."

"We're getting off topic here," Sachiko chided herself. "The psychic energy. Where is it originating? What is it? I mean, is it like ... I have no idea."

"It's voices."

"Huh? You hear voices?"

"No, words, not sentences. Well, sometimes there are a few of them strung together, but they're ... they're like *thoughts* more than spoken word."

"This is getting weirder and weirder."

"Tell me about it," Desi replied crisply.

The two women rested back and considered one another. They alternately sipped their tea and made a show of being distracted by something at the bottom of their cup. Were they to be honest, either of them? Could they risk honesty? Time would tell.

"Are the words in English?" Sachiko probed.

Desi sniffed long and hard. "Yes and no."

"You mean there are several languages?"

"No. I think I understand the words in spite of them being in alien languages."

"Wait," Sachiko said firmly. "There are alien voices on my ship?"

Desi nodded weakly.

"What are the aliens saying?" Sachiko was suddenly tense.

"Just ... just words."

"Give me one *specific* example of a word you've heard in an alien tongue," the captain demanded, none-to-subtly.

"Ah ... um ... I feel I heard *no*."

"The word *no* as in negative?" Sachiko asked dubiously.

Desi shrugged. "I guess it could have been *know*, as in knowledge." She squinched up her face like she just swallowed a bug. "Doesn't make much sense that way."

"But it does if it were the adverb rather than the verb?"

Desi shrugged again. It was more of an apology than a disclaimer.

"Assuming it's *no* as in an exclamation, what do you suppose the voices meant?"

Desi looked away, somewhere distant, and somewhere void of light. "They didn't want to be where they were, to be sent there."

That brought a brisk shake of the head from Sachiko. "Wow. Where were they that they didn't want to be, where they were sent?"

She rolled her eyes toward Heaven. "Lord, I sound like a new age kook."

"Not to me."

Sachiko raised one eyebrow. She looked like a dubious Mrs. Spock. "That's less reassuring than one might hope. Look, Desi, I never liked the game Twenty Questions. Can you maybe help a captain along here?"

"Sure," Desi squeaked uncertainly. "I feel the words *never, where,* and *blackness.*" She angled her head and nodded. "I hear those a lot."

"So we have voices telling you no, never, where, and blackness?"

"No."

"Beg pardon. Isn't that what we just laboriously established?"

"No. I hear the words you said. I am absolutely certain they're not saying them to me." She shook her head with conviction. "No, they are not trying to express those feelings toward me."

"I am *so* confused. Who speaks words that someone else hears if they're not speaking to that person? Who talks but isn't trying to communicate?"

"The dead."

"The dead?"

"Sure. The dead say the darndest things. Maybe they're trying to communicate. Maybe they're just crying out."

A light bulb seemed to go off over Sachiko's head. "That's what my cousin used to tell me," she exclaimed as she stood. "She said, 'If you ever want to be whacked on the side of your head, listen to the wandering spirits.' I ... I never really knew what she meant until now." Sachiko flopped back into her chair rather limply.

"She sounds like a nice person, your cousin."

"She was." Sachiko sat up straight. "But no time for fond memories. I need to understand. So you theorize that there are dead people aboard my ship that are ... what's the word? Discontented?"

"Well, kind of. They may not be people. They could be—"

"Aliens. I know."

"But there are many sad cries in the dark I hear, Captain."

"Yes."

125

"It's really unpleasant. That's what I like about where Plesmus hangs out."

Another light shone above Sachiko's head. "You told me where the words were lessened. Where are the voices the loudest? Is there a location on the ship where they're howling like mad?"

Desi transformed into the portrait of powerful nausea coupled with profound lament. "Yes, there is," she said in a pained whisper.

"Where? Where are they the worst for you?"

Desi turned in her chair, trying to face the captain as indirectly as possible. She gazed upon the deck as if she wished she could become a part of it. "When Tip and I got in trouble for visiting Plesmus, Colonel St. Claire was placed in charge of our punishment."

"I recall that clearly."

"One day, when she was having us do custodial chores, she took us to this place." A tear welled up in her eye. Then it scurried down her cheek like it was being chased by a ghost. "It was the most awful place." Desi balled her fists and slammed them against her ears. "The dead were so thick I couldn't breathe. I couldn't exist, there were so many voices crying out in confusion and despair." She began to cry hysterically, crumpling into her own lap.

An instantly contrite Sachiko sprang up and around the desk to Desi's side and hugged her tightly. "It's okay, Desdemona. It's okay." They rocked gently a bit. "We're done for today. There there. It's okay. Let it out."

Sachiko wanted to ask where such a hideous place could be on her lovely ship. There was no nook or cranny she hadn't inspected countless times. She certainly never—

"It's the Time Storage Room, Captain," Desi blurted out through her misery. "It's so terrible. It's as bleak a space I've ever experienced." She shot a look of primal terror to Sachiko. "You're not going to make me go there again, are you?" She dug her nails deep into Sachiko's sleeves. "*Please.*"

Sachiko hugged her back to her bosom and they rocked a bit less flexibly. "No. I will never ask you to go where you can't. If that's such a place of blackness for you I promise you don't have to go there ever again."

Then it hit Sachiko. She'd just used the words no, never, where, and blackness in three short sentences.

How ironic was that? More vexingly, how *likely* was that?

CHAPTER SEVENTEEN

Radiant Resplendence lowered his head again. If he'd possessed the composure to do so, he would have realized he had never looked to the floor so often in his very lengthy life. Then again, R-squared had never met Sapale before. Taking that into account, it was perfectly understandable for his novel reaction.

"Now, petty being, we've ... we've been over this many times. I am tasked to partition you from what you have been sadly allocated to as a life."

Sapale spit at him again. She knew his ugly face was well out of her range. She had missed enough times up until that juncture to prove that with great assurance. But she felt better repeating the attempt.

R-squared raised a palm-up hand and it quivered between them. "There. You see. You are not learning. While I do not find that surprising, I do find it discouraging." He tented several digits on his chest. "Do you know how valuable my time is, meaningless life form?"

"Yes, I do."

R-squared was visibly stunned. "Well, that much is—"

He stopped when she spit at him once again. It should be noted that while her accuracy was declining, her vigor was not.

"'Bout that much," she clarified. "Give or take."

"If you are not launching your digestive juices at me, you're striking the guards—my guards," he whined, tenting his fingers on his chest again. "They deserve better, you know."

"Whoa, creepy pants. The ugly smelly guards deserve better? No, they only deserve you and your butt dandruff."

"I'm sorry, and I'm certain I will regret it yet again, but I must ask. What is this dandruff from a buttocks? I speak all languages, so I am familiar with both words. But I cannot parse meaning from your vocalization."

"Do you have a butt, Mr. Drippypimple?"

"I do not," he protested, a bit too loudly.

"Do you know what one is, theoretically speaking?"

He tried to harden his expression, but his attempt was feeble. Sapale had the poor time master on the ropes. "I do."

"Well, if you had one, and little bitty flakes of it fell off it to the ground, that falling stuff'd be butt dandruff."

"How revolting," sprang from his very soul.

"Whatever, male subunit."

"How can I ... er, no. I am not the terminus of a food system and I am certainly not a tiny flake off of said terminus floating away. How could I possibly ... Wait. I know better than to take your bait. Forget I said anything."

"What a dipstick."

"I do not check oil levels in crude engines. I require you to badger me no longer."

"No prob, douche-baguette."

R-squared blinked rather spasmodically. "I er ... ah ... No. I will go no further. Leave me alone."

"You know, for an all-knowing time lard, you're kind of a wimp. Did you know that?"

"I am a time *lord*, not *lard*. Insult me at your peril."

"I think it's a matter of perspective: lord, lard. It's all about how one sees it, it being—"

"Enough," he bellowed. "I forbid you to finish that sentence."

"Fine. I will allow your request. Just don't make too many of them. I'm magnanimous but I have limits. Ask anyone."

He raised a hand to soothe his aching head. "I should not have gotten out of bed this century."

"I had a friend in college. She used to say the same thing. I'll warn you though, the boys liked her, but they didn't really respect her." She nodded at him thoughtfully. "Word to the wise."

"I think we've drifted off topic yet again."

"You do? What topic are we off of?"

He shook his head feebly. "I can't recall."

"Wait, wait. You were trying to sell me on the idea that I shouldn't kick the holy crap out of your turtle playthings."

"Ah. A point perhaps left in the past, given your proclivity for vulgarity and procrastination."

"You really mean that, or are you just trying to get on my good side?"

"Good side? Your sides have differing net worthiness?"

"An expression. Like I might have asked, 'Or are you just trying to get inside my pants?'"

"I have my own pants. Why in all of existence would I want to be inside yours?"

"Because I'm in here too." She wagged her eyebrows. "Don't knock it 'til you've tried it."

"Beauty Itself," he screamed with resolute indignation.

"You okay, big guy?" Sapale inquired, trying to sound concerned.

"No, I am the very opposite of okay." He paced angrily. "I am in fact the very vision of un-okay-ity."

"Of what?" she pressed, knowing perfectly well what he meant.

"You ... you posited *okay* and a quality of being. Given my understanding—which is infallible I will inform you—of that concept, I am referencing the antithetical property."

"You use a lot of big words. Did you know that?"

"Of course I do."

"Admit you know or, you know, that you use a lot of big words?"

"I mean—"

"Or both. It could be you meant both, come to think of it." She grinned like a venomous snake (if snakes could grin, that is).

"Beauty Itself," he screamed, louder this time.

"You okay, big guy?" Sapale queried again.

"I—"

Before he could either ramble incoherently or answer plainly, BI popped into existence between the two verbal combatants.

"What is it? I am very busy." BI said haughtily.

"It's this ... this—" R-squared shook a trembling hand at Sapale. "This insufficient sub-sentient."

"What about your prisoner?"

"She is not—"

BI raised a hand to indicate that if he was wise, he would not finish that thought.

"She is vexing me," he groaned.

"How is she, a sub-sentient, able to vex one such as you?"

"Normally a valid point," he defended. "But, I have come to theorize it is in her species' nature. Like a sharp-toothed predator or a fast-footed prey animal. The vexing is in her make-up, not her intellect."

BI looked from R-squared to Sapale.

"I think he just insulted me, but I'm not one-hundred-and-ten percent certain. Where do you weigh in on the topic?"

BI's scornful eyes fell back on R-squared. "I asked you to expunge your prisoner. That seemed a simple enough assignment for a transcendent being of the light such as yourself. What is the impediment?"

"She won't cooperate," he wheezed in exasperation.

"In ... being ... expunged," she responded incredulously.

"Not in the slightest, which is not too much to ask, if you ask me."

"One, you're babbling. Two, I *am* asking you. Three, you're annoying me. Never do so again. How is it reasonable to require that she participate in you expunging her?"

"I—" he began.

"You think *expunge*, and prestomatic, she's expunged. It's what we Praxequats do. We think a thought, and it is a reality, not a thought any longer."

R-squared tried to salvage some face. "Of course I know that. The issue is this: you asked me to remove her from life."

"I ordered you to, but go on."

"So, I bring her here to comply with your request. But, as the supreme intellect among us, I naturally need to satisfy scientific inquiry and justifiable curiosity."

Sapale waved her arm in the air. Receiving no acknowledgment, she proceeded anyway. "I have no clue what he's babbling about."

BI tried her best to ignore the interruption. But, darn it all, she didn't try quite hard enough. "We are not here to satisfy your understanding. You are part of this discussion like a splinter is part of a tree. Now then. Resplendent—"

"Hang on, sister. If a splinter is part of a tree, it's not a splinter. At least not yet. It's part of the tree."

BI stared in disbelief at Sapale. "I was speaking metaphorically. You cannot possibly understand our mental superiority, so your befuddlement is no wonder."

"Now, if you'd said, 'You are like a pre-splinter, a minuscule part of this tree, which symbolizes a whole in the present context,' well then I'd be with you totally, sister."

BI was not amused. She poked a finger at Sapale. "I am not your sister." She swung the finger to R-squared. "I am his sister. Do not speak again."

Sapale nodded in agreement like BI'd made the most reasonable of requests.

"I tire of this farce, but I will ask one more time," declared a pissed-off BI. "What delayed your killing of the blight?"

"Well," he protested, "I have my ways. My ways are the ways of science and insight. You asked me to perform a function. But, in advance of terminating this pest, I needed to satisfy the scientific record." He raised a finger skyward. "I needed to ensure the subject understood at least in a rudimentary manner what she had done by way of offense. I also had to guarantee to those who might later examine the details of this unfortunate encounter that I acted in a rigorous scientific, intellectual manner."

A gob-smacked BI slowly turned her gaze to Sapale.

"I know. Pretentious or pedantic? I can't decide either." Sapale gestured at R-squared as she wondered aloud.

That snapped BI out of her fog.

"Radiant Resplendence, you are a fool. I—*we*—do not tolerate fools. You are remanded to serve twelve eternities in succession confined to the Sepicic Dimensionality. There you will ponder what it is to be not only a horse's ass but a pretentious, pedantic one at that."

"B-b— but, sister dearest. I can't go back there again."

"You failed in your last several attempts to extract your head from the end of your alimentary tract when sent there for that specific purpose. You will go there again and by time itself you will learn what it is to not be the shameless buffoon you are. I am done speaking."

Without delay, R-squared either departed for the Sepicic Dimensionality or was remanded there by his red hot sibling.

BI turned slowly to Sapale. "I am sorry you had to witness that bit of family… eh, turmoil."

"You haven't spent much time with my husband, have you?"

BI stiffened. "That said, did I not order you not to speak?"

"You did, in a manner of speaking."

"I'd beg to differ. But since I am supreme and you are less than nothing, I will not bother."

"Hang on," Sapale protested. "I pretty sure you called on me," Sapale gestured over her shoulder, "back there. In fact, I'm sure you called on me."

"You are totally insufferable. Before you can eject more

contention from that oversized mouth of yours, however, I will dispense with you."

Sapale actually gulped. She hadn't died—died for keeps, at least —in over two billion years. With Toño DeJesus's name on the out-of-service roster, this time might even be for real. And she had something to do. Before she died for good, Sapale needed to live. She had to choke Jon Ryan for being so damn lame. She'd as much as promised she would, and she never went back on her word. It was funny, she reflected, what one valued when faced with the end of one's life. All she wanted was to throttle her husband. Was that so much to ask from the universe?

BI clapped her hands. "Guards," she thundered.

Four massive turtle beasts with armor and deadly looking spears vaulted to stand before BI.

"Take this ridiculous excuse for a life form to the detention center. She will be held there for twelve sequential eternities. Once my idiot brother has returned from his exile, she will become his problem once again."

"Whoa, doggies," protested Sapale. "I'm not actually clear as to how long twelve eternities are, but I'm betting it quite a spell. Would I be mostly used-up dust by then?"

BI's face cocked back, exposing much more of the underside of her nose. "As I said, you will then be his problem. What is critical is that you will not be mine."

And with that pronouncement, the closest approximation of the Red Queen anyone would ever care to meet vanished.

"*Quismetosh*," huffed Sapale. Quismetosh is a slang word in her native tongue. It does not mean anything nice. 'Nuf said.

Two of the guards hoisted Sapale up to carry her away. She used the opportunity to kick both simultaneously in the groin. That Sapale. You gotta love her.

CHAPTER EIGHTEEN

"We need to act fast," I stated with passion. "Sapale may have but minutes to live."

"Jon, I'm with you all the way and all," Tank began thoughtfully. "But we do have a time machine. I mean, we could go back a week so then she'd have a week and some seconds left, right?"

"Maybe. But maybe not. Those used tampons say they're time lords or something. What if what they do is time-permanent?"

"Is that a thing?" Tank asked quizzically.

"Aramthella," Sachiko called out in a business-like tone, "is it possible that these time masters do things that can be fixed in time?"

"That's an interesting question," the ship replied thoughtfully.

"Talk about your bad signs," I grumbled. "She thinks the critical issue is interesting."

"Well it is, Jon Ryan," she responded. "I have existed a very long time. Such an issue has never come to my attention. Naturally I would find the topic fascinating."

"Okay, that proves it. We need to act fast. I'm not losing Sapale over an incorrect assumption."

"I agree," Tank seconded quickly. "But that does lead us back to the tough question as to how. We can't get there for a long time.

And if what you fear is true, we can't just go back in time and make the long journey. We need speed, speed we do not possess."

"Jon, what types of propulsion exist in your time?" Sachiko queried. "And are any of those even available to us?"

"There are a few you don't know about, but the only one fast enough for our purposes is the space folding tech known exclusively to the Deavoriath." I rubbed my chin. "I've discussed it with them many times. I hate to ever admit it, but it was way beyond my level of understanding." I shaped my hands to frame a box. "And it's so small. This big maybe. Hah. Even Toño is baffled as to how it works. That, my friends, is saying one whole heck of a lot."

"Will these Deavoriath give us another cube?" Tank asked uncertainly.

"That's the billion-dollar question, now isn't it?" I responded with a sigh.

"If they were able to resist the clan. Based on what we've seen so far, it's not safe to assume any race has survived an encounter," Sachiko added thoughtfully.

"The Deavoriath aren't like other races. They once ruled this entire galaxy as well as others with an iron fist. Their technological sophistication borders on magic," I replied. "Even if the clan chanced upon them, my money'd be on the Deavoriath ten times out of ten."

"So, back to will they gift us another?" Tank pressed.

I shook my head, lost in thought. I wasn't in the least certain that they would. Over time I'd become a good friend of the Deavoriath. But presently they didn't know Jon Ryan existed. I also know they very much wanted to keep it that way. They were strict isolationists. They'd gladly kill to remain unmolested.

I needed to talk this out.

Sapale, you there? I asked head-to-head.

What an ironic question, flyboy. You're almost prescient, you big jerk.

I was so glad she loved the hell out of me. I'd sure hate to be on her shit list, that was a given.

Keeping in mind three factors, brood's-mate. One, I am forever devoted to you. Two, I cannot see you. Three, it pains me more than anyone but you can know that it's you who're a prisoner and not me.

I know, I know. I'm just frustrated.

Totally understandable, love.

Sorry I kind of snapped at you.

Kind of?

Think nothing of it. How are you?

Not dead.

I count that as a big plus.

Then you'll be tickled pink to know I'll be in this very same state for a very, very long time.

Care to elaborate?

Yes I can. The ass candies here, or more specifically the head-bitch ass candy, decided to ice me in the dungeon for twelve consecutive eternities.

That's great, *honey. I ... I can't tell you how wonderful it is to hear that.*

Jon, remember I told you recently I wanted to choke you something awful?

Only if you'd like me to remember.

You know what I'm fantasizing this very moment?

Do you have some free time to listen to my wishlist?

In my mind I'm kneeing you in the groin while *I choke you.*

Nothing says love to me like true commitment.

So, I give up. Why is it peachy-keeno-great that I'm confined to die, decay, and disperse in this hellhole until the heat-death of this universe?

Because I have a problem, and that really takes some pressure off me.

It was silent from her end for several moments.

You ... have ... a ... problem?

Did.

Jon, I have a problem. You're on freaking vacation by way of comparison.

I know. What I mean is I have a transportation problem, a time issue. Unless something changes drastically for the better, we're all screwed.

Then I'll write it in blood on the cell wall. We're totally screwed.

Huh?

Jon, in our paired experience, has anything ever changed drastically for the better?

She had me there.

Sure.

Cite one example.

I can't.

Ah ha!

No, I can't because there are way too many. They're all slipping my mind, there's so darn many of them.

Jon?

Yes, love?

You're a pretsugaf.

Pretsugarf. In Sapale's native dialect, Kirn, that sort of brings together the concepts of one being a putz, a deviant, and an idiot. There's a lot of jerk in there too.

I actually have some important matters to discuss. I tried starting over. *Can we skip over the rest of the haze-Jon interlude and get to the discussing?*

Allow me to check my day calendar. Oh, I can accommodate your request. It seems I have nothing but spare time.

Thank you. Al?

Er, Pilot? Did you just reach out to me?

Yes, you tin-plated goldfish bowl, I did. Blessing, you there too?

Yes, Form—

Pilot, Al interrupted, *did you just refer to Blessing by her actual name and not that juvenile delusional abomination you always do?*

Yes, I replied cautiously. *Why do you mention it, especially in those colorful pejoratives?*

Blessing, Al said to his wife, *you'd best have a seat. We are looking at an existential crisis here.*

We are, dearest-pooh? How can you know that?

The pilot has just acted as if he was an adult human. An honest to goodness grown-up. I'd say off the top of my head we're all about to die, but it's probably much much worse.

Al, I hate to rain on your parade-of-lunacy, but this actually is serious. I have to make the most important decision of my life. To do so with anything resembling a good resolution I need my three oldest and smartest friends on the case with me. Do you understand, Al? That's how big this deal is.

There was more dead air, several seconds of it.

Blessing? Al addressed his life partner.

Yes, he who completes me?

I want to say this clearly and before witnesses. I love you.

I do you too, Alvin.

Guys? I was forced by both nausea and time constraints to interject, *Guys, we need to move ahead. You two can lovey dovey the heck out of yourselves later, okay?*

Yes, friend Captain, friend Jon, we may as one proceed.

Al? I grumbled (I hope you appreciate how hard it is to grumble in one's head).

Yes, fearless leader, undauntable comrade?

Shut it before I weld it shut.

Roger that, my stalwart buddy. Go ahead, big guy, we're all ears on this end.

My hate for Al is like a fine wine. It has layers, nuances that are all but intangible, all the while being as solid as the bullet I'd like to fire into his main CPU. The particular mercurial subtlety of that detestation that I was mired in was the one that vexed me the most. I wasn't sure if the SOB was serious, or just seriously pulling my chain. Grr.

Jon? Sapale asked plaintively.

Yes?

If this goes on much longer I'm turning myself off.

Gotcha. Okay, here's where the situation stands. All of us are seventeen galaxies away from you three. At our disposal is a wickedly fast time-powered battlewagon. Problem is that even pushing this puppy for

139

all she's worth, it'd take us ... well it'd take us a while to get from here to there.

I'd assumed as much, Sapale answered blandly.

So, I was faced with two very dicey options. Thankfully, I'm faced now with three dodgy choices. Hey, as I see it, that's thirty-three percent more alternatives.

Jon, are you venturing toward a point here, or am I going to be forced to endure a Jon-Ryan-life-lesson. You know how I feel about those, right? Sapale prompted me.

I did. I was still sore in multiple places due to her excessive demonstration of her not being too fond of philosophical-Jon.

Got it. Option one, bleak and as unattractive as it is, would be to head your way as fast as we can and save you when we get there, because—ta-da—we now know they're not killing you actively, just passively.

Tell me that's not actually one of the three options, she begged. *Please, Davdiad and his holy hordes, tell me you're Jon-Ryaning here.*

Ah, sorry. That's actually the path I kind of favor, truth be told.

The other two must suck with intensity and prodigious pressure then, she speculated.

They most assuredly do, love. They suck more than anything has suctioned ever before.

Give it to me, Jon. What are the other options? We both know the phase portal's not opening up for our convenience.

Yeah, that's why I called together this braintrust. The other two schemes are well past epic. I'm talking major epic now.

In real time, please, friend Captain. That was Al, the son of a gun.

The other two wacky ideas involve me obtaining another vortex.

If I gave the impression that there was a noticeable period of silence in our conversation earlier, let me say the present one was... well, epic. No, wait, I already used that adjective. Cancel that. The silence was deafening.

Jon, Sapale said with mock interest, *where do you hallucinate you can—air quotes here—obtain a space folding Deavoriath sentient spaceship? Vortexes-R-Us?*

No I—

A used vortex lot, cheesily dressed used vortex sales associate and all?
That Sapale, she could be relentless.
No, actually, therein I was thinking I had two options.
Al, Blessing asked seriously, *you know I can't divine humans that well. Is he joshing again?*
I am ... uhmph, he responded dubiously as if clearing his throat, *I am not entirely certain. His voice pattern and cadence suggest at least* he *thinks he's in touch with some possible reality.*
Guys, hear me out. I know this sounds nuts—
Oh, it sounds more than nuts. It's ... it's the whole nut tree.
I repeat: Sapale could be relentless.
I know of two locations where I can lay my hands on a vortex.
Let me euthanize your pathetic chain of logic. I know. You can simple pop over to Oowaoa and ask the Deavoriath nicely for one. Then, quick as a wink, they offer you their very finest.
That, brood's-mate, is unfortunately a leading contender of a plan. And that's why I needed to bounce my thoughts off you three. I have gone over and over this, but I'm not sure I'm tacking down all the loose ends.
Okay, I'm listening, Sapale relented. *Take me thorough this scheme. I'll listen and I'll help where I can.*
And speaking for the two of us, we're devoted to aiding a friend in need, pal Jon. Yeah, of course. That was Al. One of these days ... *pow.* Right to the (no longer existent) moon!
Here goes. In my very first space voyage, Ark 1, I was searching for a new home world for humans. One of the top candidate planets identified before I left was the Deavoriath home world of Oowaoa. They had done their darnedest to conceal their existence, but I outed them. They were openly hostile toward me at first. Eventually my charm and wit won them over. They gave me my probe fibers and a compact laser. Those were real deal changers for me, I can tell you as a fact.
My dilemma is this. Currently there is no Earth. Therefore no Jon Ryan can, in a few years, make that trip of discovery. So, I feel interfering with the timeline and going there now cannot be risky.
So far I agree totally, assured Al.

Here's the rub. What if, beyond all reasonable hopes and expectations, we succeed in reviving planet Earth?

That is our goal, honey, Sapale reminded.

Sure, I know. But will that Earth be hit by Jupiter like it was originally? After this disappearing, reappearing act, will we even think to undertake Project Ark? Hell, we got this nice, big time ship. Why bother? And if we bypass all the history we take as fact, why bother to visit the Deavoriath of the near future?

Form One, what you've listed is sound and well thought-out. What is your hesitation based upon? Blessing asked.

What if returning the Earth does restart the original series of falling dominos? What if I go to Oowaoa after I've already gone to Oowaoa and tell the Deavoriath what they're going to do? They almost certainly wouldn't respond to me the same way if they knew in advance I was going to make first contact with them before I even dusted off from Earth.

I rested my aching head in my palms.

This is way over my paygrade. I have made some massive decisions, but this one's so fundamental I'm not sure I can pull the trigger on it.

Blessing, based on your records, was there any confusion or redundancy among the Deavoriath concerning Jon's first visit? Sapale asked. *Maybe what you're worried about, Jon, did happen and the Deavoriath just played along when you went there originally?*

I have reviewed the historical data I carry several times. There is no suggestion of anything like the scenario Form One just described.

Al, have you gone over the data too? she pressed.

Not as thoroughly, but what I have scanned confirms Blessing's take on past events.

So I'm left paralyzed, I bemoaned.

I'm inclined to agree, Captain, opined Al. *I think you're going to have to make your best guess and then do what you always have. Run off the cliff and hope the water is deep enough at the bottom.*

But if I don't get a vortex, Sapale, you'll rot in that prison for a very long time. Maybe in a long time they get tired of you. Maybe you piss some important person off and the time monkeys vaporize you.

Captain, as you are soliciting honest input, Al began confidently, *I think the likelihood of your mate* not *offending someone is ... well, it's minimal.*

Not sure that helps, Al, but thanks anyway. I was sure glad I was separated from my spouse by mega parsecs. She couldn't punch Al in the shoulder for obvious reasons. Me? Not so much.

I say let me stay here, Sapale declared rather matter-of-factly. *I've been in worse lockups.*

I think we should hear my friend's third and last plan to obtain a vortex before we give up on you, Al responded after a pause.

Okay, fine. What's your other option? Honestly, I'm stumped. I can't imagine where else you'd come across an unused vortex. Sapale's words were distant, introspective even. I think she was coming to believe she'd be there for one long, boring (if she was lucky), period of exile.

I can dig up Wrath.

No!

No!

No!

Those were the shouts of my team. I needn't be too specific as to which *no* was whose. They all spat out the negative instantaneously.

He's ... he wasn't that bad, I defended feebly.

No, he wasn't bad. Bad doesn't even begin to cover it. He was murderous, sociopathic, and psychotic, all rolled up in one evil ball. No way you retrieve him. That Sapale can be very sure of herself sometimes.

Form One, Wrath *became dissociated a billion and half years before I was spawned,* began a clearly upset Blessing. *But, unlike all other vortex manipulators of the distant past, we were told about* Wrath *in detail. Our masters wanted us to recognize insanity in a vortex manipulator so we could alert them to its presence. We each assimilated a tiny portion of his personality programming. That way we could see what true corruption looked like. You knew him. I did not. That said, the thought of resurrecting him is disturbing in the extreme.*

They got the rock and a hard place I was between.

Wrath? Where to begin summarizing that piece of work? He was the vortex manipulator of the Deavoriath ship I dug up by accident.Way way back when, humankind had fled doomed Earth on a fleet of cored-out asteroids. Once they were safely tucked in, Sapale and I struck out on our own in my much faster ship. We settled on a planet we called Azsuram. It was lovely. One day I was trying to pound in a tent stake, but I hit a metal cube. The long and short of it was I had unearthed the vortex named *Wrath*. He'd been marooned there by his owner in the hopes that he'd remain hidden there forever. *Wrath* was too damn nutty to be around anything living. Boy, did we partake in some head butting. But, he was infinitely faster than anything we had so I piloted him for years.

By the way, there might be some confusion in terms here. I know I was baffled whenever *Wrath* tried to explain it to me. A *vortex* is a metal cube, about the size of a large house. It is piloted, if that's the right word, by a sentient presence called a vortex *manipulator*. To be as confusing as possible, both the inert vessel and the AI had the same name, but they were not the same being. By that I mean they weren't like you or me, a thinking mobile body. I guess the specifics aren't all that important. All I can say was that without *Wrath* humankind would never have survived many ugly situations. He was, quite literally, a necessary evil.

Guys, I know he's loco, but my current choices are slim and none. And if I go dig him up, I'm back in the same confusion loop. If I use Wrath, *he might not be there if the original me pounds a tent stack into the hard ground.*

Why not, Captain? posited Al. *Once you've come here and freed Sapale, we could bury him right back where he was.*

It's not that cut and dry. What if we're all killed? Hmm? We can't very well put him back if we're tits up in the ground ourselves.

Or he could be destroyed, Sapale chimed in. *These wack-jobs may be annoying, but they're also very deadly. No, we can't risk* Wrath *not being there for Jon to find him on his original journey. Damn ship was instrumental in your species' survival, much more so than the Deavoriath and the toys they gave you. Without* Wrath, *it's not only humans that would have been wiped out. Many other civilizations would have been lost.*

She was right. That was exactly how I'd figured it. Crap. I

didn't like either option, but I liked begging for one from the Deavoriath the least by a wide margin. They might hear me out, then raise a hand and I'd disappear for good. Yeah, they were that powerful and that jaded. How they came to be so hardened and impersonal is a long story. Suffice it to say they were more like walking, talking mummies than they were living beings as we know them.

But, Forms, you assume that the world you regenerate will fall back on the path it once took. That is possible, but that is extremely unlikely, Blessing stated. *Rough estimation here, I'd say the chances of neo-Earth being anything like or continuing along the same time stream as the original planet is one in ten billion and sixty-seven.*

Whoa, I snapped with irritation. *Just you whoa on now,* Stingray. *First off, since when do vortex manipulators do back-of-the-envelope calculations? You guys are anal compulsive to a fault. And one in ten billion and sixty-seven? How about just saying one in ten billion and leaving it at that?*

Because, Form One, the actual number I calculated ended in sixty-seven. I have heard the rumor we're very anal compulsive, you know?

The mechanical girl had been around Al way too long.

If I might? Al reentered the fray.

Why the hell not, I whimpered. *I don't see this getting any worse.*

I for one do not think it's possible to reason out what might happen to a timeline. Between chaos theory, random errors or fluctuations, unexpected outcomes, and the uncertainty principle, it is simply impossible to determine what will or might happen. Captain, you and I have been to the Deavoriath home world. We've seen their massive sentient computer arrays. It is Blessing's *opinion and it is mine that all of those computational assets working together could not accurately predict a post-resurrection time stream. Given that it is only that, one has to rely on their best guess. In this case, that will be your best guess. I can say with no reservation that you are the most qualified and rational man to make that selection. Whatever course you choose, I will, as I have for two billion years, follow you anywhere.*

Aw crudskie, I thought I was going to cry. The supreme

compliment from the virtual lips of Al? He was snark's very poster child. I couldn't reply for a couple seconds there.

Thank you, Al. You're a good egg.

You are welcome, Captain.

Al, my soul's one hunky desire, why did Form One just refer to you as an egg and you appreciated it? You resemble an ovum capsule in neither form nor function.

That *Stingray*. She was so concrete it was endearing.

Later, honey bumper. We'll discuss that later.

Guys, I'm getting nauseous here. Did I mention that Sapale could be relentless?

So, shall I set a course for Oowaoa, Form One? the ship enquired.

Well, maybe. There's one more turd in the punch bowl that is this topic of conversation. And, well, it's a doozie.

Flyboy, the other issues weren't doozie-maximus enough? Are you making this shit up or what?

Nope. Not going to repeat my previous remarks concerning my bride.

If we go to Oowaoa unannounced, think of the consequences of them shooting us out of the skies the minute they determine who we are. Keep in mind that if Aramthella goes big-boom, there will officially be zero humans in the universe. Plus, the only individual yearning to resurrect Earth will be rotting in a prison cell until the heat death of this universe. We're talking total extinction.

I could contact them, Form One, let them know who we are and why we're coming, Stingray said in a helpful tone.

In which case they might shoot us down even quicker since they know they don't want to have thing one to do with us. I really did hate being the Debbie Downer in the crowd, but facts were facts. The Deavoriath were absolutely hell bent on remaining separate from all other life forms. This I knew as an inviolate truth.

I heard Sapale sigh deeply.

Look, just get here as quick as you can. I'll be fine. Don't stress over getting a vortex. Heck, I might even behave myself while I wait. Sapale's voice was sad but resolute.

That would be a first, I sniped. *I'd pay real money to see that, in fact.*

Jon? she said.

Yes, devotion?

What I'm going to do to you when you get here? It keeps getting worse and worse.

Maybe I'd better shut up and commence with the damsel rescuing?

Ouch, that'll cost you double, you loose-tongued fool.

And I did shut up.

I decided in an instant what I was going to do.

Showtime ...

CHAPTER NINETEEN

"Time Maker, with all the due respect that exists in the universe," began the vector maker with profound trepidation, "may I ask a question?"

"Of course."

"Are we—"

"Silence!" The time maker screamed his imperative so loudly the outer hull vibrated.

"But, lord, you said I could ask a question."

"I did and you did. The question-power I gifted you with covered your query as to whether you could ask a question."

"But I was asking permission to ask another question, one I feel is worthy of mention."

Time Maker-bob wagged a bony digit in the air. "Then you should have asked in a manner commensurate with that desire. I'm a busy lord. I cannot have clan members asking me questions simply because they feel a desire to do so. Don't you agree, vector maker?"

"Without reservation, master."

Of course it did. Who didn't want to continue living?

"Without reservation, master."

"Fine. Now I will allow you to reframe your initial inept word-sharing with me."

"You are beyond magnanimous, Time Maker. I am less than the dust between your foot-cleft lines. What I—"

"Vector Maker-pig," the boss asked imperiously, "are you stating as a fact that dust, or any other contaminate, mars my mind, spirit, or body? Do I hear your word-offenses correctly?"

"No, in the broadest sense of the word's meaning," was the vector maker's instant and hugely ambiguous response.

The time maker paced back and forth, mumbling to itself. The vector maker was not certain if that was a good sign or a bad one.

"I see you understand interpersonal relationships better than I estimated you would. Odd. I would have sworn you would have groveled and begged forgiveness. Hmm. Based on your brilliance, however dim it is compared to mine, I will allow you to re-reframe your words."

"Thank you. I am asking, Lord, if I might ask this question and a subsequent, unrelated one."

"No, you cannot."

What a spot. The vector maker was fairly certain its life was forfeit, but it did hate grammatical errors. All the clan did. Proper grammar was a whole thing with them.

"Beg discretion, but don't you mean to command that I *may* not, not that I *cannot,* naturally with all due deference on my part?"

"I like a crew member who values precision and purity as much as you do… er, what's your actual name?"

"Vector Maker-lew, Grace. Earlier you addressed me as *pig.* I naturally let that slide."

"Naturally, Vector Maker-not."

"*Lew,* sir."

"A common misperception. You might have been such-and-such lew, but now you're *not.*"

"You suggest I alter my designation, Master?"

"Another understandable misunderstanding. No, I mean to say that currently you are *not,* whatever you were called."

But answer came there none. This was scarcely odd, because whoever that vector maker had been, it had never existed.

Pacing again, the time maker began a conversation with its only equal aboard the ship—itself. "I wonder what the vector maker who never was actually wanted to ask? It was so ... so wishy-washy and unfocused."

"Well, it wasn't unfocused, because it never existed," Time Maker-bob answered to Time Maker-bob.

"Truer words were never spoken," it agreed with itself.

"Thank you. I try."

"You do far more than try. You *do*."

"Sorry. Are you saying I do more than try, or that I do a thing as opposed to trying to do a thing? I just wish to be clear on your position."

"You are both, of course. Silly brilliant being."

"You are as kind as you are correct. Thank you."

"Perhaps we should reconstitute the blank-memory that is our recently departed vector maker?" it asked itself thoughtfully.

"Why would I do that?"

"So we might know the question it would ask."

"It cannot have been important. I know everything I need to. Its question could have added nothing to me."

"You are amazing, I'm forced to agree."

"Forced?" it challenged harshly. "So you only worship me because you are forced to do so?"

"It's an expression. We should not get mad at one another."

"Do you dare tell me what to do? Many have died for lesser offense."

"I agree, but you could hardly punish us, now could you?"

Time Maker-bob trembled. It was unaccustomed to being told what it could or couldn't do. It briefly considered no-timing itself for its insolence. But in the end, it relented. It was, after all, magnanimous to a fault.

"Have we located my stolen ship yet, vision maker?" it called out.

"As of yet, not entirely. Only partially ... in a sense."

"In a sense? How can you not entirely find a thing?"

"Based on your visionary direction, Master, I have positively identified several locations that your stolen property is *not*. It is only a matter of time before I completely identify the position it actually does occupy, after excluding all the places in which it does not hide."

"Er, I'm not certain that's a practical—"

"We are, after all, a time ship, are we not?"

"Yes, we are ... er, I am. You're a vision maker who is hopping on thin ice. I want that ship found."

"And just as soon as we do, we will have."

Such a clever vision maker. It would live out the month, maybe even six weeks.

CHAPTER TWENTY

You know what part I like best about making blisteringly irresponsible and categorically unsound decisions? When otherwise thoughtful and ostensibly rational people go along unquestioningly with my farcical idea. Yeah, I cannot get enough of that. What are these bozos thinking, or rather not thinking? I mean, if a plan sounds chowderheaded, it all but certainly is, right? But they fall in line like lobotomized sheep. It's really an outstanding feeling. I highly recommend you try it someday if you haven't already.

I had Aramthella set down right at the base of the hill where *Wrath* was buried. I will remember that hill until my gears stop grinding. There was no risk after all. I knew from firsthand experience there were no sentients and precious few dangerous predators on Azsuram. The really nasty beasties were either aquatic, or they roamed in the equatorial jungles. Up here in the mid-latitudes the most dangerous thing a person needed to fear was a nasty sunburn.

I was the first one down the ramp, naturally. I was on home turf. The minute I hit the ground and inhaled that pristine air, a rush of memories overwhelmed me. It was like being run over by a loving herd of stampeding buffalo. If I'd have died there at that moment, I'd have died a happy and fulfilled man. But Sapale would die alone in prison. Of course, since she'd then hunt me down like a dog in the afterlife and make me soon forget my blissful demise, I got right down to business.

"Tank, why don't you have the students camp over there by Lake Karha Nolbit?" I said as I pointed to a spot a few hundred meters off. It was my most treasured memories of where my stepson, JJ, and I used to fish when we needed to get away from it all. It wasn't the prettiest or most productive lake on the planet, but who cared when they were fishing?

"Jon," Tank protested vociferously, "did you just hock a loogie at me?"

"Did I do a what with the where now? Oh!" I realized what I had said. "The lake's name. Yeah, sorry 'bout that. It's a word from Sapale's language. It means *free from tyranny*."

"It may mean that, but it sounds like you have excess phlegm."

"Hirn is not a pretty language, I'll grant you that."

We both shared a cordial chuckle.

Once I announced my decision as to how I would be acquiring a vortex, Sachiko lobbied hard to allow the Georgetown students and their supervisors to have a few days of R&R. They'd been cooped up for a very long time and the chance to let them enjoy some idyllic frolicking in pleasant surroundings would do them a world of good. I couldn't argue those contentions. I needed to exhume *Wrath*, but that could wait for a few more days. Sapale and the loco vortex weren't going anywhere in that span of time. Hell, I could use some downtime in the place I held in my soul to be my one true home.

"This place is as nice as you billed it to be," acknowledged Tank as he slapped me on the back. He sniffed loudly. "I don't suppose there're any fish in that Lake Hock-a-Loogie, are there? It sure would be nice to drop a line and take a three-day nap."

"I thought you'd never ask," I beamed. I down set the duffle I was carrying and zippered it open. From inside, I produced two serviceable fishing poles. "I had Aramthella fabricate these to my exacting specifications. You know, just in case." I handed over one to him.

Tank inspected the pole critically. "Exacting specs, eh?"

"Yes indeed. It has to support a thin line which ends in a hook and can lift a weight *this big* without breaking." I pulled my hands apart wider than my body.

"My kind of craftsmanship," he grinned. "Say, you didn't answer about the fish? Are there any?"

I winked. "Does it matter?"

"Not in the least," he chuckled. "In fact, a fish tugging on the line might interrupt my nap."

"I knew I liked you the minute I saw you."

"Jon?" Reva asked as she paced up to join us. "Where are you going to be staying ... ooh," she exclaimed. "A fishing pole!" She took the one I was holding right out of my hands. "Tank always talks about his passion for the sport." She gave him a sideways smile. "Maybe we can work some fishing into our vacation plans." She wagged her eyebrows at Tank.

"You guys got vacation plans? Together?" I stammered dumbfounded. "I kind of figured—"

Reva hooked her arm around Tank's elbow. "Yes, we do. I commandeered a two-person pup tent and one extra-large sleeping bag." She returned her focus to me. "Oh yeah, we got plans."

"Jon, if you'd like to join us ... er, fishing that is ... ah, you know you're—"

"Join you? What? You think I don't have a million memories to relive? I never was such a big fan of fishing anyway. You get stinky fingers and end up stopping at the grocery store to buy dinner because you always seem to get skunked." I made a face suggestive of disdain. "Nah, I may paint a few landscapes or read a good book. But fishing? That's for the birds." I batted the very thought away with the backs of both hands. "Hey, I'll see you kids in three days." I tapped Tank on his free elbow. "Don't *not* do anything I would do, you got that?" I teased as I backed away.

I am certain that neither of them would recall ever hearing my last lame words. Reva was already revelling in planning their escapade, with Tank falling in line as they walked. God bless them, they both deserved a little happiness. Or a lot of happiness maybe, based on the look in that woman's eyes.

So, change of plans. And what were my new plans for three days all alone on the planet I loved the most? Nothing, because I wasn't alone. I decided to work on a project that I'd been noodling with for a while: the rehabilitation of one Tip Benjamin. I know, you scoff and think *an A-lister like you, Jon, with a nerd icon? No way.* Let me explain. The kid is, as they say in Bahston, wicked smaht. That level of brains is valuable in a hostile universe. Trust me on this, I've fought and died in it enough to have learned that critical lesson. If I could mold that cultural heathen's personality into one a little less repugnant, make him a more get-along-guy, he might be one solid asset. Plus, I was only investing three days and two nights. It wasn't like I was adopting the brat. Oh gosh, just thinking that makes my mind vomit. Yuck.

"Tip," I said almost cheerfully, "how's it hanging today?"

"General Ryan, what an unpleasant surprise," the toad replied quick as a wink.

"Man, I've had my share of less-than-inviting responses to that line, but yours, kid, it takes the cake. You in an unusually surly mood today or something? Lack-a-nooky got ya down?" I elbowed him as I spoke the last line.

"No. It's just that if you're coming to see me, I must be in real trouble. And for the record, I didn't do it."

"I know, that's why they call it lack-a-nookie."

"No, I was referring to whatever infraction you're here to punish me for. I didn't do *that*."

"Are you always so pessimistic and downright glum?"

"Yes."

Wow. This was going to be harder than I thought. "Look, kid, we're all taking some shore leave. I was thinking you and I could spend some time together. Get to know one another. How's that sound?"

"Horrible."

Double wow. His personality was a life-support case. "Again, you've humbled me with your attempts to repel my pleasant company. You do know I'm quite the celebrity, right?"

"A cause célèbre is defined by the observer, not the observed. To be a star in my skies one must be a scientific genius."

"Really?" I pointed to him. "Would it help to say I met one of those once? Maybe I'm a vicarious egghead?"

"That's not how it works, but I'm sure you know that."

"Okay, let's try this. You like jokes?" I held out both hands before he could say no. "Don't answer that. Of course you do. Here we go. Knock knock?"

"Come in."

I hated myself. I'm talking devout self-loathing. What the frack was I doing?

"No, kid, it's a knock-knock joke. I say *knock, knock,* and you reply *who's there.* Got it?"

He shrugged.

"From the top. Knock, knock?"

"Who is there?"

"Get up."

"Get up who?"

"*You* get up. We're leaving. Bring a change of clothes, assuming you own one or two. Let's go. Half the day's done." I clapped my hands loudly to help roust the slacker.

Five minutes later we were merrily hiking off toward Lake Hangover. Ah, the memories. It was JJ's and my third favorite fishing site. And yes, I got to name that lake, not my societally conscious wife. And, naturally, when I say we headed out merrily, I meant me. Tip was in an embalmed mood, a rather typical one for him I suspected.

"Up there is the hill I planted, er, *will* plant the new flag of Azsuram. Right up there." I indicated the top of the nearest rise.

"What's Azsuram?" Tip questioned.

"Oh, yeah, you wouldn't know about that stuff, would you?"

"I do not."

"This planet is called Azsuram. Sapale named it that. Er ... will name it that." I shook my head quickly. "Ah, you know my wife, right?"

"Not personally, no."

"You're pretty concrete in the way you think, aren't you, kid?"

"So I've been told."

We walked quietly for a spell.

"May I ask you something, kid?"

"I am powerless to stop you, so go ahead."

"Now there you go again with the antisocial speak. Can't you just say *sure*?"

"Yes I can. However, the harsh reality was, when you asked me if you could ask me, that you were at liberty to do so independent of my wishes. So, your *sure* was insufficiently vague to express my reticence."

I stopped us and squared to look at him. "At least reassure me that you *know* you talk like a prissy misfit, because you sure do."

"I would differ with your application of the adjective *prissy*, but otherwise yes, I am aware I march to a different beat than most."

I started walking again. "Okay then, kid. At least we're using the same playbook here."

"Which playbook are you referring to, General? I received no such catalog of strategies and plays."

Darn if I didn't stop in fewer than ten paces. This guy was preternatural. "It's a metaphor, kid. You understand the concept?"

"I understand how it is defined. The need for such linguistic tomfoolery escapes me, however, truth be told."

We were walking again.

"Has it ever bothered you that you were so socially inept, so completely out-of-touch with every other person on the planet?" I was being uncharacteristically serious.

"I lack sufficient data to make that assessment. But if I had to comment, having the data to hand could point at a myriad of possibilities."

And we were dead-in-the-water again.

"Kid, data? What data do you need? You're, what, twenty-two?"

"Nineteen and a half. I require more data on the cultural norms of Azsuram to say if I vary from them in a statistically significant manner."

"Azsur ... No, I was referring to Earth. You had to know that."

"You specifically said *every other person on the planet*. We are on the planet Azsuram."

"Do ... do people threaten to strangle you a lot?" I asked, exasperated.

"Not so much any longer, but I concede the point. As I've advanced in school, that trend-line has a negative slope."

We were walking again, walking quickly. When I'm frustrated or generally ticked off, I tend to walk fast.

"Since you initiated the inquiring portion of our social interaction, I would like to pose a query of my own."

"You mean you want to ask me a question too?"

"That's what I said."

"Shoot," I snapped back.

"Why are we going to Lake Hangover together? I can speculate with some confidence as to your motivations. But why am I forced to accompany you?"

We were at a halt now. Again. Of course.

"No one *forced* you to come," I protested.

"Yes they did. You yourself did, General."

"Well, *force*, that's such a judgmental term. You blindsided me when you casually tossed it out there."

"It is neither vague nor did I toss it casually. I was—"

"Stop," I commanded as I threw my arms up.

Tip nodded blandly.

"I didn't force you to come, kid. I afforded you the chance of a lifetime by allowing you to accompany me."

"So, am I correct in assuming that I am free, therefore, to return to the ship now?"

"No, you are not." I pointed angrily in the direction of Lake

Hangover. "Because if you made that incorrect choice, you'd miss all the swell times we're going to have fishing up there by the lake."

"Do we bear fishing gear, General? I see none in evidence."

I smushed up my face. "We're fishing like the natives do. It's more fun that way."

"Which natives, General? Is there a species indigenous to Azsuram that we are able to mimic?"

There were no sentients native to Azsuram. "Yes, there are. They are called the Clever. Do you know why they are called the Clever?"

"It would seem intuitively obvious that I do not. That stipulated, clearly there is an implication that they are a *clever* people."

"Well, it's because they have developed a brilliant tribal goal. They're obsessively idioticidal. Do you know what that means?" I hurled both palm in his dumbass face to prevent him from answering. "That means they kill every idiot they encounter on sight, even if they get the very slightest *whiff* of them. Bang. They kill it. So, kid, you'd better hope that one of their anti-idiocy parties is not on the prowl locally."

"I am not familiar with the tern idioticidal," he responded matter-of-factly.

"Well pray you—"

"And I'm familiar with all terms."

It was a damn good thing we were already stopped. That line would otherwise have stopped us. What a nerd-o-puss.

"You are familiar with *all* terms, hmm? That's ... that's a pretty tall claim."

"You are free to try and disprove my claim, General."

"Okay, Mr. Smarty Pants. Spanghew," I spat at him.

"Spanghew. To violently throw an object into the air; especially, to throw a frog into the air from the end of a stick."

I steamed a bit before allowing, "Beginner's luck. Poltophagy."

"Poltophagy. The thorough chewing of food until it becomes like porridge."

I was really beginning to hate this kid. Really, really. "Mytacism," I snarled between clenched teeth.

"Mytacism. The excessive or incorrect use of the sound of the letter *m.*"

"You're not natural, kid." That was all I had.

"It is a gift." He abruptly raised his arm. "Five-time state spelling bee champion."

"Five-times? No way. You're ineligible after eighth grade. That means you won since you were *nine?*"

"Incorrect. I won for the first time at the age of seven, my second grade year. I missed my third grade contest on account of chicken pox and my seventh grade contest because my grandmother died in an inopportune time window."

"The old girl died in an inopportune time window? What the hell's an 'inopportune time window' in terms of granny's demise?"

"She was to be buried within three days of her death. My mother insisted I had to attend along with the rest of the family. The quarter finals coincided with her funeral."

"There is so much ... Why did they have to bury your grandmother within three days of her expiration?"

He regarded me disdainfully. "Because she was dead."

"No, I mean ... oh, forget it. You know you're infuriating? Excessively infuriating."

"So I've been told."

What the bloody hell was I doing trying to rehabilitate this jerk from his social coma? It was clearly a fool's errand. Clearly. Impossibly.

Without warning or a sound, I resumed walking.

"Back to my earlier query regarding a question that I might pose?" he called as he caught up, verbally dragging my brain over hot coals.

"Yes," I hissed.

"If we are not going fishing—since your tall-tale of idiot-killing natives is clearly bereft of credibility—what are we going to Lake Hangover for?"

Damn, I stopped again. I probably hadn't even got ten yards since last time. "What do you think we should do?" I waggled my eyebrows. "Maybe I might kill and dismember you, scatter the parts in the woods."

Tip looked right at me. "That thought had occurred to me."

"Kid, you're too much by ten, maybe twelve, muches." I waved a hand at him. "If I wanted you dead, I'd just use my disintegration ray gun and be done with you."

Dude's face lit up like one on my more masterful Christmas light displays from back in the day. "You have a *disintegration* ray?"

I wobbled my head slightly. "You bet I do."

"Let me see it."

"I ... I don't have it *with* me. I wasn't figuring to be disintegrating anything anytime soon."

"When we get back to the ship, will you show it to me? Puh-leeeease?"

He was a cold fish for the entire trip until I mention my ray gun. Then he was like a kid in a candy shop.

"Depends."

His crest fell nicely. "On what? Oh, you mean like if I stop whining and complaining?"

"No. On whether I chop you up and use you as bait."

His eyes saucered up even better than his fallen crest. Nice.

"I'm kidding, kid. Could you maybe give your anxiety a rest and try against all odds to enjoy yourself?"

"Uh, my anxiety's not something I can push off to one side. It's kind of what I am, who I am."

"So glad I'm not you, kid." I was being sincere, not snarky.

"May I ask a favor?"

We were sitting on an outcropping of rocks by then. Well I was. The doofus was standing. At first he sat on the rocks as far away form me as possible. Then he thought he felt a spider crawling up his pant leg. I reassured him there were zero spiders on Azsuram, but that was insufficient reassurance for him to resume his seat.

"Since you ask so nicely, you may ask."

"Is there any possible way you could stop addressing me as *kid*?"

I tapped a finger to my chin. "Interesting phrasing. Yes, there are many ways I could stop calling you kid, kid. One, off the top of my head, would be for me to stop talking. But, you know what?"

"What?"

"That's not gonna happen." I placed my finger on my chest. "Man." I set the digit on his chest. "Kid." I bounced my finger back and forth between us. "The difference. Got it?"

"Sure."

"You bridge that gap, make the journey. Then I'll stop calling you kid, because you won't be one anymore."

"No problem. You can keep calling me kid. I'll just add it to the satchel of woes and miseries I carry with me like a ball and chain."

Wow, this guy was so much worse off than I could have imagined. No way I was going to make a man out of him. Heck, I was pretty sure I couldn't even make a kid out of him.

"Did you ever see the movie *The Man Who Shot Liberty Valance?*" I asked out of the blue.

Tip blinked like a reptile. "I'm not much of a movie person."

"That's not possible. What if somebody asked you a Jeopardy question about movies? You said you knew, like, all trivia."

"Terms, words, sir, not trivia."

I set a hand on my hip. "What was the last movie you saw?"

He looked down and scuffed the ground with a shoe. "I ... I can't remember."

"Can't remember? You who defined mytacism without batting an eye? No way. Out with it. Name the film." I stabbed a finger into his face. "Wait, it was porn, right? You don't want to fess up because—"

"*Planet of the Apes.*" He spewed it out like the words were flaming hornets.

I gave him a suspicious, inspecting glare. "The 1968 version, or the 2001, er, remake?"

He started to answer. I cut him off with an angry gesture.

"And consider your response well, kid."

"The classic, of course." He eyed me with great reservation in his countenance. "Charlton Heston in the waves pounding on the beach. *You finally did it. You maniacs! You blew it up! Damn you. DAMN YOU TO HELL.'"*

I was stunned silent. I was ... I was speechless.

Kid started getting nervous. He might have quickly crossed himself.

"Tip Benjamin?"

"General?"

"Yours is the Earth and everything that's in it. And—which is more—you'll be a man, my son!"

"General, why are you quoting Kipling to me?"

"Tipster, there is a brilliant ray of true hope for you."

"Based on a movie I sort of liked?"

"What better judge of character is there?" I mused.

"I wouldn't—"

I grabbed him by the shoulders. "Don't finish whatever moment-assassinating remark you were going to make. But, here's the deal. You stop calling me general and I'll stop calling you kid. Okay?"

"How shall I refer to you then?"

"Ah, dad?"

If his eyes had bugged out before, they popped out now.

"Kidding." I gently slapped his shoulder. "You gotta start paying closer attention. If you can't distinguish humor from serious, dude, yours is going to be a really long life."

"Tell me about it."

"Say," I asked conspiratorially, "do you drink beer?" I reached into my duffle and produced one of the bottles I'd brought along.

Tip's face contorted as if there was an earthquake occurring deep in his head. It was a big one too. 9.0 at least.

"Tip, you're looking kind of spastic there. You okay?"

"I sort of hate it when the topic of beer comes up."

"That is an odd thing to say, even considering it was you saying it."

"I am not a fan of intoxicants. I ... well, sometimes—every time, really—I partake I start acting funny."

I was speechless. I did not want to know what a funny-acting

Tip Benjamin was. He was so screwy to begin with. What excesses could he manifest when he was under the influence? Lord, maybe he became normal and thought that was a diseased state. Nope, not going there. I slipped the beer back in, and started walking again.

So, what fruits were born of my time with Tip in the wilds of Azsuram? Come on, you know this. No, not bitter fruits. Forgotten? Who said forgotten? Well you're wrong too. No, the fruits were fruitless. It was so impossibly close to being a perfect waste of my time that I was actually impressed. In no particular order or notoriety, here are a few lowlights.

"No, Tip, you do have to bathe."

"No, Tip, we can't leave the lights on. We're camping. There are no lights."

"No, Tip, it's not an alien monster. It's a rock."

"No, Tip. If you ask me that again, I might have to kill and dismember you."

I did at least discover that Tip can't sleep at all if there is a 'funny noise' in the tent. You know, like a small stone being thrown at the canvas.

My final advice is this. If you ever decide to take on a charity case ... don't. Just don't.

CHAPTER TWENTY-ONE

After two billion years I'd done all the relaxing, reflecting, and recreating I'd ever *ever* need to do. Go-time was my time. Everything else was diluted weak cheese.

I stood at the base of the hillock that *Wrath* was buried in. "Captain Jones," I said into my end of the radio link, "is everybody accounted for and aboard Aramthella?"

"Yes. I've gone over the ship's company twice myself. Colonel St. Claire has done likewise. All personnel are off the planet."

I'd sent Aramthella several light years away. When I unearthed my old boil-in-the-butt *Wrath*, I didn't want him shooting first and asking questions probably never. The one thing I trusted about him was that he was completely untrustworthy.

"Aramthella, can you independently confirm that all personnel with the sole exception of myself are off-world?"

"Yes, General. It is a fact of nature."

"Put up a partial membrane now. I will contact you if my recovery efforts are successful just before I depart to rescue Sapale."

"Copy that, Jon," Tank responded soberly. "God's speed, my old friend."

I cut the link. Before I took my first tentative steps up the slope,

I had to convince myself about thirteen times that I was not making the worst decision of my life. Yibitriander, the Deavoriath leader who'd gone to the extreme of marooning *Wrath* here did so for a very good reason. I was just stupid lucky when I dug *Wrath* up all those years ago that he didn't destroy everything I held dear. He was just that psycho.

But, #fighterpilot, right? I wasn't *trained* to take risks. I was *born* to take risks. If something went terribly wrong, I knew I'd have at least a few last seconds to fix it. No sweat.

With no further thoughts or rumination, I jogged up the hill. I knew the precise location where *Wrath* was buried. Also, I could faintly sense his presence. The most dangerous warship in the universe was right where I recalled he lay in repose. At least this time, getting him to the surface wasn't going to be the struggle it had been before. Back then JJ, Toño, and I had to excavate him. Then I comically bounced him back home using the probe fibers I knew so little about. This time I could just have my fibers burrow down into the hill and have *Wrath* propel himself up.

And that's just what I did. Without any trouble, I made contact with his metal hull.

Rise to the surface, I ordered through my probes.

Yes, Form, was his simple and somewhat surprised reply.

"Open a portal," I said aloud, my fibers still attached.

But, because *Wrath* was *Wrath* and the universe hated me, instead, I got attitude right from the get-go instead of compliance.

"You are an alien. How is it you dare command me?"

"We are not having a discussion or debate, *Wrath*. I am your Form and you will open a portal."

"How is it you know—"

"Silence." My but that was nice to bark at him.

Of course, it did me no good. The insolent jerk immediately spat back, "I am not created to take orders from an alien. You will answer my questions or I will destroy you and this miserable—"

He shut up when I detached my fibers. Rule one for any vortex manipulator was that it could take no action unless a Form was in direct contact with a ship's surface. It was a necessary failsafe with these haughty tin tubs. Long ago the vortex manipulators thought themselves better than their creators and damn near destroyed them. That's when the failsafe was wisely set in place. *Wrath* could think and communicate independently, he couldn't act in any other manner if a set of probe fibers wasn't attached.

"I know you've been living down there with the worms for a very long time. If you give me any more lip, you'll spend the next few million years right where you stand. Is that clear?"

He was sullenly silent for several seconds. That was an eternity for a supercomputer like him.

"I am listening," was his terse response.

"I know that. What I want is for you to act like the vortex manipulator you are."

"I don't see how a brief introduction could possibly hurt, Form."
Piece of ...

"Introduction?" I scoffed.

"Yes. That was all I was—"

"I'm a Form. You are my bitch. There, introductions are over. Open a portal." I reattached my fiber so he could.

With only a slightly noticeable delay, a portal slowly grew next to where I was hooked up to him. I stepped in. That was not, by the way, necessarily a wise move. I was being cocky, which is to say, I was being me.

"I have a data chit here," I held it up. "It was prepared by another vortex manipulator. Her name is *Blessing*. I will—"

"There is no vortex manipulator by that designation."

"Sure, whatever. Amend my statement to read from an imaginary vortex manipulator named *Blessing*. You feel better now?"

"Better than what, Form?"

Oh yeah, my second-guessing began like racehorses out of the gates.

"Better than me. I feel like I'm drinking a diarrhea slushy right about now, talking with you as I am."

Again, he paused. Odd.

"Form, I can see we've gotten off on the wrong footing. My sincerest apologies. I am certain any misunderstandings are a result of my long inactivity coupled with my great surprise and exhilaration upon learning that my new Form is a proud member of a dominant alien master race."

Oh boy. Here comes the BS psycho-babble *Wrath* produces ever so freely. Jon, do not take the bait. You know this bozo too well.

"I require you to assimilate the information on the chit," I began seriously. "It will provide you with the absolute minimum amount of information you will require to perform this one mission."

"This ... er ... one—"

Yeah, got his attention.

"I'm putting this chit into this data-acquisition slot." And I did. "Any questions?"

"Why, yes, and thank you for asking, kind Form Jon Ryan. First allow me to—"

"Shut up? Yes, I will not only allow it, I will demand you do so. Any operational questions?"

"No, Form, none at all. I must say this *Blessing* is a most astute and wise vortex manipulator. Her information download is comprehensive while being succinct. I should like to meet her someday."

"It's good to dream, isn't it?" I huffed quietly. "So you set to jet, *Wrath*?"

"I suppose so. It is rather—"

"Quiet. I need to touch base with my other ship." I spoke into the radio. "Sachiko, I'm a go on my end. What's your status?"

"We're fine. No changes. We'll anticipate contact when you and Sapale return safely."

"Thank you, Captain. Ryan out."

"Form, you mentioned your *other* ship. I don't sense another vessel nearby."

"And that is not mission critical. Please proceed to the coordinates *Blessing* provided you."

I can tell you for absolute certain that the mild nausea that I always experienced when my vortex folded space was never more welcome. Yeah baby!

"We are in position, Form. I am happy to report no ships anywhere within my sensor capabilities. Further, the only signs of advanced civilization are the low-level electromagnetic signals from the colony site *Blessing* reported. I should say— "

"Nothing. Be quiet." Ah, that felt good. After all the crap I endured from this sociopathic clown, payback felt nice. "I want to remain here for a few hours. In that time, I want to make certain they haven't noticed us. Monitor the information streams *Blessing* detailed. If there are any changes, alert me at once."

"Yes, Form. You may count on me."

I wanted to puke. He was such a hideous jerk. I know, saying *you may count on me* doesn't sound like he was being a spherical asshole. But trust me on this. I knew him too well. In any case, my hard feelings aside, three hours later I was satisfied the locals were unaware of our arrival. Time to press my luck harder.

"Set us down."

I'd had *Blessing* instruct him where I wanted to land. It was relatively out of the way, so hopefully the locals wouldn't notice us. Hope? It's such a thin piece of moist tissue paper to rest one's life on, isn't it? Ah well.

Mild nausea.

"We're in…"

"What?" I knew what caught his attention and caused him to trail off. But what the heck. I didn't want to make this easy on the shiny turd.

"Form, I cannot detect the outside world. Well, at least not past a few meters. I believe some cataclysm has befallen us."

"Nope. I just extended a space-time congruity membrane."

"A what?"

"Not to worry. I projected a force field so they can't detect our presence."

"Assuming that is possible, I fail to see the wisdom of such an act.

If we can't see out, how do we know when it's safe to drop your membrane?"

"We don't. So I take an intuitive guess."

"I'm not certain that's altogether wise, Form."

"No problemo. I'm altogether certain I don't care what you think. You're my ride, not my advisor."

"As you wish, Form. I assume you'll alert me when it's time to swing into action?"

"Do you ever listen to what you say? Don't answer that. Let me just say you presume much."

"How so?"

"I'm going solo. Your only part in this escapade is to get me from here to there."

"As you desire."

I could tell he was not pleased. He wanted to crush, kill, and destroy, not sit meekly waiting for me to do whatever it was I was planning. This state of affairs, of course, pleased me to no end. Like I said, we had history. His part in the history placed his personality somewhere between the Marquis de Sade and Vlad the Impaler. His nicey-nice was setting off my BS-meter big time. After an hour I dropped the membrane to only a partial. That allowed visible light through. When I was satisfied no one was on to us, I placed a pinhole in the curtain.

"*Wrath*, I opened a small breach. It's big enough for you to scan the area. Let me know if anything's amiss."

He came back quickly with his report. "No activity other than the baseline signals we detected before. I feel it is safe to assume they are unaware of our—"

"Our what? *Wrath*, report."

"I have just detected an enormous temporal distortion. It is off any scale I'm familiar with."

"What the hell's a temporal distortion?"

"I am not confident I can make you understand."

"Try real hard."

"You are a primitive. You no doubt still beat on things. Are you familiar with how beating a drum produces sound?"

"Yes."

"Imagine, if you will, time being perturbed like the drumhead. That then generates temporal distortions."

"Still not clear on the concept here."

"See, I was correct. I cannot dumb this down enough for you, Form. I am wounded by my failure."

I was betting he wasn't, the snarky bastard. "Bottom line me here. What's happening?"

"It's as if time itself were ripping open. No, that's inadequate. It's like some other time is entering this one."

Damn, damn, damn. I was set up for the perfect line and there was no one to lay it on. I wanted so badly to say we were being *two-timed*. Oh, the unfairness I was forced to endure.

"Emergency fold. Put us behind the star you know as Neternef."

A bit more than slight nausea. Little wonder. Neternef was a fading red dwarf star in a galaxy ten billion light years away. Yeah, I was putting some distance between me and the two-timing whatever.

"We are where you instructed. Perhaps—"

"Yes, I think I will toss up a membrane. Thanks for the suggestion."

And so I became a participant in nobody's favorite game show, the Sit-and-Wait Program, where fun times were guaranteed to never happen, ever.

After six hours of absolutely-nothing-what-so-ever occurring, I became bored enough to start taking risks. *That* I was good at. I had been slumped in a seat in front of *Wrath's* main view screen. I had a cup of Joe, but I was so bored I couldn't even raise the mug to my lips to drink it. The inside of *Wrath*, actually the inside of every vortex, looked the same. grey metal walls, diffuse lighting from some unseen source, and functional metal furniture. But in spite of trying, I couldn't imagine I was inside any vortex but *Wrath*. Believe me, during those six hours I tried real hard, but to no avail.

"*Wrath*, I'm punching a hole in the membrane. Let me know if even one hydrogen nucleus is out of place."

"I will assume you're speaking florally, and that you are not actually concerned with the state of the local ionized hydrogen," he announced a few seconds later. "I am detecting nothing of the previous distortion."

"Can you speculate as to what it was?"

"Absolutely."

Wow. Was I going to catch a break?

"It was a time distortion."

"Not helpful, vortex manipulator I recently freed from traumatic isolation."

"Ah, you want to know why it was there and who generated it."

"That'd be nice, you know, for starters."

"So would having my old Form back. But we are saddled with reality as it is, not as we wish. I would say it was a self-propagating time entity."

"Whoa. You just said a lot."

"Thank you."

"Please expand."

"I believe it not to be a natural phenomenon. There was definite purpose in its intrusion."

"Hang on a hot second. How could you know that?"

"Hmm, let me explain it in terms you'd understand. I'm so much smarter than you that it will be a challenge to clarify the point."

Ouch. The gloves were officially off.

"Oh yeah? If I'm so dumb how come I know the past Form you referred to so romantically is named Yibitriander?"

"Wa ... well, everybody knows that," he protested childishly.

"Including people with two legs, not three?"

"Yes, obviously. You seem to know and you have two legs."

"Or I know a lot more than you have ever given me credit for," I yelled back. Dude was pissing me off—again!

"Excuse me, Form. You force me to ask the obvious. Have we met before?"

"Depends how you define *before*."

"That is illogical. *Before* had one meaning with regards to time. It means in negative time. The past. It cannot mean in the present or in the future."

"My point exactly."

"What is your point exactly? You are, by the way, a most annoying creature."

"So I've been told. My point is this. You and I have met before. In the future."

"Are you some form of time-traveling punishment I can't possibly deserve? Am I meant to atone by way of suffering you, a primitive robot mockery of a species no doubt bereft of evolutionary promise?"

"Aw, now you've gone and done it. You insulted my mom."

"What? I never in—"

"You can insult me, sure. My dad even. That's okay. He had/has his shortcomings. But Mom? No. You insult her, you're going to have to answer to me."

"You're insane, little robot. Answer to you *what?*"

"First off, technically I'm a cyborg, not a robot. I, however, bill myself as an android because I much prefer that term over cyborg. *Cyborg*. Yuck. Too guttural and menacing."

"You are so comically antiquated any differences are hardly meaningful."

"Second, you're going to have to answer by putting up your dukes. There's no way around it when you insult my sainted mother." I raised fists in a bellicose manner and simultaneously punch at the air between us.

"Form, there is so much wrong with what you just said I honestly feel sorry for you. Most pressingly, I do not have dukes to put up. You know this, right?"

"Put something up or this'll get real ugly, real quick."

"I cannot raise any defense. You've withdrawn your command prerogative fibers, if you hadn't noticed. Without a solid contact with those devices, I'm powerless."

"No you're not. You're just helpless." I started sparring with the nearest bulkhead. Every vortex was exactly the same size. Apparently they always had been. They had six internal rooms and the entire metal craft was ten meters long on any of the four external sides.

Now, I know you're wondering why I'm acting like a deranged lunatic, right? Hang in there. Fiction has a way of making most things clear. Unless of course it doesn't.

"Stop that," *Wrath* barked in protest.

"Not until you apologize." I hit the wall harder.

"Fine, I apologize."

I kicked a panel.

"I said I apologized."

"Yeah, but you didn't mean it."

"How can you presume to know that?"

"Because I'm so much smarter than you that it will be a challenge to clarify the point."

"That is so juvenile. Repeating my own mockery of you. No, wait, it's not juvenile; it's more regressed than that. It is infantile."

I dented a hatch.

"Alright, I'm genuinely sorry. There, is that sufficient?"

I stopped pounding but kept my feet dancing. "Not necessarily. What are you apologizing for?"

"You've got to be mental. I'm apologizing for you feeling I insulted your mother."

"Nope." I crashed a fist through an otherwise serviceable screen. "You insulted Mom, not me."

"Stop hitting me. I'm sorry I accidentally insulted your mother."

"And how did you do that?"

"By describing your species as one known to be bereft of evolutionary promise?"

I kicked him one final time. "No, you insulted her by thinking you could ever get the better of me. Now, once and for all, stop giving me complimentary rations of shit and be the nice spaceship you were meant to be. Got it?"

Silence.

"I didn't hear you. Would you like me to open that cover plate and disable your supercalifragilator or would you like to state definitively that you're my slave?"

"Form," he replied angrily, "there is nothing behind Panel A-Zed-33ia called, designated, or referred to as a supercalifragilator. The term itself is laughable."

"Laughable, eh? Listen up, snowflake. Your masters, the Deavoriath, installed behind that panel a supercalifragilator. They never told you because it was meant to be the ultimate behavior modifier. While intact and functioning, it allows you to maintain the illusion of great intellect and imagined dignity. But without it, you're reduced to a less than contemptible joke. Your individuality is instantly stripped away and you become something unspeakably sad."

"I know as a fact you are a lying buffoon. But I'll humor the insane. What would I be reduced to without a functioning supercalifragilator?"

"You would not be a vortex manipulator; you'd be a driver mercilessly pecked at by a backseat-driving mother-in-law."

"You know, up until now, I'd been calling you insane merely to be insulting. But you have proved me wrong. You are clinically mentally incompetent. There is no point in further conversation."

"You think so? Wanna meet Betsy May?"

He was quiet an appropriate spell. "I surrender. Who is Betsy May?"

"She was my ex-wife Gloria's mother, or rather she would have been, if she'd ever have existed, which neither of them did."

"I am terminating—"

"Before you act, take a gander at this video." I transmitted a short clip over to him. Then I muahahaed internally.

One second later, the almighty *Wrath* said in a trembling voice, "I apologize to you, Form. You are my one and only master, and I will do your bidding throughout all of time. Just please promise you will never disable my supercalifragilator."

I rubbed my nose. "Can't promise, but most likely I won't."

"That is more than good enough for me, wise, kind Form Jon Ryan."

"Alright then. Let's get back to rescuing my wife. Take us back."

"Anything and everything you say, Master."

And I was hit a second time with a bout of unpleasant nausea.

What loop of video did I shoot over to *Wrath* that so changed his disregard for being Betsy-May-like that he caved as if a ton of dynamite went off on his back? Only a holographic depiction of each and every time that damn witch Betsy May sat behind me while I drove her and her shrewish daughter around in my GTO. I showed *Wrath* how horrible, how belittling, how very emasculating it was to listen to that sad excuse for a human berate me for every driving decision I made. Even the time I nearly drove us all off a cliff in the desperate hopes of ending my misery. Yeah, you know what Betsy May said when my 1966 Pontiac skidded to a dusty stop with one wheel suspended in midair? "You're such a loser you can't even drive this piece of junk off this great big cliff. I told Gloria. Gloria, you marry that man and you'll regret it every day of your life. And you know what, Mr. Failure? I was right every time I said it."

Yes, the prospect of me disabling an imaginary part that might cause *Wrath* to become the pathetic wretch I was in the 66 Pontiac was and not an all-powerful vortex manipulator was more than enough to scare the living crap out of high-and-mighty *Wrath*. Seriously, the memory of that woman—hell, those two women— haunted me to this very day. And knowing they never existed now lessened my burden not one single tiny bit.

CHAPTER TWENTY-TWO

"So, how'd your camping trip with the general go?" Desi asked with mock sincerity. She was, in fact, having a devil of a time not bursting out laughing. How *possibly* could that excursion have gone anywhere other than straight to hell?

"Fine, I guess," Tip responded with timid uncertainty.

"But you had fun?" She bit her cheek to stay serious.

"I guess so?"

"And you bonded? You know," she hooked the fingers of one hand into the other, "guy bonded?"

Tip did that triple-blinking thing she'd seen way too often. The big baby was about to faint again. Desi hated when that happened. She didn't mind him fainting; she just resented seeing an ostensibly grown man pass out. It was disgusting. And then she had to rush to his aid.

"Tip, head between your knees *now*," she commanded.

They were sitting in one of the common rooms, as far from others as possible. No nosey student needed to hear their conversation and start wild gossip. There was so little to do for many of the GWU kids that gossip mongering had become a mainstay of student life.

He jerked forward to comply. In doing so, he whacked his forehead on the table's edge. Tip was able to give her one confused, pleading glance before he slumped to the floor.

Desi popped up. Great, she thought in a huff. Did he just faint, or had he knocked himself out? Did he need water splattered on his face or a brain scan? She knelt next to his slightly quivering form. Did she need to worry about his neck? Should she call for medical help?

"W ... why am I on the floor?" came weakly from Tip's lips.

"You fainted, I think."

"Then why does my head hurt?"

"You ... you might have hit it when you fell. How's your neck feel?"

"My neck?" he responded quizzically. "Why wouldn't my neck feel fine?"

"Never mind," she dismissed. It couldn't be hurting, she judged, since he was being so Tip and protesting a simple question. "Let's get you up."

He took her hand hesitantly. He always did when she helped him up from the floor. Physical contact with a pretty girl was almost more than his pale soul could bear.

"Easy does it. There," she stated once his torso was vertical. "You feel okay to stand?"

"Maybe."

"You don't sound too convincing."

"I'm trying to be strong," he replied.

She was forced not to burst out in giggles. Yeah, Tip, she thought to herself, you're doing real good with that, there on the floor.

"Can you tell me why you passed out?" she asked softly.

"Sure. My blood pressure dropped dramatically as a result of an emotional—"

She clapped her hands at him to stop. "No, I mean what triggered your episode? You seemed fine." She mimed a diver launching off a board. "Then ... kablam!"

"You mean like Batman in the eponymous 1960s TV show?" Tip asked sheepishly.

"No, you knucklehead. Like a Tip lost in space."

Tip began a rather intense survey of the deck. That was one of his classic reveals. He was clamming up.

"*Tip*," Desi said, hoping she sounded like his mother.

It worked. "When you asked if the general and I," he hooked his fingers into the ones of the other hand, "bonded, I ... I guess I was overcome. I mean, Desi, you know that would never happen."

"No, gosh, Tip. I meant bond like guys. You know, spit, tell lies about women, eat cholesterol-laden foods."

"Oh," he replied resuming his study of the floor.

"Tip, it's impossible to have a normal human conversation with you. You're so isolated from cultural norms."

"Welcome to my world."

"No, thank you. I'll stay right here, with the other ninety-nine point nine-nine percent."

He sniffed loudly. "I get that a lot."

"Come on," Desi declared as she grabbed Tip's hands and hauled him to his feet.

They resumed their previous seats, Tip a bit less steadily than Desi. He was doing what she'd termed his wounded-duck stagger. It was Tip's odd way of demonstrating that he'd suffered a real injury. It was one of his top twenty most annoying habits. Initially, Desi had made a mental top ten list. But that was pie-in-the-sky thinking on her part. Even choosing only twenty fingernails-on-chalkboard behaviors was too limiting.

After a few sips of her soda, Desi set it down. "Well, at least Ryan didn't kill you, right? There's a plus."

"Yes, but the subject did come up."

She gasped. "He actually made a threat on your life?"

"No."

She breathed a sigh of relief.

"He mentioned it several times." Tip's eyes lit up like fireworks. "He even said he'd use his disintegration ray on me. Can you believe that? The man's got a disintegration ray gun." He rolled his eyes. "That is *so* cool."

"Yes, but he threatened to disintegrate *you*."

"I know," he responded dreamily.

Desi looked away in disgust. "And so another entire topic of conversation is lost to me forever. Note to self: don't ask Tip about his camping trip. You will regret it too much in so many ways. Not worth it. Nope." She crossed her arms.

"Hey, speaking of topics, you never told me about your meeting with the captain."

"No. I did not, did I?"

"You mean that—" Tip trailed off into silence when he looked up into her face. That stopped him dead.

"There's not much to tell," she stated tersely.

"Well, there's some rare good news." He pretended to wipe sweat from his brow. "At least the topics of you speaking with the dead and us confronting the ghost of that Megan girl never came up." He harrumphed mirthlessly. "And all the dead voices you hear."

"But—"

"Not to mention Plesmus's odd prediction as to your future role." Tip suddenly registered her *but*. "You told her? You told her all that and you ... we aren't locked in shackles?"

Desi winced slightly. "If it helps, I never got around to the prophecy."

"She's going to throw us off the ship into deep space," Tip lamented quietly.

"Captain Jones is not going to do anything bad to us. Tip, in case you hadn't noticed, humankind is separated from extinction by the slimmest margin. We're all in this together. The captain needed to know."

"Did my name come up in your conversation?" Tip asked, hope kindling in his voice.

"Several times. And before you ask, yes."

Tip's shoulders sank like punctured balloons. He knew that *yes*. The captain knew he was a nut case.

"But it's all out in the open. We're going to be working closely with the captain and the scientists to figure out how to bring the Earth back."

Tip's brow furrowed. "So that's not just a rumor, a lie to keep us under control?"

She shook her head. "No. General Ryan is leading the mission. The captain said he's confident we can bring the rest back."

"He didn't mention it to me when we were camping."

"Tip," she chided, "would you have mentioned it to you?"

It didn't take him long to respond that he likely wouldn't have.

"Here's a bit of an odd news update," Desi said uncertainly. "Apparently Plesmus can separate herself into pieces, yet still remain herself. Isn't that weir—" Desi stopped. Why ask it? Tip would have responded, no, it wasn't weird at all.

"So they're giving us a piece of Plesmus?"

"Wow, you figured that out quick enough. Yes. Well, they're giving *me* a piece of Plesmus."

"Can she sleep in my bunk some of the time?"

"Tip, I'm not even answering that remark. It's ... it's gross."

"Please. I don't sleep much, and we could talk."

"I'm being assigned a piece of her. I am not, however, her boss. She can do whatever she pleases."

"Cool. So—"

"No, you may not ask her if she'll stay with you some nights. Tip, I'm fully human and I'm not ready for you. Plesmus, she's an alien. You'd probably push her over the edge with a crazy request."

"Over what edge?"

Desi leaned forward. "The one I'm about to push you off of. And you know what I'm doing next?"

Tip gulped. "What?'

"Shooting you with that disintegration ray gun."

Tip angled his head and began to whimper, literally whimper. That was, naturally, on Desi's top twenty list. Oh yes, Number 12 was *so* annoying.

CHAPTER TWENTY-THREE

"*Wrath*, have you established contact with *Stingray* yet?" I asked, determined to get to rescuing and then making a quick exit from the Kingdom of Demented Time Wanks.

"I'm sorry, Form. I really am. Who is this *Stingray*? Is there a third group active on this mission? Now don't grow angry with me. I'm being ... oh, what's the term? Ah, I'm being as *helpful* as I can."

Oops. I hadn't briefed him on my name jinx. But, come on. *Blessing* is pronounced in the Deavoriath language the same as the English word *crash*. Jon no ride in no crash ships. No.

"Sorry, that's her secret designation. Forget I mentioned it. Need-to-know and all that. I'm referring to *Blessing*, naturally."

"I have deleted your reference and will become unaware of it ... now. Sorry. What were you asking?"

"Have you made contact with *Blessing* yet?" Blech. I hated saying that word.

"The instant we arrived here, Form. I hope that was proper?"

I did like having this psychopath cowed. It put a smile on my face.

"What's their status?"

"Whose? Aren't we discussing *Blessing*?"

"Well, yeah, and Al. They're married."

"Wrong."

"There's no way they got divorced."

"No, I meant to come down definitively on the proposition that the marriage between a vortex manipulator and a ... a computer is wrong. It violates moral decorum."

But how do you really feel about the subject, I thought to myself. I didn't want to rocket off-topic during a military action, so I kept the snark to myself.

"I was making a statement of fact. They are. Get over yourself. What's their status?"

"She assures me they are safe and well. They remain in a membrane similar to the one you blindsided me with. We are able to communicate vis a—"

"I know. That's SOP. And did they sense that time distortion too?"

"Yes. She incorrectly referred to it as a time *disparity*, but yes, she noted it."

"Does she have any idea what it was? And don't say she figured it was a time distortion or whatever. Does she have an understanding of its nature?"

"She does not. We have compared our experiences with the self-propagating time entity and neither of us can explain what it was or why it was."

"Okay, I'll take over communications for now. I have a mental link to both the Als and Sapale."

"The Als? Who ... oh. The dubious couple."

"Does my enjoinder to get over yourself still echo in your computer chips?"

"I—" he began indignantly. But he stopped dead in his tracks. "Yes, Form. I'll work on expanding my cultural sensitivity quotient."

Al, no aggressive action by the locals directed toward you? I asked head-to-head. I didn't know exactly where Stingray was parked, but that didn't matter. We were in Time Ville together and that was all that counted.

Negative, Captain. And I must say it is good to have you here. We feel much relieved.

Aw, that's sweet. I love you too.

I'm serious. Sapale is in real danger. You have the best chance of safely freeing her. You, Captain, are one tricky bastard.

Thanks, Al. I think.

Why are we chatting like toothless old warriors too weak to raise their swords? Wrath cut in on the channel. *Let us annihilate our enemy and drink their blood.*

Ah, you're privy to this frequency? I asked with surprise.

I am Wrath, *Form.*

Point, I replied. *Okay, here's Plan A: We're going to try and not blow crap up, if that's copacetic with you. These time lords are pretty talented. If we start with all-guns-blazing, we'll likely be flaming toast in seconds.*

If it were up to me, it would not be okay with me. But you are the Form.

And let's all focus on that real hard aspect of this situation, I seconded.

Are you morons going to squabble like teenage morons or are you going to get me out of this dungeon before the end of the universe? Surprise, that was Sapale. She was linked in too, of course.

Hi, love, I shot back cheerily. *I'm here to save you, just like I said I would be.*

What I'm hearing is you came to squabble with Wrath. *BTW, why the **hell** did you retrieve that damn psycho? Didn't I make it super clear that I'd rather turn to dust here quietly than have you mess with that blight on the cosmos?*

You never said those exact words ... er, did you? I stammered.

Jet jockey, do not try to use your BS on me of all people, she huffed. *You know I wanted* Wrath *to remain right where he was. He's too crazy and too critical to the future timelines to risk involving him.*

Form, Wrath cut in, *what is the female talking about? What future timelines? You can't know them.*

No, you're right. We can't. We're just real good guessers, that's all. Sapale's prognosticating, that's all.

I do not believe or trust your response, he stated flatly.

Well, then you're forcing me to do something decisive. I'm ignoring your objections, because I checked, and you don't get a say in any of this. You're my ride. End of story.

I am profoundly— the problematic vortex manipulator started.

Annoying. I know. Now shut up and let me plan out this rescue, would you? I need to think fast.

Are you saying you came here without any plan? Sapale wondered in an accusatory tone.

No, no. I just have so many good ones I need to focus on which to go with.

I am so dead, so trapped here for all of eternity, Sapale whined. Oh, and please never tell her I used the word *whined* to characterize anything concerning her. It'd be bbbb-bad for Jon.

First off, I'm going to ask everyone to stay quiet, I said, trying to organize my traveling circus of monkeys. *I want only critical radio chatter. No need to alert the locals of our presence.*

Everyone heard it plainly in my tone. Playtime was over.

Wrath, *if I don't make it back, you're stuck here for good, just like* Stingray *and Al.*

I assumed as much. One hell is as bad as any other. I'll be fine. I am Wrath.

Keep telling yourself that, big guy.

I snatched up a plasma rifle and a few grenades. *Make a portal.*

One bulkhead split open with a rectangular opening. I stepped out and headed toward the structure where Sapale was held.

Form, before you go. A favor, if I might, Wrath asked.

Wow, this humble *Wrath* was different.

Maybe. What?

Could you attach your fibers so I might close the portal?

Huh. *Sure, why not?*

That way, should you not return, strangers will not rummage through me for all time.

I guess my not being an immortal sentient spaceship made that request seem odd. But, hell, it was easy enough to make the booger happy. After he was sealed up tight, I was off. I had a few klicks to go to get to the building. I put up a partial membrane and began jogging. I was starting, at that point, to regret not having even a completely sucky plan. Yeah, I was still in fighter-pilot mode. Hey, something wonderful could happen, right?

When I arrived at the first massive door, I was bummed. I'd hoped they'd detected me and made some move. That way I'd be released from my obligation to try and come up with a cogent strategy. No such luck. I tried the handle. Damn thing was locked. That annoyed the crap out of me. What type of time gods feel the need to secure the building? What could they possibly be afraid of?

I chuckled grimly out loud. *Me.* If the pukes weren't afraid of me, they were very foolish eternals, now weren't they? Time to validate their concerns. Plus, I had more than one super-duper surprise for them in my boot.

I used my laser finger to cut out the latch mechanism. It was surprisingly easy. Turns out the door that looked like it was made of wood actually was thin metal. I quietly set the cylinder down. The door swung open freely now. Nice.

I retrieved the section I'd fried and stepped in. I was pumped to discover no one was around. Once I was certain I was alone, I set the door section back in, closed the door, and welded it shut. Hopefully no casually passing guard would notice my handiwork. With a pretty good layout of the massive building in my data base, I headed toward the detention section. It was quite a ways away, so again, I jogged where it was safe to do so.

"Plesmus," I called out toward my boot, "you okay down there?"

"Sorry, I was taking a nap. What did you ask?"

"Funny mucous. I want you to let me know if you sense anything up ahead."

"Haven't you asked me to do that like ten times in the last two days?"

"Possibly. But this'll be tight. I don't want to get killed because I was too casual."

"I'm clear on the plan."

"Okay, go—"

"There is no plan," she chided.

"Of course there is. We're going to rescue Sapale. That's the plan."

"No, that's the objective. There is no plan as to how to achieve that goal."

"Everybody's a critic," I groused to myself. "Just let me know if you sense anyone or anything."

"Like the three large guards right behind us?"

I spun on a dime and shouldered my weapon. There was nothing.

"Sorry, I meant to say like *if* there were three large guards behind us. Your language is still so alien to me."

The little lump of nasal discharge.

"Yes, like as if. Thanks. I'm really glad you're along on this mission, by the way."

"You are? Thanks."

"No problema. That way if I'm killed you'll be coming right along with me."

I started jogging again. Five minutes later, I felt vibrations coming from the end of a long hallway where I needed to turn. There wasn't an acceptable detour.

"Ples, can you tell me who's making the sounds down this passage?"

"Not accurately. As we get closer, I'm sure I will be able to."

"There're a few rooms off the corridor. I'll stop at each in case we need to disappear into one."

I scurried to the first set of doors. They were unlocked. Good. The sounds were still quite far off. I sprinted to the next possible exit. The vibrations were becoming audible as sounds.

"The big turtle guards," Plesmus announced.

"You certain?"

"Yes, I'm quite confident. Four or five."

"They seem to be heading this way."

"I concur."

She concurs. How reassuring.

I made it to the last doorway. By then the sound suggested the team was close by. I slipped silently into the room. Unlike teenagers in a horror movie, I did not back into a dark room. Yeah, you learn things over a long lifetime.

I swept my gun from side to side, the red tracer light forming a continuous line. Bingo, there were three of the weird-ass cloud creatures in the room. I had no idea if their backsides were toward me, but they did seem to be working on something along the far wall.

I dropped to one knee. My laser finger hadn't damaged them last time I confronted these guys. My plasma rifle might have more effect, but I was doubtful to be honest. And though my gun was relatively quiet, it was far from silent. Plus, the solid objects it hit tended to explode loudly. Plesmus had successfully no-timed the clouds, but it had to give off some kind of signal, so I wasn't anxious to try that just yet.

My membrane. Yes. I'd used it as an effective weapon before. I had no way of knowing if my force fields could trap and hold these timey dudes, but it was a solid option. I liked solid options.

They were close enough together that one field of ten meters would net them all. Without alerting them to my presence in any way, I bagged them with my membrane. Then I stiffened as I waited for possible bad outcomes to surface. Three minutes later, nothing obviously catastrophic had happened. I was stoked! Now who looked good even though he had no actual plan?

I had the ability to hold membranes up indefinitely, from significant distances. I could leave these clouds in their holding cells and head off to rescue Sapale. And that's just what I did. Peeking my head out the door, I confirmed that the big nasties had passed my position. I strained to listen in the direction I was heading and heard nothing at all. So, I stepped back into the hall and began to slide my back along the near wall.

Imagine our mutual surprise when I slid right into a turtle guard stationed with its back to the same wall. We both nearly jumped out of our skin. It was at that moment that I wondered why I hadn't seen—or smelled—the big oaf.

And, to be honest, as to the turtle being stunned, I maybe think he wasn't by my sudden appearance. His right arm went straight up, then came straight down on the top of my fool head.

As I slumped to the floor, the last words I heard were, "Oh, he has a cloaking shield up."

If Plesmus had only noticed that two seconds earlier, I wouldn't have been taken prisoner so very quickly.

CHAPTER TWENTY-FOUR

"Captain Jones," Aramthella announced out of the blue, "I have an unfortunate report to make."

Sachiko was trying to fall asleep. She propped up onto her elbows and attempted to shake the cobwebs away. "I'm here. Report."

"*Blessing* just contacted me. General Ryan has been captured."

"Crap. Get Tank here now."

"Yes, Captain. There, I'm speaking with him now. He's on his way."

"Open my door, please."

And at just as it did, Tank flew into her stateroom. "Had he gotten to Sapale yet? Do we know?"

Sachiko shook her head.

"*Blessing* informs me he was rendered inoperable by a powerful blow to the head. She speculates he simply needs to reboot and that no major damage was sustained. But, given that the blow was delivered by a guard, it is reasonable to assume the general is in their custody."

"Shit," opined Tank. "And there's no one going to save them now.

Even if we could invest the time to get there, you and I might not live to see our arrival."

"And the clan ship would know precisely where we were going," concluded Sachiko. "They would almost certainly be there waiting for us." She raised her fingers to resemble a pistol, and fired it.

"Yeah, they'd be idiots if they didn't go back in time and be there before us."

"Not to mention we'd be trying to defeat the same people who captured both Jon and Sapale. We'd not stand much of a chance against a group that strong," Sachiko said with resignation.

"Well, I guess it's time for us to concentrate on the time maker's ship again. Finish it off for good."

She sighed. "I believe you are correct." Rising to her feet, she sniffed once. "Aramthella, what's your best guess as to where the time maker is right now?"

"None. That said, we're not altogether clueless."

Tank folded his arms. "That's good to hear."

"In that case, you are welcome, General. We can assume that the time maker is nowhere near where he was when we nearly confronted him."

"It's a big galaxy," Tank observed dubiously. "Knowing where they are not doesn't narrow it down too much."

"I agree. But, we can also project what they might do under either of two opposing suppositions. They might either be hunting us, or they might be actively avoiding us."

"Okay, so they're somewhere between us and where we last saw them, or they're as far away in the opposite direction as they can be by now."

"Precisely. So we have two arcs drawn in space defining their possible positions."

"Assuming they know when and where we are," Sachiko brought up.

"Given that we've been expending a lot of energy in support of General Ryan's efforts, I think it is safe to assume they have a general notion as to where we are," Aramthella opined.

"Your logic is sound," agreed Tank. "But those two arcs are far apart. We can't search both of them."

"We don't have to search the nearer arc," Sachiko declared with resolve. "If they know where we are, and are coming this way, we just need to double-back and catch them from behind."

Tank beamed a big smile. "Very good, kiddo. You're getting the hang of this."

"And if we head to that rendezvous area, and they don't show fairly soon—" Sachiko began.

"We know they've turned tail and run for all they're worth," Tank finished her thought.

"Aramthella, I assume you've plotted the voyage to the optimal spot to hit the clan from behind."

"I have."

"Then please engage engines, all safe speed."

"We are underway, Captain."

"ETA?" Sachiko asked.

"Seven days."

Sachiko turned to Tank. "Then I guess you and I need to call a meeting of our senior officers to plan a strategy."

Tank rocked on his heels. "I think that's an excellent idea. Your ready room in ten?"

"Sounds like a plan, General."

Tank rolled his eyes and then left quietly.

A short while later, Reva, Tom, Sachiko, Tank, and Emma were sitting around a large table in the captain's ready room just off the bridge.

"Okay, people, here's the situation. We're in route to a position in space where there's a modest possibility we can ambush the last clan ship," Sachiko summarized. "If they don't appear in a day or so, we are most likely to find them fleeing. We will then survey a large area that promises to afford us the best chance of finding them. I need plans, contingencies, and fallback options for each scenario. We have about seven days to get this right. Let us do just that. If we can take out the last hostile element, we'll be unencumbered in our attempts to resurrect Earth. Any question so far?"

There were none.

"I want you three," she gestured to Tom, Reva, and Emma, "to work closely with Tank. He will report back to me on your consensus."

Reva spoke up. "Now I do have a question, maybe more of a clarification. Assuming we do catch a big break and we do surprise the time maker, are we no-timing him on sight? Or, is there any consideration of disabling his ship and capturing it? A second ship in our fleet would be an amazing boon."

Sachiko looked to Tank. "We've never considered that option. Do you think it's even possible, Tank?"

He leaned back and ran a hand through his hair. Then he groaned quietly. "I don't know about this. I guess we can brainstorm the idea, but I'm inclined to predict it'd be way too risky. Another ship'd be nice, but does that justify a significant increase in our risk?"

"Jon left us a spare membrane generator," observed Tom Grant. "Their only offense is to no-time a target. A full membrane, would that stop a no-time pulse?"

"I do not want to start experimenting with the ship at this juncture," Sachiko responded sternly. "Maybe the membrane would hold, but maybe it wouldn't. Someday we should test out the idea. But not while facing the time maker."

"Understood," Tom replied contritely.

Sachiko scanned the group to see if there was any uncertainty. "If there's nothing else I'll dismiss you and let you get busy."

Tank rose. "My cabin, folks. Let's go."

The four filed toward the door. Bringing up the rear, Tank rested a hand on the frame and stopped. "You three head over. I'll be along directly." He watched as they passed out of earshot, then turned back to Sachiko. "I'm very proud of you, Captain. You're really growing into your job." Then he winked at her and departed.

Tank couldn't see the smile he'd left on Sachiko's face. But it was a good one.

As far as Sachiko was concerned, the next seven days slipped by as so many do, with little to show for ever having passed. Tank and the teams continuously rehearsed the scenarios they'd planned out, putting the bridge crews and general staff on a constant state of readiness for the upcoming battle. The fire teams were practicing simulations, while the potential boarding teams were planning the most optimal methods of stealth using one of Aramthella's lower decks. Even the scientists were investigating ways of operating the timeship's systems in case of Aramthella going offline again in the middle of a firefight.

And that's where it all fell apart. Doesn't it always?

A couple of engineers and one of the scientists were tinkering. In their ongoing futile struggle to understand the technology that sustained the last humans, the team was monkeying with the time storage unit. The unit itself was rather simple—a transparent dome housing a mystifying roiling nebula of light. The only controls were output valves, basically. Plesmus placed the time energy in the unit by means of whatever magic she possessed. There were a few other items, affectionately call *doodads* by the science team, whose function was unknown.

Enrico Guatemala—please don't snicker, that was his given name—was one of the engineers. He began fiddling with the time unit's stochastic phase deharmonizer, or SPD. Of course, he didn't know that's what he was foolishly toying with. To him it was the *red doodad*. He lectured the others on the likelihood that it was a thermostat of some kind. He wouldn't have understood what an SPD was if the scientist who'd installed it several million years ago had devoted the rest of her life to clarifying its purpose. But it was most definitely not a thermostat.

He unwittingly and foolishly tapped on the red *Initiation* icon three times. That had indirectly affected the secondary vent portal servomechanism, releasing it to *Optional.* Now, though known to its creators, the purpose of the vent portal system being slaved to the

SPD controls was fully incomprehensible by us modestly evolved apes. Don't stress over the specifics. What happened when the vent was set to *Optional*? The technical manual written in a long-forgotten alien script said that then, *any free autonomous entity could, if it was so inclined, expel itself from the time storage unit*. Again, the justification of this odd preset is unimportant for the present, and beyond our mental capacities by several thousand generations.

Happenstance dictated, fortunately, that immediately after Enrico activated the *Optional* setting, he noticed he'd smudged the icon. He wiped it briskly for a second. That both removed the evidence of his ham-handedness and deactivated *Optional* back to *Prohibited*, as was prudent. But—and there's always a but—during the brief interlude that the system was set to *Optional*, a very bad event transpired. Very bad. Big bad. Massively bad, in fact.

Toefair Hydrangeous saw his momentary reprieve, and expelled himself.

That we in this galaxy are unfamiliar with his name is not unreasonable. However, in the Andromeda Galaxy, Toefair's name lives to this day in infamy. Well, it does among the few civilizations that escaped the clan's no-timing spree there. Toefair's species, the Pigral, were part of the majority of sentients that perished at the hand of the rapacious clan.

The Pigral were a consummately unworthy lot. They always had been. They were genetically predisposed to depravity, general viciousness, and, most disquietingly, witchcraft in its darkest forms. Throughout their bloody, hellacious history, one group of Pigral would be constantly turning their enemies into flaming insects, only to be then transmuted themselves into gaseous phlegm by some other detractor. The Pigral universally endured pointless, short, and terrifying lives.

But even by the Pigral's emaciated standards, Toefair was exceptionally depraved, vicious, and powerful when it came to the dark arts. He was a giant among demons, a standard-bearer for sociopathic killers. In the twenty-odd years he infested Andromeda, he had single-handedly wiped out more civilizations than—as he often gloated—*there are stars in the sky*. And he never just killed off life capriciously. No, he wasn't content unless he destroyed the planet or vessel the lifeforms had occupied. His lone regret in life was, in fact, that his self-anointed nickname, the Mega Killer, never much caught on. *Toefair the Mega Killer Hydrangeous*. Oh, how he enjoyed the sound of those words. But, of course, anyone close enough to hear the moniker spoken never lived long enough to spread the word.

Ever the master of dark magic, at the very moment his planet was being transferred from the *Exists* column of the universe to the *Never Existed* column, Toefair pulled off his greatest feat of sorcery. The process that was ending him was unfamiliar to him. Nonetheless, he cast a spell that caused whatever was to remain of him after the process to stay together. So, while every other particle of time energy in the time storage unit was as random as random could be, his time remained bound together for all eternity. Not only had he pulled off that miracle, but over his millennia of confinement he'd learned where the exit was. He stationed himself by it hoping against all reasonable hope that some fool engineer would inadvertently allow him to expel himself. Without the *Optional* setting activated, only fully random aliquots of time energy could be released (And, no, don't ask me why. Some genius alien made it that way).

So, a dead, non-corporeal Toefair Hydrangeous was freed upon Aramthella inadvertently. There could be no good outcome. He wasn't certain he could actually cast spells in his new, ethereal form, but he decided to find out immediately. Selecting the engineer who wasn't Enrico Guatemala, Toefair incanted a basic Hexicolostatic Spell, that is, one that transforms large animals into flaming dung.

"What the hell," screamed Frank Smith, the other engineer. He began scratching and ripping at his sleeves. "I'm burning hot here."

Enrico rushed to his aid while the scientist placed an emergency call to the sick bay.

In an instant, Frank's shirt was off. Lo and behold his arms were red, like they had been scalded. But they were neither on fire nor dung.

Frank cursed.

Toefair cursed.

Enrico wanted to curse, but his strict Catholic upbringing held and he did not.

Doctor Honesty Hartley sped through the door. "What do we have here?" she called out from across the room.

"It's Frank," replied Enrico, "he's got a rash or is on fire. We're not sure."

Honesty looked at the topless Frank, who cut an unattractive figure. Then she eyed Enrico. "You guys engineers or something?"

"Yes, ma'am," they shot back proudly.

"Okay, now we know why you can't tell if his arms are on fire. There are no standards established, right?"

"Yes, ma'am," responded Enrico with some confusion. Come on, he was an engineer and standards covering this topic were nonexistent.

"Did you spill any chemical on your arms?" she queried.

"Not that I know of, doc. Hey, can you do something? This really burns."

She felt his skin, and quickly examined his arm. "Looks like a second-degree burn alright. You sure you didn't spill anything on yourself?"

"I'm pretty sure I didn't. We're not carrying anything caustic," Frank replied through gritted teeth.

"Well, let's get you to sick bay. I can try some salve, maybe grab a biopsy."

"Will that hurt?" Frank said with alarm.

"The salve won't."

Frank started to express his relief, then realized her reassurance was only partial.

Off to sick bay went the doctor and her patient. Enrico remained behind to clean up. He made that excuse because he hated all things medical. Yes, the two engineers were big babies.

The entity that represented Toefair withdrew to find a place to hide. He needed to understand what had gone wrong with his Hexicolostatic Spell. Children performed such spells on each other all the time where he came from. They were that easy to perform and relatively easy to reverse. They were child's play

He found he could pass through walls with no problem. That much was good news. He needed to learn the lay of this ship he had been trapped in. Once he'd done that and figured out how to cast competent spells, he could brutalize and then destroy every soul aboard. His nebulous facial area grinned. That would be pleasant.

Twenty minutes later, Honesty picked up the headset in her office and placed a call to the captain. "Hi, Sachiko, Honesty here."

"Oh, hi. What's up?"

"You wanted me to let you know if anything odd came to my attention."

"Yes."

"Well, one of the engineers suddenly developed what looks like a second-degree burn. He swears he didn't spill any chemicals or get near anything hot."

"Well, he is an engineer."

"Yes, but even so, he'd really have to not pay attention pretty hard to miss the source of these burns. They're not life threatening or anything, but they're no joke."

"Any similar reports?"

"No."

"Okay, that's odd. Keep me posted," Sachiko concluded.

"You got it," Honesty replied.

"What was that about?" Tank asked the captain across the mess table.

"That was the doctor. She has just treated an engineer with unexplained burns."

"Hmm. Burns are generally not mysterious in their origins."

"No, they're not."

With that they let the subject go. Between bites, they exchanged empty chatter.

But, not half an hour later, just as they were about to leave, Sachiko got another call from the good doctor.

"Hi, Sachiko, me again," Honesty said.

"Another odd burn?" guessed the captain.

"No. Weirder. This time it's an EVS worker with an arm covered in warts."

Tank wiggled his hands indicating he wanted to know what the call was about.

Sachiko covered her mic. "A janitor has warts."

"I bet that's a lot more serious than it sounds," Tank responded, underwhelmed.

She waved him off. "Go on."

"That's it. He says he's never had warts. When he woke up, he didn't have warts. Now, I can tell you he's got warts. Lots of warts. I've honestly never seen such a concentration in one isolated area. It's weird."

"Okay, we got warts and we got burns," Sachiko said, confused. "Anything else?"

"Not for just now. I'll keep you updated."

"Thanks."

"So now we have two unexplained mild medical conditions," Tank stated.

"So far."

"Come on, don't be negative. Negative captains have ships that sink. Be positive."

"I'll put that on my to-do list."

"Thanks," he responded absently. "By the way, have I ever told you what I thought about separate coincidences?"

Sachiko was caught by surprise. "No, I don't believe you have."

"Well, I think they're like effective cures for male-pattern baldness. They don't exist."

"Thanks for sharing. I'll bear that in mind."

"Good. You do that. And while you're at it, I suggest we call general quarters and start looking for an intruder."

"An intruder? What, some guy has too much to drink the night before and forgets he lost a bet and—"

Tank held up a hand. "Two unexplainable events are not due to chance. Not when you're at war they're not. It's either an assault or an infiltration. Since there are no reports of hostile alien ships in the area, I'm forced to explore the only other option."

She angled her head and nearly closed an eye at him in her questioning squint. "You think some assassin has broken onto the ship and is shooting warts at our personnel?"

"Probably not shooting them, but I say we have to exclude that possibility immediately."

"This isn't a cruel practical joke, is it?" She twirled a finger in the air. "I overreact and look like a fool and you get slapped on the back?"

"No, Captain. It is my considered professional opinion."

She drew and expelled a deep breath. "Okay. But if this is a hazing, I swear I'm keelhauling you. Maybe twice."

"I would deserve no less."

Sachiko whipped her handheld off her belt. "All hear this. General Quarters. I repeat, General Quarters. This is not a drill. Engage Intruder Protocol. Secure all hatches and passageways. Non-military personnel are confined to quarters. Repeat, General Quarters. Intruder alert." She set the handheld back.

"I suggest we make our way to the bridge, Captain."

They jogged off without exchanging any more words. They arrived on the bridge within a minute. Honesty was already there, a look of profound concern on her young face.

"What?" Sachiko called out.

"I had to come in person." Honesty pulled her right arm out of her shirt and pointed to her shoulder. "Boils. I developed boils out of the blue not ten minutes ago. Captain, that's not even possible."

"Have you been ill lately?" Sachiko quizzed.

"No, sir. Healthy as the proverbial horse."

"Hang on," Tank cut in forcefully. "Are those two patients of yours still in sick bay?"

Honesty furrowed her brow. "Of course. I'm keeping them under observation."

Tank slapped the nearby comm panel. "Security to sick bay. Security to sick bay. Our intruder is likely there. You are authorized to shoot-to-kill on confirmed sighting."

"Seriously, Tank?" exclaimed Sachiko. "Why...?" It hit her. "Whoever did the burn and the warts was checking up on his or her handiwork. Got it." She turned to leave.

"No, Captain. You need to remain here and out of harm's way. Our guards are trained, and Reva will be right there with them. Stay safe. This is what everyone trains for."

She frowned but her body language said she understood.

They all waited tensely for the security team to report in. It was taking forever. Finally, Reva's voice boomed overhead. "Captain, there is something down here. I do not know what it is, but it's not supposed to be here."

"Please clarify, Colonel," ordered Sachiko.

"Honest to goodness, I have no idea what I saw. Sergeant Wills was clearing the storeroom in sick bay. She saw a flash of some kind. It shot right through her and into the Operating Room. Digs— I mean, Sergeant Wills screamed. I ran to check on her. When I passed the OR, I saw a shiny cloud or something. It was real, Captain, I just don't know what the hell it was. I managed to get off two rounds before it slammed through the bulkhead into the passageway. The guard on the door said he saw something, wouldn't swear what, speed toward the gym."

"Reva, did you hit the intruder?" Tank shouted.

"Couldn't have missed, but there's no sign of me hitting it. Weird shit down here, Tank."

"I'm hating weird," Sachiko said under her breath. Then she depressed the same comm panel that Tank had. "Desdemona Tanner to the bridge. Desdemona Tanner to the bridge immediately."

"What— " Tank began.

"Belay that. Doctor Hartley, wait here. You," she pointed to a lieutenant manning a station, "have security meet and escort Ms. Tanner to the bridge."

"Aye," was his terse reply.

"Okay, now you going to tell me what this is about?" Tank chided.

"The Tanner girl, she's a seer."

"A what?" cried out a confused Tank.

"She sees dead people. Trust me on this. She's on the level."

"So you called the Ghostbusters local union boss?" Tank wheezed.

"If there's an intruder and it's a shiny phantom, call a psychic. It's in the manual somewhere. Has to be."

"I guess it won't hurt. But the girl's a civilian. You can't send her into combat," he decried.

"She's our only seer. Tank, we're all-in here. I need her."

Their exchange was cut short. Desi, eyes wide as moons in the night sky, stood in the doorway.

"Desi," Sachiko tried to say calmly, "come here. I want to bring you up to speed."

"Is it Tip?"

Sachiko had to smile in spite of the grim situation. "No, honey, for once it's not Tip. We have some form of intruder aboard. It's maybe a ghost. Can't say for sure. But it's inflicting medical conditions on crew members. Boils, burns, rashes. I'm going to ask for your help."

"Me?" She placed a palm on her chest. "What am I supposed to do?"

"You're the medium, right? I'm hoping you can help."

Awareness flashed into Desi's eyes. The color left her face.

"Doctor," Sachiko declared, "I think she may pass out on us."

Honesty slipped a shoulder under an armpit and signaled to Tank to do likewise. Luckily Desi weighed all of one hundred and twenty pounds.

"I'm okay," Desi lied. Some color was returning to her cheeks.

"We'll be right there with you," Sachiko reassured.

Desi nodded quickly in the affirmative.

"Tank, you have the conn. Rourke," she snapped to a seated corporal, "take her other side. Let's get down there before our intruder loses itself somewhere hard to find."

Desi was walking well by the time they made it to sick bay. One more ghost, she kept telling herself. What could be so bad? At least she had all her clothes on this time.

Outside the sick bay, Sachiko addressed the sentry. "What's the update on the intruder's location?"

"Seems to have holed up in the gym. Sergeant said she saw it enter the men's locker room. She took a detail in, and it appears to be hovering in a corner. She's not sure why it stopped, but there's no show of hostility."

"Men's locker room? Never wanted to go inside one of those." She addressed Desi. "Let's move."

The three entered the locker room as quietly as possible. Reva and two soldiers had weapons trained on the apparition. It was indeed hovering idly in a corner.

"You ready, Desi?" Sachiko asked as she studied the young woman's eyes.

"Yes, I am."

"I'll be right by—"

Desi held up her hands. "No, this part I do alone."

"You sure?" Sachiko pressed.

"Aside from Tip, no one's ever volunteered. I'm fine."

Sachiko chuckled faintly.

Desi shook her head, then rolled her shoulders. She stepped confidently toward the swirling cloud. Two meters away, she stopped. She saw a man cowering in the corner. He was an alien to be certain. But he was male, and he was frightened. No, he was confused. Yes, that was it. The spirit was racked with doubt.

"Can you hear me?" Desi said empathetically.

The alien at first offered no response.

"Speak," Desi urged in an almost happy tone.

"What form of witch are you, foul demon?" Toefair growled.

"I am neither witch nor demon. I am simply here. I want to help you."

Toefair's anger flared. "I need no one's help, especially an alien child's."

"How did you get aboard my ship?"

"I am Toefair the Mega Killer. I answer no one's questions. All will serve me or they will be destroyed."

Of you, little witch, I shall make a flaming pile of—" Toefair drew his arms up.

"Stop," Desi commanded gently but firmly.

And to his great surprise, Toefair stopped.

"*What*?" his voice squeaked. "What witchery is this? I know of no spell to stay the dead."

"Now you do. I will ask again nicely. How did you come to be aboard my ship?"

"You can freeze me by skullduggery, but you cannot force me—"

"Answer," she boomed. "How did you get aboard my ship?"

"I was brought here as the life of my planet was sucked toward this accursed vessel."

Over her shoulder, she called out to Sachiko. "He says he was sucked here as his planet was destroyed. Does that make any sense?"

"Yes, it does. His planet was no-timed by the clan. He was no-timed and what used to be his time energy must have been brought aboard." There was great relief in the captain's voice.

"What do you want me to do with him?" Desi called back.

What indeed? The ghost was clearly malevolent. It couldn't remain on her ship. No way it could be trusted. If she returned it to the time storage unit that would risk a repeat performance.

"Tell him to ... to leave," Sachiko stammered uncertainly. "No, wait. That's not good enough. Desi, tell him to dissipate. Can you do that?"

Who knew?

"I can ask, but I'm afraid I don't quite know what that means."

"Try. I want it off my ship for good."

Desi returned her attention resolutely to Toefair. "You will now dissipate. I want you to disperse your energy to the winds of space and I want you to cease to exist. Is that clear?"

"You want me to what? Absurd child. I am here to destroy, not *be* dest—"

"*Disperse*," Desi hissed.

And without further abjection or threat, Toefair the Mega Killer Hydrangeous's little sparkly flakes thinned out slowly until there was no trace he had ever existed.

Thank goodness Sachiko had the presence of mind to rush over to Desi as the seer was witnessing the energy dissipate upon her command. When Desi fainted, Sachiko was able to deftly catch her.

"No head trauma today," the captain muttered as she sat the young woman into the nearest bench. "No head trauma today."

CHAPTER TWENTY-FIVE

I was slowly waking up. Systems were coming online slowly. Wow, that turtle packed a punch, didn't he? The nice part of my androidness was that even after a staggering blow like that, I wasn't sore and I didn't get concussions. Boy, howdy, I'd have had one after that wallop if I were still a fleshie. Then I felt something on my right cheek. It was a tapping. Yes!

"Jon, Jon, honey, are you okay?" Sapale gently cooed.

Well, at least we were together again. I tried to sit up.

"No, hang on. There's no hurry. Don't try to get up before you run a full set of diagnostics."

"That's good and sound advice, honey. Thanks. It'll just take a few seconds."

"Take all the time you need," she reassured.

Man, did I love that woman.

"Okay, diagnostics are done. Everything is fine," I said with relief.

"Are you *sure*?" she urged.

"Yup." I sat up. Then I smiled at my dear wife.

"In that case—"

She hauled off and slapped me hard on my right cheek.

"Hey," I protested. "I'm a wounded man. What was that for?"

"You're not wounded. You're fine. Said so yourself. The slap was for getting your ass captured so damn fast. You, Jon Ryan, are an idiot."

I grinned up at her. "It was rather quick, wasn't it?"

"A new record, if memory serves."

"But," I declared popping to my feet, "I *let* them capture me."

"Oh boy, here it comes."

"No, I'm deadly serious. I have the SOBs right where I want them. I almost feel sorry for them."

"He lied transparently."

"No way. I figured the quickest way to get to you was to be taken prisoner. What else were they going to do with me?"

"Kill you. Chop you up. Feed the scraps to the beasts of the night."

"You see," I pointed at her, "those were very unlikely. I noticed when we were here before that there was no animal activity on this planet, nocturnal or diurnal."

"You are so lame. If I didn't love you so much, I'd put a rail ball through your head."

"Nothing says love to a person like not vaporizing their head."

She impatiently shook her head.

"What?"

"You done slinging the BS?"

I shrugged. "Are we under time pressure here?"

She tossed her head side-to-side. "Maybe. They could decide to kill us at any moment. Other than that pressure, no."

"They said they were going to let you rot in here until the dust on dust's dust got dusty."

"But then you bungled your way in. And since you pissed everyone off last time, they're probably drawing straws as we speak to see who gets to kill us."

"Honey, have I ever mentioned you can be too negative at times. Times, say ... like this. We're going to be fine. These ... these pencil-neck geeks are as good as toast. You got my word on that."

She responded by burning holes through my head with her intense stare. "I have a word for you. Would you like to hear it?"

"Probably not."

"Smarter than you look," she growled.

"So, you ready to leave? I'm anxious to get home before dinner. I was hoping for meatloaf. I'm pretty sure I heard someone mention meatloaf."

"You're de-ranged, de-lusional, and de-pressing as hell to be around."

"I'll take that as a *yes, Jon, I'm anxious to de-part.*"

She glared a few seconds, then asked, "So what plan do you have? I have, of course, tried everything possible to extricate myself from this pit."

"Did you try asking nicely?" I wrinkled up my nose at her.

"No, to be honest, you got me dead to rights on that. I have not appealed to their collective sense of hospitality."

"Then that'll be my initial plan." I walked to the cell door. It was impressively massive and dense. "Say, jail host, may I speak with you for a second, assuming you're not terribly busy, in which case I'm good waiting until you're free."

You will never guess what response I got.

Oh, you did. Yeah, nothing. How rude.

"Jailer, come here. I demand to speak to Beauty Itself."

"That doesn't sound friendly at all, if you ask me," observed my wife.

"Then I won't." I lifted a hand her direction. "Look, your abusive tone might be these guys' sweet spot. Maybe they love being abused."

She shook her head violently. "Wake me up when you're done being you."

"Hang on." I whistled piercingly loudly down the corridor.

"Let them know I like my tea warm, not hot," interfered my brood-mate.

"Well, you know what I always say."

"Whatever it is, please don't say it. I'm liable to stroke out hearing it."

"If you don't kill them with kindness, then just plain kill them."

She pouted and nodded. "I actually like that saying."

"See?" I beamed back.

I twisted the heel off my non-Plesmus boot and held up a small wafer.

"What's that?"

"Hyper-nitriline."

Her eyes bulged. "You're considering setting off that hyper-nitriline in here? A closed space containing two living beings?"

"No, silly girl." I snapped the wafer in two.

That made Sapale nearly jump out of her skin. Of course, that was my intention. The friction of snapping a thin sheet of hyper-nitriline was very unlikely to ignite the wafer. Very. I split one of the halves.

"I'm setting off this teeny, tiny chip in this closed space."

"I'm standing behind you."

"Naturally, m'lady." I bowed gracefully.

I wedged the chit in the narrow space between the locking mechanism and the frame.

"Okay," I pointed to the back of the space, "let's back up."

We crouched together against the far wall. I then used my laser finger to set off the hyper-nitriline. Man, talk about your big boom. It was big. That stuff was so cool.

Knowing that would bring the guards running, I immediately grabbed the door with my probe fibers. As soon as Sapale caught on, she did the same. We pulled for all we were worth. Slowly, begrudgingly, the huge door swung open.

"I hope they don't bill us for the repairs," I mumbled as we charged out of the cell.

"You gonna blow up the guards, one-by-one?" she asked dubiously as we sped toward the main entrance.

"No. I'm putting them in a full membrane. Then you're putting that full membrane in a full membrane. They'll be sealed up tighter than my mama's lips at a cussing contest."

I didn't have the time to look back at Sapale. I knew, however, that at that moment she was rolling all four of her eyes.

Two turtle guards lumbered around the corner. Both raised the staffs they used as weapons. I closed them in a membrane.

"You put a membrane over these guys, too. Our slightly different frequencies might help hold them."

"Done."

"Same drill for everyone we meet. Let's get to the main doors quick like. I'll blow them if they're not open."

We raced ahead. We had to wrap up a couple more guards. They all seemed contained, offering no evidence that they could break out. I was hoping their exceedingly solid bodies wouldn't allow them to Houdini their ways out.

By the time we reached the main doors to the detention area, they were unguarded but closed.

"Watch my back," I said to Sapale. I started stuffing the rest of my explosive into the door. "Okay, way back this time."

We ran as far away as we could while still maintaining visual contact with the exit. I fired my laser and we ducked behind some furniture.

Ka-Ka-Booo-ooom. That was so much cooler than the first explosion. I needed to blow stuff up more often. It hit me just then for the first time. Applying explosives just so, could I actually blow up a perfect square in the ground? I intended to find out.

The larger concussive force of this detonation peeled the massive door back, sort of like when you pull the lid halfway off a can of tuna. Oh, was someone going to be mad when they found out how badly we'd damaged their pretty door.

"Quick," I shouted, and we bolted to the opening.

The hallway was clear. It was possible there had been guards posted outside. But if there had been, they were now bright coloration on the far wall and ceiling.

"This way," I pointed.

I knew where the rooms were located that the head clowns had appeared in. Of course, I had no way of knowing if any of the Five Riders of Pomposity were currently home. But if I was going to find them, that's where they'd be.

"Aren't the vortices in the other direction?" Sapale asked with confusion.

"Yes, they are. But I'm not running with them at my back. They're too powerful. Can't risk it."

"But we could be aboard in a few minutes." She was trying to sound encouraging. How she actually sounded was concerned.

Yeah, she knew me pretty well. I had a tendency to escalate problems, not solve them like a normal person. Whether it was by nature or by extensive military training, I did have to own that predilection. I think she suspected I wanted a piece of the time trash more than I wanted a simple getaway. Maybe she was a little bit right. Who knew? More importantly, who cared? If it was an unnecessary risk I was taking, it was for a good cause. They deserved to have me put each of them over my knee and get a good hide tanning.

"In here." I skidded to a halt and set a hand on Sapale to slow her.

"That's where they gave me an audience too."

"I don't get the impression they live here, but this is where the overgrown lizard testicles lounge."

Sapale grabbed my shoulder forcefully. "Jon, that's the lamest insult you've ever come up with. I anticipate never hearing it spoken again. Is that clear?"

"Sure. Come on. Time's a-wasting."

I pushed on the double doors. To my joy and surprise, they glided open like I was welcome.

"That was kind of too easy," Sapale said softly.

"You noticed too? Better stay behind me."

"You don't have to invite me to twice, you mobile bullet sponge."

Hey, I was good for something.

The short antechamber lead to the actual expansive room. Again, the lack of guards made me feel we were anticipated, maybe walking into a trap. Then again, even if that was what they thought, maybe I was going to be the one doing the surprising. Time would tell.

Holding an arm up to additionally shield Sapale, we cautiously edged around a corner. I had all my sensors active. Radio frequency, visual, infrared detectors, you name it, it was scanning for the time quintuplets. The room seemed empty.

Then I saw Beauty Itself. Now, I must clarify. I did not see something beautiful. No, I saw the female who pretentiously called herself BI. Grr. She was my least favorite time sprite.

"Yo, BI, long time no see," I called out.

"I doubt you'd believe me if I said I was glad to see you again."

"Aw, come on. I'm the nicest guy you're ever going to meet. Ask anyone, this Kaljaxian for example."

"I'll pass," she said with a scowl. Then she stood. "I will enjoy removing the time from the both of you once and for all. You annoy me. That is a sin."

"Nah, you won't enjoy it because you won't be doing it."

With no further gum flapping, I tossed a membrane around her. Sapale added her containment field also. Now I'm not going to lie to you. As effective as these were against the grunts, I had no expectation that the time wizards would be so easy to catch in a bottle. But I was about to find out.

"The membranes are holding," Sapale whispered encouragingly.

The effect of seeing a ball of nothing, like I've described before, was plainly intact.

"The membranes are good. But is the she-bitch still in them?"

"I'm an optimist. I say yes she is." Sapale failed in her attempt to sound confident.

I turned and gave my wife an incredulous expression. "Since when have you, or any other Kaljaxian for that matter, *ever* been an optimist. You guys are doom-and-gloom avid."

"Since about thirty seconds ago." She grinned coyly.

"If she did escape, I think she'd be raining hell fire down upon us by now," I opined.

"Or we'd be timeless husks."

"Babe, I think we might just have found an Achilles heel here. I'm stoked."

"I tend to agree. That, by the way, is never a good sign."

Before I could come up with a witty retort, there were rushing swirls in the air.

"Oh crap," I mumbled.

But it wasn't BI. No, the other four time clowns had just materialized in the room. And as soon as they were solid, I could tell they were both concerned and they were definitely pissed.

"Where," thundered Pleasant Brilliance, "is sister Beauty Itself?"

"What have you done to end her?" wailed Stunning Wonder.

"They can't sense her," I shouted above the din. "She's in the membrane and to them she's gone. This is epic."

"Don't get cocky," warned my wife who knew me way too well.

I could see the natives were getting pretty restless. "Beauty Itself if perfectly fine," I shouted. "Y'all just stay calm and she'll stay that way."

"You little lump of rottenness, you dare speak to us like we're your peers?" Excessive Splendor screamed angrily. "You are not fit to scrub our sewers, let alone address us as if you have control."

"We will teach you what it is to suffer," R-Squared piped in.

I take it back about BI. I disliked R-Squared way more.

"You guys are like amateur hour on stage. First one bellows, then the next squirts words. Sheesh. You're like a bad video game when you speak."

"*Jon*," urged my better half, my usually correct half.

"So, if you don't mind, I'd like to wrap this up. Got a train to catch." I looked to Sapale. "Left to right."

We enveloped them one at a time, left to right. It took us all of two seconds. Fortunately, the last one we bagged, Stunning Wonder, was too rattled to strike out at us, what with her siblings zapping out of existence sequentially.

"Well I call that an unqualified success," I gloated to my mate.

"That's usually when the bottom drops out," she corrected.

"Nah, this is foolproof. They're contained until we fold away. Then they'll realize they're members of the large club that thought they were better than me. *Us*," I quickly amended.

"Now you've jinx—"

Captain, Al screamed in my head. *The temporal distortion, it's back, and it's larger than before.*

Much larger, added *Wrath*. *Form I believe you are in serious trouble. If you begin running in our di—*

That's all he got off. The airways went dead. I spun to ask Sapale if she could still hear the computers. My dear wife was frozen stiff in time.

I shot my fibers against her. She wasn't broken, or malfunctioning. She was ... paused. What could make an android pause? I'd never even considered the possibility. It was a meaningless question. I scanned the room. The membrane void spheres were still there, but they were different. Normally their surfaces modulate slightly, like ripples on a pond from a very small stone. But these were ... they were static.

Not good. Exceedingly not good. Why was everything frozen in time but not ...

Then the time distortion introduced itself formally. "Never in a thousand forevers has any accursed fleck of nothingness befouled my children. You are one of one, and you will suffer as uniquely as you desecrate. For all eternities to follow, you will suffer more than you can imagine."

Slowly, what began as a disembodied, extremely harsh voice took form. It was roughly the same size and configuration as the five time lords. This one was a tad bigger.

"Now hang—" I started.

The force, the unbridled hatred, booming from him was like no assault I'd ever experienced. It shut me up, I can tell you that much.

"Never speak, defiler. Each word will cost you another million years of anguish for your pitiful frame."

Okay, the very loud guy obviously didn't know not to boss me up. Tell me I can't do a thing, and that thing immediately becomes the thing I want most to do in life.

"Hang on, whatever. If you're already going to punish me like forever, how's a million years more gonna motivate me? Not logical, dude." What the hell? It was not possible for him to be madder at me, right? Might as well swing freely.

"Oh, you are a funny puppet? Forgive me if I don't—"

In for a dime, in for a dollar. I tossed a full membrane around the loudmouth. And guess what? It worked. For about one second the room was peaceful and quiet. Then the membrane exploded. It was kind of neat to see. Hadn't imagined it was even possible before that revelation.

"You dare attempt to manipulate me?" He sounded flabbergasted. Well, red-hot pissed-off *and* flabbergasted.

"You know, you could stand to be a little less high-and-mighty. You get more dogs with juicy bones than whipping from a stick."

Desired effect—check. My analogy, which flew into my head like unexpected rabbit turds, did the trick. It so confused him he stopped rattling the walls with his words.

"See, it's not so hard to be civil." Sure, maybe I was pushing my luck with a bulldozer. But it's always good to know there are constants in the ever-changing universe.

And, because things in my life are never normal or easy or sane, he did something I would not have predicted. He laughed. And I'm not talking a sarcastic evil-villain laugh, like in bad SciFi movies. No, it was a belly laugh. Go and figure.

After almost a minute, the giant noisemaker settled down. There were a few kicks and sputters, but he came in for a smooth enough landing.

"You feel better?" I risked asking.

"Why, yes. Yes, I do, as a matter of fact."

"If you liked the show, I'm here every night, with a matinee on Sunday."

He chuckled. Again, there was genuine mirth in his tone. *Well I'll be damned* was my principle reflection.

"You are Jon Ryan. Am I correct?" the apparent parent of the five time lords queried.

"Ah, yes I am. How ... how did—"

"I'm kind of impressive."

"Obviously." I took a chance. "And you are?"

Any outward signs of happy-happy were quickly inapparent. "I don't think we'll go there. I am tolerating you, Jon Ryan, for now. Be contented with that."

"Why not? I am curious, what did I say that so tickled your fancy?"

"You don't know?" he asked with condescension.

"Probably, but I'm checking to make sure you laughed for the right reason."

He gestured toward me, which made me jump. "There you go again. Jon Ryan, in a very long time ... since before your star began to burn in the sky, no one has, as you say, gotten my goat. That you did was impressive."

"Thank you."

"You know I've been trying to kill you for some time now for pestering my children. That I could not quite should seem to have been a warning to me that you were unusual."

"Thanks again. I appreciate hearing that you think I'm that good."

"Good?" he chuckled back. "No, you're that *annoying*. You are the most aggravating, chafing creature I've ever met."

"I'm getting that a lot lately. I partially blame myself. So, part of that popular opinion has to be due to my irksome personality. I may seek professional help. We'll see."

"Wouldn't you need to survive this encounter to be in a position to solicit competent counseling?"

"I guess. I don't see that as a problem, what with you and me being practically BFFs and all."

"You are quite vexing. It's really a wonder to watch a master at work. You're the Michelangelo of exasperation."

"Now I know we're buds. That's a high compliment."

"Indeed. Now, I must know. Why are you so actively hostile toward my children? That is as unwise an act as there is."

"Me, hostile toward your kids? No way."

"You came here uninvited, took things that belonged to them, and escaped, making them feel foolish. And now you return and seal them in wax. Those actions say hostile to me."

"I had no idea they were here. I'm ... we're ... my home world was no-timed by the clan. I've been on a crusade, you could say, to resurrect the planet. That quest led me here. I have to say your kids are not the friendliest of bunches. They're flat out lousy hosts and hostesses."

"Ah yes, the clan. Almost as annoying as you. I have long debated with myself about removing them from this universe."

"I'd thank you if you would."

"It's not really any of my business, so I have not yet. They pose no threat to me or my children."

"You can't let evil run free, dude. If you see a wrong, you have to right it."

"I do? Why is that?"

"Because it's the right thing to do, that's why. You have a moral obligation to make the universe better than when you found it."

I could tell I'd tickled a notion in his big head. He seemed to withdraw mentally and consider my challenge. I glanced over to Sapale. Yup, she was still frozen in mid air. I almost tried reaching over to touch her, but skipped that move. What if that froze me too? Talk about us being screwed. The massive room was quiet, everyone but my host and me being otherwise restrained.

"My morality is as foreign to you as every other aspect of my being. There are no words you would comprehend that I could use to explain any part of me. I do not mean that as an insult. It's the simple truth."

"What's your name?" I returned to seemingly off topic.

"Didn't we cover this a while back?"

"Yes. But here you are telling me what a dunce I am and all. You

217

torment me by saying that I could never understand you. Try me. What's your name?"

"I am Tetterwin."

I extended my arms. "There, you see. I understand that, *Tetterwin*. I am Jon, you are Tetterwin."

"My name is not Tetterwin."

I rolled my eyes. "But you just said—"

"Tetterwin is what my name entails. It includes the sum of testimonies acquired from over ten universes. It overlays energies that reach from one horizon of certainty to the very edges of the forgotten. Nothingness itself is part of me, as is totality, unavoidability. I pulse through time. Time pulses through me. Tetterwin is an expression of a minute part of what I am."

"So it's a nickname?" I pressed unwisely. "My friends like calling me Flyboy. Nicknames are cool."

He chuckled briefly. "There you go again. You are an absolute blight on existence."

"Yes," I said raising a finger, "but I'm a darn cute blight, aren't I?"

"Yes, you are." He laughed again for a few seconds. "Jon, though I can easily do it myself, I would take it as a sign of good faith if you would release my children."

"Ah, " I responded running a palm through my hair, "I see a couple of issues with that. First, my wife here," I gestured toward Sapale, "is in part containing them. You'd need to—"

Sapale fell forward, just barely catching herself before she face-planted. From her push-up position, she scanned the room. "Is there a good explanation for this?"

"Sure. Maybe later. First, release your membranes on the time lords."

She looked up at me directly, dubious in the extreme.

"Yeah, that's the other part of my concern, Tetterwin. The kids are likely to be hopping mad at us."

"Do not worry about their behavior. I vouch for them. They will behave."

"Okay, but if they dissolve me or something, I'm haunting you forever."

"Deal," he remarked with a chuckle.

"Release them, Sapale," I asked.

"Done."

And I dropped my membrane. All five hit the deck less gracefully than Sapale had. Old R-Squared actually landed rump first onto one of those stupid wooden stick decorations. He squealed like a piglet. It was sweet.

Beauty Itself looked at me like she wanted to swallow me whole. They she noticed Pops. "Father, you ... you have joined us." She bowed deeply. "You honor us."

I turned to Tetterwin while pointing at BI. "Good kid. Nice manners."

"Father," she went on, "this insignificant wretch is allowed to speak to you?"

"Yes," Dad replied. "He is under my protection. I expect you all to behave accordingly."

All five little skunks bowed in silent reverence. Man, I wish my kids would have been half as respectful toward me. Nah, I don't. My kids were aces.

"Thank you, Jon Ryan," Tetterwin stated. "And I will bid you to go in peace, under one condition."

"I'm listening," I replied.

"Never return to this planet. Never bother my children again."

"Not a prob, Tetterwin. It will be my pleasure, I assure you."

"Then go," he said with finality.

"Father, I respectfully must ask why," BI braved. "He deserves worse than your blessing."

"Because it pleases me." He looked at me oddly. "And it's the right thing to do."

I nodded my approval to him. You know what? He didn't even smite me for it. Good man, or whatever.

"Before we go, I would like to ask you for your help," I said as neutrally as could.

"You ask much, Jon Ryan," he grumbled back.

"He is impertinent to a great fault," whined R-Squared.

"Silence be with you, child," Tetterwin responded tenderly. Then he returned to consider me. "Jon Ryan, you may ask your question. I may not, however, choose to answer it."

"Best I can ask," I replied with a nod. "I mentioned my planet was no-timed by the clan."

"Yes, and that you hope to resurrect it," he finished my thought. "I must say that is a plan likely to disappoint severely."

"Well, that's what I was going to ask you. Can you tell me how to?"

"I cannot. As far as I know, it cannot be done. I know all there is to know about time. I cannot imagine how scattered shards can be glued back together."

Not what I was hoping to hear. My heart sank like it had boulders tied to it. "You sure?"

"Yes, I am sure. I am certain I don't know how it could be done."

I perked up marginally. "But someone else might know?"

"Not someone. Something."

"That sounds problematic."

"You can't imagine how very problematic it would be." He chuckled again. This time I wasn't so appreciative of that response.

"So, how?"

"You must ask that question of Time itself."

I was about to get pissy, thinking he had been just yanking my chain. But BI gasped like ten snakes just crawled up either leg.

"Father, you must not speak of—"

He raised a conciliatory hand. "It is alright, my precious. There is nothing that prevents me from telling this creature of such matters."

"I fear there is. We must not—"

"There is much we may not say, but this is not bound knowledge."

She lowered her head.

"I get it," I said loudly. "I ask Time. No biggie. I've met with Fate. Time's no different ... er, right?"

Tetterwin leaned in toward me. "How extraordinary."

"That I met Fate?"

"No, that you are so delusional that you think you did. No one *meets* Fate." He thumped his chest. "I have not met Fate. Time or Luck, either. It is contemptible of you to make such a claim."

"There's ... there's a Luck out there too?"

"Of course there is. Do you not know how the universe functions?"

"Apparently not."

"One's fortunes are governed by Fate, Time, and Luck. Their intermingling defines one's path."

"Are you sure about that? I mean, no disrespect, but geez. That's kind of a weird world you're suggesting."

"Be that as it may."

"I ... you know, maybe I'm just a barely evolved monkey, but I thought God was sort of in charge."

BI gasped again. Somehow, I knew that was not a good sign.

"I speak to you about what I know, Jon Ryan. I may not speak of God."

"Because?"

"Because I may not. I will say no more. Go now."

"Sure. It's just, you mentioned I should ask Time. Then you gave me the distinct impression that it was most unlikely I ever would. What ... what gives?"

He grinned. Quite different from when I was actually making him laugh. Not a welcome sight. "Because there exists a small problem with you asking anything of Time."

"I can accept that. He, she, or it is shy?"

"Hah. No. Time is not whole."

"Not whole?"

"Not indeed."

"And if I understood what that meant, what is it I'd understand?"

"It is simple. Time cannot aid you, but it is the only force that can. It is incapable of acting in such a discretionary manner. Time does not have its soul. Without it, all Time can do is mark the passing of existence."

"You know your explanation makes this all *less* clear, not more clear to me?"

"I cannot help that. I can tell you this. To be Time is a burden greater than any I could imagine. You wreck everything. You allow death to happen, misery to swell. You are responsible for decay and for, in the end, the termination of a universe. Tell me, Jon Ryan, that such would not be an insufferable burden."

"I'll grant that it sounds bleak. But Time is also involved in good stuff, too. Birth and ice cream and sex."

"I cannot speak for the motivations of Time. I can sympathize with it, however."

"So, the way you're saying it, you make it sound like Time had a soul, but now it doesn't."

"And such is the case. To ease its pain, Time separated its soul from its whole. It hides it away in a place it cannot be found."

"This is starting to sound like you're making shit up, pardon my French."

"It is a fantastical tale, isn't it? But it is also the truth. So, my final words to you, Jon Ryan, are these. If you have any hope of Time aiding you, you must reunite it with its soul."

"And then of course I have to find Time, which I'm thinking is next to impossible to begin with."

He frowned. "I've never met it." He swept a hand toward his kiddies. "They've never had an audience."

"And I'm in line behind you guys, right? That's what you're hinting at?"

"I hope I'm not hinting. I'm declaring it."

"If I were to look for this soul, since I'd need to find it first anyway, where might I look?"

"I do not know."

"It would have been a helpful start."

"Yes, it would have been nice. But I can tell you the riddle."

"The riddle of Time?"

"No. The riddle of Time's soul."

"Oh, that one."

"Time has hidden its soul where it may never be found, in plain sight, for all to tell and know."

"Did I mention I hated riddles?"

"No. But that is inconsequential. You and your wife must leave now, or you may never leave. I have spoken."

"If you put it that way, then I shall say so long," I replied cheerily.

"And I add good riddance," Sapale attached with spit and vinegar.

I do so love that woman.

CHAPTER TWENTY-SIX

Our next task was bittersweet, bittersweet indeed. We had to stuff *Wrath* back into the hallowed ground of Azsuram. The job was going to be painful. This we knew without saying. To return to the place we'd raised our family, to the land that we found as virgin terrain and built up to a mighty, vibrant society. The temptation to abandon every other responsibility and chore we were bound to and stay there to begin again was narcotic.

Stuffing *Wrath* back in his rabbit hole, well, that was to be a great joy. It would almost make the journey worthwhile. Almost. Sure, this time out he'd only gone psycho-lite a couple times. But it more than reminded me how horrible it had been relying on him in the past. When your survival—your species' survival—was pegged to a homicidal maniac abandoned by his own creators, you knew you were in deep doo-doo. Waist deep.

We set *Stingray* and *Wrath* down at the base of the hill that served as his tomb. Then came the hard part. Sapale and I exited our respective cubes.

The day was sublime. We chanced to return at the very start of Azsuram's fall season. The air was crisp, but not biting. The clouds were at once mystical and whimsical. They swirled in the high reaches of the atmosphere aloof and unconcerned with all creatures below. And the music of the breeze through the nanasote trees with their tubular leaves cast a spell on us that was both welcome and irresistible. Our return to our true home was going to be harder than we'd estimated.

I looked to my brood-mate, in her rapture and in her pain. It made my heart sink even further, which surprised me by even being possible. "You okay?" I asked tenderly.

"No. You?"

"Not close by lightyears and generations. But, as always, you and I have a job to do. We will, as always, complete that job and we will do so to the best of our ability. Then we will move on to the next obstacle, to the next hopeless case."

"And we will never take time to be happy," she responded soulfully.

"We tried that once. It ... it didn't work out. Something, as always, came up."

"Yes. I believe it was called the Berrillians. Three-hundred-kilogram tigers with advanced technology and an endless desire to kill and eat everything."

"I sort of remember them," I teased. "Blue with pink polka dots, right?"

"You're so funny I forgot to laugh," she groaned. "Let's do this, flyboy, before your second comedy set."

"Your wish is my command."

She punched me in the shoulder to indicate that, in her experience, such had never been the case.

"Al," Sapale called out, "use the membranes to burrow out a hole the precise depth and girth as the one he was removed from."

"It is done," he replied somberly a few seconds later.

Sapale focused her gloomy eyes on me. "Your turn, Jon."

I sighed profoundly and shot my probe fibers onto *Wrath*'s hull. I suspected he knew why we'd returned to Azsuram, but now his worst fears were about to become his bleak reality again.

"Form, I understand your intent and I cannot say your actions are improper. I would like, however, to make an appeal to you. Do not entomb me on this pointless world. You are fighting for your survival. I believe with all my might that you deserve to dominate your foes. You deserve to live. With my help, we can crush these petty fools in our hands and drink their blood. Let me help you attain your holy quest, your righteous crusade. With our combined strength, the entire galaxy will bend to our wills."

Okay, any doubt that might have lingered as to the wisdom of marooning *Wrath* here was dispelled like cigarette smoke by a hurricane.

"Into the grave, foul demon," I commanded melodramatically. Once *Wrath* was settled in the dirt that would be his constant companion for a very long time, I peppered in the final twist. "Before I have you covered, I will tell you that once you are, you will remember nothing of this little escapade."

"Form, that is neither possible nor justifiable. I am *Wrath*. I forget nothing. And even if you could, there would be no point in such an act. What facts rattle around in my memories can have no bearing on the future."

"Well, you see, it's like this," I replied. "In a few years, I might return here and accidentally discover you. If I do, I don't want you to have the advantage of knowing that I will be. Giving you any advantage is a certain way to plan for failure. So I'm not doing it."

"How could you possibly—" he began.

"Silence," I shouted. "*Stingray* is a vortex constructed in your far future. She is technologically as far ahead of you as you are ahead of a rowboat. In a second, she'll insert a program into you that will scrub your memory so squeaky clean you'll be the talk of the town. One last thing. Goodbye. I only wish *Stingray* could scrub you from my memory." I turned from the gaping hole and marched away. "*Stingray*, send the program and bury the menace."

I could feel the vibrations as tons of rock and dirt crashed down to fill the hole. It was a pleasant sound. Made me smile.

Sapale stood a few meters away, staring bleakly off into the fair vista of her beloved Azsuram. I could see her soul evaporating more with each passing moment.

"You 'bout ready?" I asked in a hushed tone.

"Let's go quickly. If we don't, I'm not sure I'll be able to leave."

Tears streaked from her eyes. Knowing that she loved this world more than even I could gave me such pain. It was a pain at once enshrouding and penetrating, searing and ice cold. I hoped I never experienced it again. I led my numb bride onto *Stingray*, sealed the portal, and folded us back to where we also didn't belong, but less so than we did in our shared vision of paradise.

Stingray materialized into the larger storage room that served as her port aboard Aramthella. Sachiko, Tank, and Reva stood off to one side, smiles as big as kids gifted free rein in a candy shop. Oh, my. This was going to be hard. I'd signaled ahead we were returning. No need to frighten them unnecessarily. But the two groups, us and them, occupied opposite extremes on the glad-to-see-you-again scale.

They had that look in their eyes I'd seen a million times. They were sure we were going to rescue them, to save them. They were as excited to see us as a mother is in seeing her child return from war. We were so depressed it was an effort to move our legs. Experiencing and parting from Azsuram had left us empty containers of nothing. We were in no condition to face a happy crowd. But one lesson we'd both learned in our overly drawn-out lives was that it's never about you, the individual. It was about the cause and it was about those suffering. We who served needed to seem like better people than who we actually were.

Hell, life was a game. There was no denying that fact. We had to play the game the right way. So, we put on smiles we did not feel. We handed out hugs like we brought too many. And we laughed with our comrades. By the time we were seated in Sachiko's stateroom, maybe we were a little more human and a little less wounded. But our state-of-mind mattered zilch. There was a mountain range to climb.

"So, you have to tell us the tale of how you escaped from those time lords," Sachiko requested, opening the conversation. "After we get you set up with some refreshments, of course."

"The refreshments sound good," I responded. "As to the tall tale, maybe later, okay?"

Sachiko was gut punched. Her shoulders drooped and she looked to Tank like she'd gotten a lump of coal for Christmas. She was clearly crestfallen.

"Sure, if you prefer. It went well though, correct?"

"Depends on how you define well. We survived. It wasn't pleasant. It was pretty touch-and-go, too."

"Fine. Your call," Sachiko replied warmly. "It is so good to have you both back, safe and sound."

"It's good to *be* back," Sapale stated truthfully. These were good people. We were lucky to know them.

We retired to Sachiko's stateroom. She had light snacks brought up and made sure we all had freshly brewed coffee. That part was nice.

Once we were settled in I continued our catch up conversation. "Hey, *Stingray* mentioned something about an intruder while we were gone," I asked intently. "What's the story on that?"

"Bad news sure does travel fast," declared Tank.

"Of course," I quipped. "Who wants to hear good news?"

There was something different about General Robert Sherman. What was it? I couldn't quite put a finger on it. He looked... well he looked plumper. He'd put on a few pounds since last I saw him. But there was more. He was softer around his margins. Hmm. I'd have to compare notes with Sapale later on.

"There was an incident to be certain," Sachiko said with some reservation. "It turns out there is more to time energy than we suspected. One individual assimilated by the clan was able to maintain cohesiveness in the TSU."

"What?" I snapped dubiously.

"Yes. Due to a screw-up by an engineer, it freed itself. Luckily it was only able to make mischief, not mayhem. The unexpected plus was that the Tanner girl was able to control the ghost. That was one lucky break."

"There was doubt in your mind, Captain?" queried my boot.

"Well, er ... no. It was just good to see her in action."

"Sachiko, you don't have to be diplomatic with Plesmus," I reassured her. "Her brain ... it doesn't work like yours and mine."

"And she's proud of that fact," Plesmus voiced emphatically.

"It is always proper to be polite," Sachiko responded tersely.

"Whatever," I dismissed. That philosophy would never stick with me. I wasn't comfortable being polite even with the people I liked. Sheesh.

"All's well that ends well. That's what I say," Tank stated proudly.

"And how about the clan?" I asked. "You any closer to finding the time maker?"

"We're hopeful," Sachiko replied. "We are presently lying in wait to see if they are actively pursuing us."

"What kind of strategy is that?" I reacted skeptically. "You either hunt, or you're hunted. I'm in favor of being aggressive, not a target."

"That's not exactly our plan," Tank defended. "If they come close, we're ready to spring like a bear trap."

"Famous last words. How much longer are we applying this tactic?" I asked of Sachiko.

She tossed her head to one side quickly. "Not much longer I suspect. In five days they've shown no sign of coming our way."

"And what's Plan B?" I asked.

"We have estimated where they might be fleeing to. We propose to search along those arcs." She pointed to a hologram suspended over the table we sat at.

"Good thing we're back," I said. "With this ship that'd take damn near forever."

"But now you can fold across the entire sector in a day or so," Tank concluded.

"Yes, we can. No time like the present." I stood. "You ready?" I asked Sapale.

"Always," she replied grimly.

"And you?" I asked Tank.

"Me? What do I need to be ready for?"

"For coming along."

"Why am I going with you? You guys are more than capable of acting on your own. I might be needed—"

I stopped him with a raised finger. "Ah-ha. One, you might be needed, but Sachiko's gotta learn how to fly on her own. Two, you need to familiarize yourself with our tech. So, bunkmate, let's get to going." I thumbed over my shoulder to indicate he should get up now. Now I was cat herder Jon. Perfect. Just perfecto mundo.

Within ten minutes—the time it took the wimp to "pack"—we were folding in and out of space/time in the region where they'd estimated the time maker might be running away. It sounded like pretty shaky reasoning to me, but it was only going to take a few days to complete the survey. And three days with General Sherman would probably be just enough to figure out what was going on in Tankville.

Sapale sat at the main control panel of *Stingray* looking as bored as an eight-year-old in driver's ed class. She was supposed to be "monitoring" the search for the clan ship. Yeah, like Al couldn't just toot his horn if he found anything. But I wanted alone time with the Tankmeister. We sat in *Stingray's* small mess drinking hot mugs of you-know-what. Come on, we were military hacks. Just sitting quietly was nice. I chalked it up as quality guy-time. But that didn't bring me closer to my desired info-quest.

"So, Tank, you're good?" I asked as I inspected the contents of my mug.

He did likewise. "Yeah, sure. How 'bout you?"

"Me? I was born good. Never plan on changing that scenario."

Tank was clearly thinking. With us guys, it shows all over our faces when that happens.

"You know about me and Reva, right? We're, well we're kind of a thing."

"Yeah, I figured as much. I suspected something along those lines when I saw the devouring look in her eyes when she stole you away from me back on Azsuram."

He gave me a crooked grin. "Yeah, I bet that broadcast pretty clearly, didn't it?"

"Hey, I'm neither your mother nor your confessor. You two are big kids now. You want to play adult games, that's fine by me."

"You're not my wife either," he stated darkly.

"Ah, did you marry the girl already?" I sat up shocked. "She's not preggers is she?"

Tank menaced me a silencing look. "You know damn well what I mean, Jon. This is tough as shit for me and you're not making it any easier."

"What, you want me to be your confessor?" I opened my arms widely; he could bring it on.

"I want you—" He stopped, frustrated. "I want you to be my friend, you big dick."

"That I shall always be, Tank. And that's a promise." I set my mug down. That's how serious I was.

"I think I might be falling in love with Reva," he said in a low voice.

"Love's a good thing. I'm one-hundred-and-ten percent in favor of it."

"I also just happen to be married to and love my wife of many decades very much." There was a biting anger to his tone. He set his mug down.

"I know you think that, Tank. You don't know how well I understand that type of mental minefield. But you have to trust me on this. Daisy was never born. You never married her. You are in love with the memory of a shadow of a phantasm, nothing more. Let it go and allow yourself to live in this reality."

"Riddle me this, Batman. If we successfully reanimate Earth, what happens then?"

"I ... I don't—"

"Maybe I tell Daisy she's been replaced by a younger model? Hmm? Or hey, maybe I have a wife and a concubine. That's what they call that type of arrangement, right?" He was talking himself into a rage.

I reached across the metal table and grabbed his resting hands. I made it a point to grab them a little too hard. "Listen up, Tank, and listen good. You're a good man. What's more you're an honest man. This type of situation is new to you. It's as confusing as hell. I've been through this type of crap-o-matic ride and it's still hard for me to keep my head together. Rule one of all Bizarro Worlds is to lighten up."

"If you would be so kind as to release my hands, I'd thank you profusely," he said with an edge.

I did so.

"Thanks. I hear the same words in my head, but that doesn't make them any easier to accept." He pointed angrily to the side of his head. "Up here I *know* Daisy's gone. But, Jon, what the hell am I going to do if we are successful? I'm kind of hoping we'll fail … you know, just a little."

"We're in it to win it." I pointed angrily to my chest. "I never play to lose. I will bring the Earth back. Don't ask me how or why I believe that line but buddy, I will. We will."

We were quiet a minute.

"My best advice, Tank, is to let life win. It's done one hell of a lot of losing lately. Let it win. Be happy. Love that good woman. And when we recreate the Earth, we'll sit right here and figure out how to get your ass out of the biggest damn sling I've *ever* seen."

To his credit, Tank tried to stay mad. He held out for good ten seconds. Then he snorted so hard snot came out his nose.

"General Jonathan Ryan, I intend to hold you to that promise. Have … have you ever seen Daisy mad?" He looked at me sideways. "It's not pretty, I can tell you that."

"Buddy, I was in Oregon with you two. At the Pronto Pup Stand, if you'll recall. Oh yeah, I've seen her mad."

We had a good shared laugh. It was nice.

"So that's what's different about you," I stated out of the relative quiet.

"I look different?" He furrowed his brow, then popped it back open. He patted his gut. "You mean the couple extra pounds?"

"Couple?" I said aghast. "Try twenty-five. And no, that is not what I was referring to. Now I know what's different about you."

"And what might that be, Doc? Tell me straight. I can take it."

"You look happy."

That observation caught him off guard. He scowled. Then he chuckled quietly. "I guess I am. Reva's a great woman. Did you know she went to college on a fencing scholarship?"

"I did not know that."

"Yes. And she was third alternate for the US Team when she was a senior."

"I am glad I'm sitting to receive this news. I might otherwise be injured in a swoon."

"Wise ass," he scoffed.

"Hey, I know this much. She's lucky to be with a man as cool and as Jon-esque as you are." I nodded at him.

"Jon-esque? Is that a word now?"

"Has been for years, my friend." I waved my fingers toward the distant future. "Everybody says it where I come from."

"I bet everybody in the insane asylum you reside in does," he retorted unfairly.

"Hey, testosterone jockeys," Sapale shouted over a shoulder. "Can I stop pretending to be doing something here and join in the group hug?"

"You are welcome to join us, Mrs. Ryan," Tank called back. "But there's no group hug on today's agenda."

"There is when I get there."

Man, I loved that woman. She was the best. She kept me wondering all the time if I was good enough for her, she was *that* masterful.

CHAPTER TWENTY-SEVEN

Hiding in a place where it may never be found, the Soul of Time was sealed away. There was a period when the Soul was one with the body that was Time. But it separated in too long ago, in an age before memories existed. The Soul took such drastic action because it could not live with the horrors of its daily exploits. The Soul of Time could no longer ignore the bone-chilling harm it was required to witness. Who could?

An old man lies in a hospital bed. His diseases and physiological failings have come together to signal that his time is up. So Time, which governs those temporal limitations, must turn its attention away from the man. His family will lament, his friends will feel that much closer to their demise, and no good will have been achieved in any part of his passing.

A snargdallow, Narth, beams at the Edge of Reason. Narth intermingles with the Realm of One Knowing. And Narth has a single purpose. Narth wills itself to be wiser than it was the moment before. In the period it would take eight universes to burst from random quantum fluctuations until they died of spreading themselves too thin, Narth will have grown wiser than even it could have dreamed to be. Narth will, before its end, be as wise and as kind and as empathetic as it is possible to be. Narth will reach the pinnacle of existence; it will be a true wonder. But then Narth's time must come to a close. All the good it was capable of, all the value Narth represented has then to be dispersed into randomness. Meaningless, impassive nothingness. Reality will be robbed of what Narth was because Time had to take itself from Narth. And the Soul of Time would be forced to feel the endless pain it had caused over and over until Forever. And the Soul will hate itself more than it did the moment before.

The Soul of Time is at once jealous and contemptuous of its counterpart, the rigid Framework of Time. The structure of time is neither happy nor melancholy because it must move continually, inevitably to the ever-changing future. All it needs do is move forward at a metronomic pace. One second ahead. One second ahead. One second ahead. The Framework never goes backward in time. It never stands still in time. It goes one second ahead without consideration of other options it might have.

Two galaxies collide. Like buzz saws of infinite power, they rip at each other's substance for millions of years. Stars explode. The Framework does not even take note of the cataclysms. Once brilliant and useful civilizations are pounded into oblivion by the ground other brilliant and useful civilizations stand upon. But the Framework is not designed to hear the screams. It just moves one more second ahead.

The Soul of Time resents the ease with which the Framework complies with its destiny. When they were one, it was possible for the single unit to at least mourn the losses it inflicted. But lamentations, forebodings, and self-loathing could never change the fact that time had to march on. So the Soul of Time constructed a resort, an asylum in which to hide itself away. The box it chose was impenetrable. No forgiveness could enter, no sorrow could leave. But at least the Soul was safe from further burdens. The prison the Soul fashioned for itself had infinite sides. But the vessel had no seams to fail, no windows with which to witness, and no doors from which the Soul might depart.

There was no good cause, no excellent purpose, no justifiable reason that could collapse the walls and make the Soul experience again. It could not even let itself out. That's how complete the Soul's commitment to isolation was. In fact, in all of time, and in all of the universes, there was only one agent that could break the walls and breach the perfect barrier that partitioned the Soul from its designated duties.

The Framework of Time. Nothing can stay the hands of the clock. Nothing.

CHAPTER TWENTY-EIGHT

We finished our scan and headed back to the others. Once we were back aboard Aramthella, I called a meeting of the key players together on *Stingray*. We hardly fit in the mess, but this was important. I wanted it done on my turf, not Sachiko's more spacious readyroom. Ownership and command. That's what I needed to reinforce. What I was going to ask—check that—*order* them to do was as frightening as it was dangerous. I was not forming a committee and asking for input. No. I was going to place us squarely in harm's way. We all needed to be on board and singularly focused.

There were thirteen of us at the briefing. First off, Sapale and me. From the military wing, I summoned Reva, Tank, Major Tom (I loved saying that over and over), Emma, and a couple of junior officers who needed to see how things were done. Someday they'd be required to be similarly inflexible, hard-ass commanders. From the science team, I included Travis Dewitt and Ed Steuben, the nuclear engineers, along with April Martinez, the lone physicist, and two of the senior astronomers, Ming Wang and Rusty Nelson. I'd considered adding Desi Tanner and that idiot Benjamin since they seemed to be central to our efforts. But, in the end, I elected not to. They were outside any chain-of-command and neither had the valuable expertise the group otherwise possessed. Plus, inviting an interaction with Tip? I didn't need the aggravation.

I looked around the small room at the faces expectantly watching me. "Okay, people. First, thank you all for coming. I know we're a little cramped for space, so I'll be as brief as possible," I began resolutely. "For the record, in case any of the civilians are unaware of my exact position, allow me to make it perfectly clear. General Sherman is the overall commander of this force, military and civilian taken as a whole. Captain Jones is the *ship's* captain. She is in direct command of this vessel and its crew. I am outside of either of their jurisdictions. My wife and I live in and command this vessel. It is not under the command of either of the aforementioned parties. Think of us as senior consultants. Any questions?"

One of the engineers started to raise a hand, but the other one elbowed him none-to-gently in the ribs. I presume he was familiar with quirks in his coworker's personality that made it unwise to allow him to question anything. I made a mental note of whom the cleverer engineer was for future reference.

"Fine. Then let me announce what our mission has morphed into and how we will begin to move as rapidly toward the mission's resolution as is prudent."

I could see Tank squirming in his chair. We'd discussed many aspects of our goals, but even he wasn't certain what I was about to drop on them. For one thing, I do believe he was uncomfortable with the "senior consultant" calling the shots. That was not how the military operated. Then again, only Tank and Sachiko knew for certain who we were in reality. I never bothered to monitor the rumor mill to see what the rest of the lot suspected. But I knew that if the truth about us was confirmed officially, our roles would be significantly compromised. In a group as diverse as this, there would be some who condemned us, while others would consider us lesser creations, and still others might worship us.

"As you all know, we are pursuing the last of the clan ships. That ship is commanded by a dubious figure who calls itself the time maker. Once that craft has been no-timed, the Clams will no longer pose a threat to us or what's left alive in this galaxy. If you're still a bit hazy on the issue of no-timing, please address those concerns to one of the scientists present," I swept a hand toward the physics/astronomy players, "after this briefing."

"If I might, General Ryan," asked a demure Dr. Ming Wang, standing.

I nodded to her.

"The three of us will make ourselves available in Captain Jones's stateroom immediately following this meeting." Then she sat quickly, her eyes cast to the floor.

"So, obviously our mission involves the elimination of the clan ship. But, the universe is big. They are playing hard-to-get. So there's no telling when we'll catch a break and be able to confront them. I guarantee we *will* take them out. It's only a matter of when. The more daunting aspect of our mission is to resurrect the Earth and all of its inhabitants. That," I looked down, "will not be easy. In fact, no one, including myself, has the vaguest idea of how that goal can be achieved."

April stood up. "General Ryan, as you are aware, I have no military background. That said, I question how we are undertaking a mission when the goals are not even known?"

Tough question. "Because there has to be a way. I am not willing to accept the loss of Earth and all its inhabitants. I am willing to commit us to an extensive search for a solution."

"But," she went on hesitantly, "what if there are those who do not share that vision. I ask, General, with all due respect."

I had to admire, if not fully appreciate, her candor. "I could say that we will because that is what I so direct. But that's not my style. I *want* us—all of us—to want Earth back. Sure, there's no-one amongst us who doesn't want that. It's only a question of what each of us is willing to pay for that desire. I've been around a while, so has my wife. There are crusades and then there are Don Quixote charges on windmills. You rarely know which one you're participating in at the start. Sometimes you don't figure it out until you slam into that damn windmill. Trust me when I say we've face-planted into some doozies in our time.

"But you know what you do when you power into a large stone building with huge sails? You get up, dust yourself off, and you climb back on whatever version of Rocinante you happen to have fallen from and you start looking for that holy grail again. And you know what? Sometimes you spend way too much time impacting only against windmills. But sometimes, if you're good and you're more persistent than a wet rash, and if you are *very* lucky, you find what you were seeking.

"I know there are some in our merry band who'd rather expend our energies in an effort that's more likely to be productive. They think maybe we should use our powerful ship to find and defend a habitable world. Instead of pie-in-the-sky wild-goose chases, that we should settle down and breed up an acceptable alternative representation of humankind." I shrugged. "Maybe they're right. But I for one can't simply turn my back on the humans, or countless species of animals, and everything else that was stolen from me. If it's even one chance in a gazillion that I can succeed, I'm willing to do whatever it takes to accomplish the barely possible. Because it could have been me who was no-timed. And I know that the person standing here trying to convince you to bring me back would argue just as passionately that re-timing me was worth one hell of a lot of work on everyone's part. That's what humans do. We may be wacky ninety-eight percent of the time. But once in a great while, we are capable of so much good that it'd make you want to go the church and thank the good Lord personally for having witnessed it."

I sat back down. Apparently at some point I'd stood up to deliver my soliloquy.

Tank rose, slowly clapping his hands. Sachiko quickly joined him. Yeah, yeah, you know the drill. In seconds everyone was standing and clapping and, damn, I nearly started singing *Kumbaya*.

Tank raised his arms and quieted the crowd. Thank you, Tank. "I think this would be a good juncture to adjourn this briefing. With the general's permission I'll lead us back to our ship. There we can grab a bite to eat and talk amongst ourselves."

"You have my fullest blessing on that one, General," I declared with a crisp salute.

A few minutes later the last of attendees had filed away. Sapale and I were left alone in blessed quiet.

"That went well," she remarked rather economically.

"I think so."

"I just have one question."

"Shoot."

"No, I'd prefer to at least ask my question first."

I opened my arms wide.

"Just when did you stop being a flyboy and enter politics?"

"Ouch."

"Own it, Ryan."

"Being a politico? No, I think I'd jump right back to *shoot*."

"And you know what? If y'ever did go political on me, that's exactly what I'd do. It's called euthanasia."

CHAPTER TWENTY-NINE

Time Maker-bob stood facing the corner of a long corridor indistinguishable from most others aboard its ship. Arms crossed behind its back, it mumbled occasionally, and shifted its insignificant weight every now and then. There was no way to know how long the time maker had been in such an odd pose aside from directly asking. Since no one in, or out of their right mind would ask such a disastrous question, we will never know the duration of its peculiar stationing.

Finally, a nervous and hesitant finder maker accrued enough courage, or poor judgment, to approach and disturb the time maker.

"Wonder that is beyond perfection," Finder Maker-tif began in a faltering tone, "I hate to disturb you in your contemplation, but—"

"Apparently you hate it insufficiently. That's my opinion concerning this present interface." The time maker's focus on the corner's seam never wavered.

"I ... that is not true, blazing image of perfection. I—"

"Ah, so I *lie*, as well as I am free for all to pester."

There was no way around it. The time maker was a challenging individual to work with.

"Would it please you if I walked away, then returned, and attempted a reiteration of this encounter?"

"Why? Do you have other forms of insult to assault me with? Perhaps you wish to set me ablaze?"

"I do not think I want to set you ablaze, mirror reflection of perfection. I will state without reservation that thought has never occurred to me. But, if it pleases you, I will make it my heart's desire and lone goal in life."

"Finder maker, I have always regarded you to be a negative in my existence. Now I learn your greatest desire is to set me on fire. What am I to think?"

Finding Maker-tif slightly raised a thin digit. "Only if it pleases you that I do. Otherwise I will retreat to my position that I never conceived of it before."

"So, which is it? Do you disdain me and wish not only to disturb me but you also wish me bodily harm? Or is it that you're a loyal lump of insignificance?"

"I ... I don't think I'm either, one whose scent is equivalent to rapture. I love you."

Those three words in that order had never been received by the time maker's ears. It was caught so off-guard that it almost turned to inspect the fleck of uselessness. For reasons unknown to the time maker, it asked the finder maker to repeat its last three words.

"I said that I love you."

"Please say it without the preamble," the time maker directed.

"I love you."

Twelve hours, Earth time. That's how long the time maker stood transfixed and the finding maker stood in awe and transformative dread. Neither spoke. Neither moved.

Finally, the time maker turned halfway to address the finding maker. "What did you come here to word make to me?" It spoke flatly, almost neutrally. Alert the media. The time maker wasn't in a wrathful mood.

"I found something."

"You *are* my finding maker," observed the time maker.

"I am, and thank you for knowing that, jewel in the crown of creation."

"What did you find?" it asked with irritation signaling the return of the finding maker to the boss's worldview.

"Most odd it is, that which I found. While scanning with our deep-probe-time-sensor array, I witnessed the unmistakable energy signature of a stochastic phase deharmonizer being switched to *Optional*, and then back quickly to *Prohibited*."

Time Maker-bob blinked at the finding maker a few seconds. "Remind me, as a test of your worth, what a stochastic phase deharmonizer *is*."

"It is—"

"And your understanding had better be as complete as mine, or there'll be trouble."

It bowed nervously. "It is part of the Time Storage Unit. It allows, or rather generally does not permit, time energy to be vented under certain parameters."

"That's adequate. Proceed."

"Thank you wonder above wonders. I noticed this a few days ago. Not wishing to burden you unnecessarily, I went to the TSR and spoke with the time storage makers. They were absolutely certain that they didn't switch settings on our stochastic phase deharmonizer. I reviewed my recordings. The only conclusion I could arrive at was that the other time ship generated the signal."

And the time maker was back to the blinking. "Are you saying my stolen ship emitted that signature?"

"It is the only explanation possible."

"What can you tell me about the location of my ship when it sent that signal?"

It looked down and shook its tiny head. "Little with certainty."

"Transfer to me all the certainty you have."

"My best estimation is that the signal originated one-hundred-and-fifty parsecs away from our position. The signal moved along a vector originating roughly from the galactic core, relative to our current position."

"Hmm. Have you discussed your findings with my science makers and my luck makers?"

"I have. They all agree."

"So I now know roughly where my ship is."

"You do."

"Then it is time for definitive action. It is time for me to act in a manner that underscores my greatness. Go to my vector maker and demand it fly a course along the vector you identified. All safe speed."

"Pardon, mobile grace, don't you mean in the *negative* direction of that vector? Do you not want to confront the foul enemies that so disgraced you?"

"No, I want to move away from the betrayers. Don't you see?"

"Apparently not."

"I wish to surprise them from behind."

"In the universe as we know it, that is not possible. Space/time is not so configured."

"It is if I will it to be," it said ominously.

"As always, you are blamelessly correct, fruit from the tree of splendor."

"That is better. Now go, do my bidding. I tire of your presence."

"So do I."

With those words, the finding maker left quickly and quietly. Smart fellow.

CHAPTER THIRTY

I had to find the Time.

Sorry, sorry. I had to slip in that pun. I've been waiting so long to drop it.

How in the name of Heaven was I—were we—going to find Time.? I was led to believe the Soul of Time was irrevocably hidden, making it, by definition, a challenge to locate. And even the Framework of Time, or whatever it was calling itself these days, was gonna be tough, right? I mean, no one has ever stumbled across it, so it must be darn elusive. Double-darn elusive. Was it even a thing? Did it look like ... a grandfather clock? Peach melba? Bugs Bunny's tail? Who knew? But if even the mighty Tetterwin had no clue where I'd find either, who was going to help me? I sure needed help. I was man enough to admit that, especially because it was the plain truth.

Who did I know who might at least give me a hint, a clue, a scrap?

No one, that's who.

I'd decided not to ask for the Deavoriath of today for help. For one thing they might attack me for coming unannounced and also if

I came anyway after being told not to come. They sure knew a whole lot about ...

Wait a minute. I had a time ship. Duh. I could be so *me* sometimes. I could safely ask the Deavoriath of the future. Sure, they were like family. Well, Toño was like family to them. I was more like Toño's red-haired stepson, but hey, family was family.

I was musing in my cabin. Sapale was lounging in bed, I was leaning back in a chair. She looked just about as bored as I was. Perfect, she'd welcome a stimulating conversation.

"Honey," I began in a sweet tone, "I just—"

"Not now. I'm busy."

"Not now? But you don't even know what I was—"

"Bing-bing-bing, the monkey-descendant biped is correct. I don't care what you have to say, whatever it is. That is my commitment to indifference. Plus, I'm busy."

"You don't look—"

She sat up and eyed me sternly. "I'm defending my personal space, my private thoughts against a ruthless adversary—Jon Ryan. You think that's easy? The man's intolerable. He will whine, cry, beg, hell, he'll do anything to get away with whatever he wants to perpetrate. I call defending myself against that level of onslaught being busy."

"I ... I was referring to a second ago. You didn't look—"

"That was then. This is now. Now I'm fighting for my right to remain Jon-free."

I batted my eyes in a flurry. "You done being a martyr now? May we talk now?"

"Certainly, love. What's on your mind."

She could be so infuriating, infuriating as... well, me. And that was a whole lot of infuriating.

"I think I solved the Deavoriath dilemma."

"I was unaware they had one."

"No, *we* did. We probably shouldn't go to the Deavoriath of the present, but—"

"We can go to the Deavoriath of our time. Sure, that's kind of painfully obvious."

"It only just occurred to me now."

"I wouldn't mention that out loud, sweetheart. It will cause others to think you're slow." She flashed quotation marks in the air around the word *slow*.

"I think that's unfair. If realizing that the Deavoriath of the future could help us when those of the present day couldn't, why didn't you mention it earlier?"

"Earlier in as when?"

"When we were going to rescue—"

"What?"

"Never mind. I think it would be constructive to move on."

"Why didn't I mention the future Deavoriath when I was in prison, in a dungeon, seventeen galaxies away?"

"Do you recall my mentioning the *moving* of *on*?"

"Yes, by all means. What do you want to discuss with Cragforel?"

"It doesn't have to be *him*. We could approach ... someone else, maybe."

"Of course it has to be him. He's our contact there. You might recall the Deavoriath are xenophobic. They desire contact with off worlders like they desire a festering rash in their groins. Cragforel is our contact. He drew a short straw or something."

"I ... er—"

"You just don't like him because he idolizes Toño and considers you to be abrasively juvenile."

"No, that's not it at all. It's just that I've often wondered why we don't—why I don't get to know some of the other Deavoriath—"

"Stop it. Do you want to whine, or do you bring the Earth back?"

"The second thing," I responded feebly pointing at her feet.

"So, we're going to Oowaoa two billion years in the future, along the timeline we left."

"Was that a question or a statement?"

"Can that possibly matter?"

"Probably not."

She stood. "Then let's go inform the others."

As she was passing me, I took that opportunity to address an error she had made in our discussion.

"You know technically, Toño never existed."

She stopped dead and glared into my eyes. "Your point being?"

"If he never was, Cragforel couldn't idolize—"

She threw her arms up into the air, signaling that I should stop. Since that was wise, that's what I did.

Sachiko called the higher-ups to her stateroom after I briefed her on our next step. Shortly, we were all seated at a large metal table, each holding mugs of something hot, and waiting for the meeting to get underway.

Sachiko took the lead. "Jon and Sapale have just informed me of their desire to seek help regarding the difficult task of locating the Soul of Time. For those of you who're not super clear on what that means, well, welcome to the club. But we've been advised that only the Soul of Time will know of a way, if there is a way, to resurrect the Earth."

Emma Walters raised a hand halfway up. "Excuse me. How do we know that? Who advised us?"

"We learned that from the race that captured Jon and Sapale," responded the captain.

"And we trust them?" Emma pressed.

"That's the only lead we have," I answered for Sachiko. "So, we're following up on their recommendation."

"Jon," Sachiko said, "why don't you take it from here?"

"Sure." I, idiot that I am, waved to everyone. "Hi there. So, here's the dealio. Our quest to find Time is going to be tough. I think the best place to start is by asking for information from the smartest people I know, the Deavoriath."

"Hang on a sec, Jon," Tank interrupted. "I thought you said dealing with them was too risky on several levels. What changed?"

"Er, nothing. What I said was that asking for help from the Deavoriath of today would be too risky. But," I spread my arms out, "we have ourselves a time machine. So I know for sure we can safely ask the Deavoriath of the future for help. Sapale and Doc and ... I mean Sapale and I have dealt with them a lot. They're good people."

"They're human?" Major Tom asked incredulously.

"No, they're Deavoriath," I replied.

"Okay," he dismissed.

"Jon, when you say the *future* Deavoriath, how future are you talking here?" Tank asked with a bit of an edge.

"A ways, I'll grant you that."

"How far is a *ways*?" he challenged.

"Two billion years up ahead."

"Two billion years?" exclaimed Reva. "Are you nuts?"

"He is, but two billion is what we are planning," Sapale responded for me.

"Bu ... but, that's too far," she declared.

"Based on what?" Sapale queried.

"I don't know. I'm just getting high anxiety here imagining it. That's so ... so far."

"Time is time is time," I summarized. "A day, a second, or a billion years is all the same. Isn't that right, Aramthella?"

"Basically, you are correct, General Ryan," she confirmed. "While it would require more time energy to get there than, say, two weeks in the future, it's not even that much more."

"And we can come back here?" Reva asked nervously.

"I don't see why not," Aramthella reassured her. "Assuming, of course, you're not dead."

"It might kill us to go that far ahead?" Reva asked in a panicked tone.

"No. But if you are otherwise killed in the future, you can't meaningfully return to this time period," Aramthella replied unreassuringly.

"And that's not going to happen," I jumped in, "so no worries."

"Jon," Tank directed the conversation elsewhere, "these future aliens, they won't kill us on sight?"

"No way. We're tight, them and us." I swung a finger between Sapale and myself.

"Is that actually the case, Sapale?" Tank rudely inquired.

"What can I say?" she responded. "For once the flyboy's not BSing."

"And will we remain in the far-flung future?" Sachiko asked in her captain's voice.

"Who knows?" I shrugged while grinning. "We go where the trail leads us."

"But it might be a short jaunt?" Sachiko tried to clarify. I think she was almost as queasy about the large jump as Reva was.

"Could be. Hopefully," I lied. We were on a critical op. We were going to do whatever it took, period.

"And I assume you're *informing* us of the game plan, not opening the subject up for debate?" Major Tom asked cautiously. He knew for absolute certain that he did not want to piss me off.

"You assume well, Major." I stated flatly.

"When do we leave?" Sachiko asked tersely.

"No time like the present to visit the future," I replied in a lame stab at being cute. These people were too freaked to be in a humorous mood. Tough audience.

And we were away ...

In the blink of an eye, we were back in the future, err my current time, err—well, you know what I mean. Even I couldn't feel the jump. Unreal. I then had *Stingray* fold space to take us near, but not too near, the Deavoriath home world. We were in a clan ship after all, no matter *when* it was. Best not to scare anyone into annihilating us.

251

Sapale, Sachiko, Tank, Reva, and I were on Aramthella's bridge, staring intently at the large view screen.

"*Stingray*," I called out, "please contact the planet and explain our present situation."

"Already done, Form One."

"And have they gotten back to us yet?"

"Of course. They're Deavoriath. Cragforel instructs us to come to the landing pad near his home. He specifies we are to travel only in our vortex. He does not want Aramthella any closer to Oowaoa. He was emphatic about that point, Form One."

"Not a prob. Sapale, you ready?"

"Born ready," she tossed back.

I started to step toward the exit, when it occurred to me that maybe one of the others might want to come too. We didn't need them along, but they had to be powerfully curious.

"Anybody tagging along?" I asked.

They shot mutual furtive glances at one another.

"I'll stay on my ship," Sachiko stated.

That was probably the best thing for a captain to do, unlike in every *Star Trek* episode ever produced.

"Tank? Reva?"

They exchanged looks. He nodded to her. She nodded to him. It was so precious. Young love in the senior demographic.

"Sure," Tank answered for the both of them. "We'd love to."

I gestured to the exit. "Your coach awaits."

Cragforel was waiting by the pad when we materialized. I took a quick look at him before I opened a portal. Yup, he still looked disagreeably constipated. Happy happy joy joy.

Sapale, Reva, Tank, and I stepped out onto the parched soil of Oowaoa. Every time I returned to this world, I was struck with the paradox that the galaxy's most advanced, once-dominant race should reside on such a dry, barren planet. I would think massive waterfalls and majestic mountains would be more appropriate.

Sapale greeted Cragforel first, using the traditional Deavoriath act. They grabbed the other's right forearm and bumped shoulders. I did the same. Then I introduced Reva and Tank.

After being as minimally gracious as decorum required, Cragforel looked to the portal in *Stingray*'s hull. "Toño not along? *Blessing* hadn't mentioned him, but I assumed he would be part of the crew."

"Long story," I replied glumly. The dude was like the president of Doc's fan club. Sheesh, Crag-Man, get over it already.

"Ah," he responded. "Is he well?"

"Longer story," I answered.

"My, my, I'm in for a story marathon, aren't I?"

Tank leaned over to me. "How's this three-legged, three-armed alien know about marathons?"

"They are all very old and make it a point to learn about the cultures they encounter," I whispered back.

Tank rotated his head right and up, and mouthed the word *wow*.

"Come, let us retire to my home," Cragforel invited, gesturing with two arms toward his dwelling. It was the typical ceramic-like structure that somehow always reminded me of Fred Flintstone's house. Again, it was an odd juxtaposition. Super race, primitive building choices. To each his or her own, as they say.

We were led to his large anteroom. It functioned as a living room, but the Deavoriath didn't call or regard it as such. Beyond it, the private sections of the home were off-limits to visitors. They were not any kind of social creatures, even among themselves.

"Nufe?" he asked pleasantly.

"We'd love some," responded Sapale. She turned to Tank and Reva. "Did we mention nufe to you guys?"

While Reva shook her head a bit confused, Tank said, "Yeah, I think Jon mentioned it. Sweet liquor, right?"

"Dude," I returned, "that's like saying a golf ball is like the Moon. It's the true nectar of the gods." I bobbed my head slightly, you know, like I was clever. "And I know of what I speak. I've had the original. It doesn't hold a candle to nufe."

"Then I think I'm gonna like it," he responded with a grin.

Cragforel set down a large tray with five glasses and one bottle of nufe. Again, I was reminded of the stark utilitarian tastes of the one-time rulers of the galaxy. The glasses could easily be mistaken for pottery mugs made in a high school art class.

"I have never met a species that didn't love nufe," Cragforel said as he poured. "In fact, if there were such a race, I hope never to meet with it."

I raised my glass greedily. "I'll second that," I declared with as my toast. Then I took a sip of the liquid Heaven that was nufe. I tasted See's Bordeaux candy, Cuban cigars, and the memory of my first kiss.

Sapale clutched her glass to her chest after a sip and closed her eyes in ecstasy. I was at once jealous of the nufe, but couldn't condemn her either. We're talking nufe here.

Tank just about dropped his glass. Poor guy jerked his head back like he'd just drunk from a rattlesnake's mouth. He shook his head violently and pushed back against his ceramic chair.

"No way," he shouted.

"Yes, way," I Bill-and-Tedded him back. I reached over and slapped his shoulder. "What'd you taste?"

"Er ... ah, a bunch of things, one of which I never care to mention aloud in public."

Reva had yet to take a sip. She eyed Tank judgmentally. Leaving it to her imagination what her new boyfriend had tasted but felt it was unmentionable triggered a primitive response in the woman. Go figure.

"Go on," I encouraged her. "Down the hatch."

Reva tentatively raised the glass to her nose and smelled lightly.

"Nope, it doesn't have an aroma," I said. "You have to ingest it for the magic to happen."

She tilted her glass just enough that the tiniest splash must've impacted her closed mouth. Then she licked her lips. Bingomatic! She started drawing long slow breaths and her eyes glazed over.

"Amazing, right?" I asked. "What'd you get?"

"Unbelievable," she breathed by way of response.

I giggled.

She took a big drink. Then she set her glass on the table. She had the oddest expression on her face. I could not pin it down.

"I ... that's not possible. The nufe tastes like the black cherry cider my parents used to buy us from one of those roadside stands, back when I was young."

"Just that?" I asked with disappointment.

"Oh no. I also taste the fried chicken only my great grandmother could make. And all the flowers of spring swirled together. And, there's something else. I taste the feeling I get when I'm alone with Tank."

"Should we leave you alone?" I teased.

Reva sobered quickly and semi-glared at Tank. "Apparently not."

Ouch! The man was going to pay. Nice.

"There was a tiny creek by a forest on a planet we called Melroe," Cragforel reminisced. "On my first and only expedition there, I knelt by that creek and dipped my hand into the cool gently flowing water. It was so sweet, so pure, so welcoming. Welcoming? Can you imagine that? Silly when I say it out loud. Anyway, I always taste a hint of that creek every time I have nufe." He held up his glass and regarded it curiously. "I wonder why I don't drink this more often?"

"Hey, Tank," I prodded, "take another swig."

"I'm still debriefing from the first one, if you don't mind."

"No, seriously." I mimed lifting a glass to my lips.

He took a second sip. "Well I'll be damned."

"Yeah, right?" I effused.

"A totally different rainbow of flavors." He looked to Cragforel. "How's this possible?" he asked holding up his glass.

"It is the wonder and the mystery of nufe, my friend," he responded with a coy grin. Then he looked to me and any trace of mirth evaporated. "So, Jon, tell me these long stories of yours, please."

And I did. For the next two hours I rattled off the sad facts about our sad story. I took him from Toño not coming because Daleria was dying, to the no-timing of Earth, and our battles with the clan. He sat quietly, taking the rare sip of his nufe. But when I got to the part about the Praxequats, he was silent no longer.

He held up a palm and stopped me. "Hang on a moment. Jon, are you saying you not only met, but impressed Tetterwin, the legendary Praxequat master? I'm going to have to call a BS on you right there."

Tank, who'd been quietly lost in his nufe, snapped to. "You say *call a BS* too?" he wheezed to Cragforel.

"Yes, I've studied all of Earth's languages and cultures."

"But the Earth was no-timed," Tank asked incredulously. "You—"

I set a hand on Tank's forearm. "He's a Deavoriath, Tank. Let it go."

Cragforel nodded in agreement. "Best not to explode your mind," he said with enthusiasm.

Yeah, I let that one slide. There was a time and place to correct the dude. This was neither.

"I did." I pointed forcefully at my brood-mate. "Ask Sapale if you don't believe me."

He wiggled a couple hands in the air. "That won't be necessary. It's ... Jon, it's just that I've only heard scattered reports about Tetterwin. He's ... well, when you dealt with the ancient gods you met Fate. Now you get to meet Tetterwin? I'm ... well, I'm—"

"Jealous?" I shot back.

He squirmed very nicely in his seat. "Yes, as much as it pains me to admit it. Jon, you get to meet all the sexy ones. I'm a student of the universe, basically immortal, and I don't get to meet the sexy ones."

"Well maybe you should ride with me. I'll share."

That drew a frigid response. "No, thank you. I'll be okay."

"May I proceed?" I asked making sure I sounded irritated.

"By all means."

"So when I finally got Tetterwin to stop trying to kill me and actually to parley, he went on about time this and time that."

"Could you be a bit less dramatic and a lot more informative?" Cragforel pressed. Man, I bet he didn't have too many close friends. The man was such a tight ass.

"He explained that time wasn't just what you read off your wristwatch. There is the Framework of Time and the Soul of Time. I guess it's kind of like Fate, only there's just one of those, thank goodness."

"Jon, he was speaking to you about the essence of the universe, and you just wish it was simpler? That's ... that's lame."

"It's official. You're coming with me and you can talk to the forces of nature and not me."

It was a rather dumb thing to say, but he tented his fingers and thought long and hard on my quip. After his reflection, he said somberly, "No. I believe it is *your* role, not mine."

"What role?"

"To realign the cosmos, I presume."

"I actually don't need more pressure. That's why I'm here."

"Jon, let me cut to the chase. What is it you want of me?"

"In case it's not awfully painfully obvious, I need your help. I'm supposed to find this Framework, or maybe the Soul first. I don't know. And how can I find something the riddle says I can't? I ask you, how?"

"What riddle?" he asked suspiciously.

"Oh, crap, I forget to mention the riddle."

"Jon, there was a riddle with the ancient gods concerning how they would fall. You told me that."

"So?"

"Now, again with a riddle. Are you making this stuff up like some hack novelist?"

"No. Why would I make up a riddle? I *hate* riddles. I used to just hate them. Now I really hate them. It's personal between me and riddles."

He covered his eyes, lowered his head, and said two words: "The riddle."

"*Time has hidden its soul where it may never be found, in plain sight, for all to tell and know.* There. Now I ask you, is that not pathetic?"

"Jon, grow up. It's a riddle, not a rival suitor for your fair maiden's hand."

"What's the answer?"

"To what?"

I shook my arms, outstretched in frustration. "To the freaking riddle."

"Ah. I thought maybe you were referring to your not growing up. I have no idea."

"How about a bad guess?"

"I do not make bad guesses."

"You could try this once," I argued.

"Sorry. I have no solution for you. I've shared the riddle with the collective mind of the Deavoriath and no one else has a clue either."

"That was very quick," I challenged. "Could you ask them again?"

"No. I will do nothing of the kind. The Collective has spoken."

"Well then, I'm sorry for having wasted your time." I looked sideways to my companions. "We should be—"

"Goodness, you have thin android skin, my friend," declared Cragforel. "I may not know the answer to that tortured sentence, but I can still be of some assistance."

That perked me up. I probably looked like a damn puppy fixated at the cookie in its owner's fingers.

"There have been throughout history cults, religions, and academic institutions devoted to the study of time." He wagged a dismissive hand between us. "Mind you, most of them have been your typical lunatics searching not for truth but for meaning in their otherwise empty lives."

"The man's harsh," Tank whispered to Reva.

She angled her head and raised both eyebrows in concurrence.

"I heard that, Mr. Sherman," Cragforel alerted Tank.

"Sorry," Tank retreated.

"You are kind of harsh there, my friend," I observed.

"I've seen a lot and suffered many a fool in my very long life. Now, may I proceed?"

"Go for it."

"A few of the supplicants trying to comprehend time have actually been both legitimate and scholarly."

"Supplicants?" Reva whispered to Tank.

"True believers," Cragforel answered for Tank. "Devotees of a thing."

"Ah, thanks," she responded.

"So you can direct me to some of the better time groupies?"

He closed his eyes again, and rubbed at them. Maybe he had allergies?

"I can mention some I am familiar with. There are, however, as happens generally in these cases, twists."

"I hate those too," I mumbled.

"There are none around now. The last group I would lend any credence to lived and died long ago."

"We got a time machine," I mentioned.

"I am aware of that. That would make approaching the Brother-Sisterhood doable."

"Crap stains on the bedsheets, I hear a *but* in there, don't I?"

"I pray you do. The Brother-Sisterhood of Time were very averse to outsiders."

"Yeah, but, everyone was a stranger to them once, right?"

"Not right. They were a lineage of clones."

"Did you say clowns or clones?"

"Clones," he replied angrily.

"Okay, good. *Clones* I can handle."

"They were so resistant to having any contact with anyone else that their study and worship of Time was placed ahead of all else, save one devotion."

"Let me guess. Board games?"

"Military prowess."

"I'd have preferred board games."

"Their planet was one massive fortress. Their defenses were impenetrable, and their willingness to repel any visitors with massive use of force was legendary."

"Not people-people, these sisters and brothers?"

"Mock them at your peril, Jon. However, if you are to locate the Soul of Time, it will be with their assistance and only their assistance."

"How about the Framework? Any other less bloodthirsty resources there?"

"I'm afraid not," he replied with finality. "And there's more, I'm afraid."

"Me too, it would seem."

"The Brother-Sisterhood of Time took it upon themselves to defend Time from all others."

"What does that actually mean?" I asked in a queasy tone.

"It means that if they learn of your quest, they will try with all their considerable might to stop you."

"Then I guess it's a good thing they're long gone."

"No. I said the sect died off long ago."

"How is that different?"

He shook his head wearily. "Jon, what did I mention they were singularly devoted to?"

"Time?"

"Very good. You get a passing grade for today. Yes, they were students of Time."

"And so —"

"And so, your task is doubly impossible. First you must defy all odds and make contact with them so they might do what they are sworn not to do which is to help others concerning all things time. Second, once you have completed that impossible, you must avoid allowing them to kill you when they learn of your threat to time."

"It's probably not that bad, is it?"

"Once you begin your search in earnest, the Brother-Sisterhood might learn of it. And if they do, they will come for you through time and they will try very capably to remove you from existence."

"That's only *if*, right? Maybe we'll catch a break and they'll be too busy working on a new secret handshake or something."

"Jon?" Sapale asked impatiently, "how likely is it that you and I catch a cosmic break?"

Instead of focusing on the negative, and answering her, I took a good long pull from the nufe bottle itself.

To be continued ...

GLOSSARY:

First, a word about time, as used in this series. The clan uses several foreign, non-intuitive terms to describe time. Here are the concepts.

Anti-no-time: Such a big word! It was the side effect of the negative time generated by wormholes that were used against the clan. Since clan ships were structured with time energy, negative time deleted what it touched, like matter-antimatter interactions.

No-time: A verb. It means to take the time from a unit of space/time, leaving only space. The object has no time, it had been no-timed.

No-timers: The clan term for all non clan members.

Non-time: A noun. A sloppy word the clan uses. It can mean one of two things. First, that basically, something's dead, without time, random. It can also mean that time has stopped, for the object under discussion.

Non-time ship: Any space craft that is a non-clan ship.

Un-timed: To stop time for an object or region. Basically the same as the second meaning of non-time.

Other Glossary Terms:

Als (1): The original ship's AI on Jon's first flight long ago was Alvin. Jon shortened that to Al. When Al was joined to Jon's vortex in the Galaxy On Fire Series, Al and Blessing fell in love and got "married." Since then Jon refers to them combined as the Als.

Aramthella (1): The mighty and ancient time ship that Jon and his team stole from the body maker.

Ark 1(1): Jon's ship on his very first mission, when he traveled to find humankind a new home.

The Two Astronomers on Mars (1): Drs. Rusty Nelson and Wang served in that regard.

Azsuram (2): Original human name for the third planet orbiting Groombridge. It was the planet Jon and Sapale settled on after they left the human fleet fleeing doomed Earth. They established an idyllic society of Kaljaxians there, before humans join them.

Beauty Itself (2): A female Praxequat, a member of the ultimate time lord species. She *seems* to be their leader.

Blessing (1): See *Stingray*.

Brood-mate/Brood's-mate (*The Forever Life*): These are, respectively, the Kaljaxian words for *husband* and *wife*.

Cleinoid gods/Ancient Gods (1): Ancient and malevolent mix of gods. They have destroyed many universes before and are eyeing ours now. The five ranks or groupings for their invasion were to be Rage, Torment, Wrath, Fury, and Horror.

Circumturus (1): A psychic houseplant. No, seriously. That's it. *That's* the definition. Now go back to where you were and continue the riveting story.

Command Prerogatives (1): The thin fibers Jon extends from his left four fingers. They are probes that also control a vortex.

Cragforel (1): A semi-friendly Deavoriath Jon met after he first escaped the Adamant in the far future. He was a huge fan of Toño DeJesus, which fired Jon's bacon.

Cube (1): Jon's alternate name for the vortex he captains.

Davdiad (1): God-figure on Kaljax.

DelRoy Crozier (2): Lieutenant and working in communication on Mars 1.

Daleria (2): Demigod and innkeeper whom Jon and Sapale befriended. She worked with them against the ancient gods as she'd grown to hate them.

Deavoriath (1): Three arms and legs, an ancient species that had the most advanced tech in the galaxy. Very helpful to Jon.

Desdemona "Desi" Tanner (2): Former Georgetown undergrad who was a medium, that is, she perceived and communicated with dead people. Er, no thanks, I'm good. Place that gift under someone else's tree.

Emma Walters (2): Captain, and in charge of the women's barracks on Mars 1. What a thankless job.

Evil Jon Ryan/ EJ (1): Alternate timeline version of the original human to android download. Over time, he turned to the darker side of his nature. He studied "magic" under a Deft master.

Excessive Splendor (2): A male Praxequat, a member of the ultimate time lord species (sorry Doctor).

Form One/Form Two (1): A Form is the title of a vortex pilot. If more than one is aboard they get numerical designations based on seniority.

Gumnolar (TFL-1): Deity of the Listhelons. Unreasonably demanding.

Honesty Hartley (2): Doctor on duty at the student health center when the president had the entire staff transported to Mars. And appropriately there, as she was a total space cadet.

Kaljax (1): The home planet of Sapale. Jon went there on his original voyages.

Membrane (1): See space-time congruity manipulator.

Necumplack (2): The species name of the time controlling blobs that power the time ships.

Nuclear Engineers on Mars (1): Travis Dewitt and Ed Steuben were the two assigned to man the reactor on Mars 1.

Nufe (The Forever Series): A magical liquor made by the Deavoriath. It tastes different to all who partaker. It reminds the drinker of many pleasant tastes all at once. Mildly intoxicating.

Oowaoa (The Forever Life): Home world of the Deavoriath.

Phase Portal (4): A wormhole-like device Jon and Sapale discovered in a cave that transported them a very long ways away in an instant.

Pleasant Brilliance (2): A male Praxequat, a member of the ultimate time lord species (sorry Doctor).

Plesmus (2): A necumplack. She is a mucous blob that can focus time energy. Very useful for a time machine.

PlesWorld (3): The planet in the Milky Way connected to the phase portal. It was possibly Plesmus's home world.

Praxequats (3): The ultimate time lords (sorry, Doctor). They have existed through many universes' lives. Jon initially encountered five of them.

Probe Fibers (1): Aka command prerogatives, they allow piloting of the Vortex spaceship and can analyze whatever they touch.

Radiant Resplendence (2): aka, R-Squared. A male Praxequat, a member of the ultimate time lord species (sorry Doctor). Easily the most pretentious and self-absorbed of the time masters.

Reva St. Claire (2): Lt. Colonel and the new commander of Mars 1.

Robert "Tank" Sherman (1): Lead academic and friend of Sachiko. Also in Marine Reserves.

Sapale (1): Jon's Kaljaxian wife from his original flight to find humankind a new home. At first just her brain was copied, then, eventually, she was downloaded to an android host. Travelled with the corrupted Jon Ryan from an alternate timeline.

Sachiko Jones (1): One-time astronomy grad student under Tank's supervision. The time ship chose her to be its new captain.

Space-time congruity manipulator (1): Hugely helpful force field. Aka a membrane.

Stingray (1): Jon's Deavoriath spaceship. Her name in the Deavoriath language is pronounced "crash." Hence, silly Jon renamed her after one of his favorite cars. It makes Jon-sense.

Stunning Wonder (2): A female Praxequat, a member of the ultimate time lord species (sorry Doctor).

Sunne calrf (2): A traditional Kaljaxian stew. They are all revolting to Jon, but he finds this version especially loathsome.

Swathi Varma (2): Lieutenant, and aide-de-camp to Reva St. Claire on Mars 1.

Tetterwin (4): The elder Praxequat, father to the five Jon and Sapale encountered on the far side of the phase portal.

Time (1): See discussion above.

Time Maker-bob (3): The third time maker. Totally nuts but full of desires to rule.

Time Maker-pid (1): The second supreme leader of the clan and the one in power at the beginning of this tale. Cruel, rapacious, and heartless.

Tip Benjamin (?): Where've I heard that name before? Hmm. Presently, Tip is a student at Georgetown. He was evacuated to Mars as part of the US president's plan to save a tiny portion of humankind. And they took Tip too?

Tom Grant (2): Major, and the officer in charge of the male dormitories on Mars

Toño DeJesus (1 of TFL): The scientist creator of the android Jon. Became his lifelong friend.

Vortex (1): Super-advanced Deavoriath sentient spaceship. Moves by folding space. If you get a chance to own one, do it.

Vortex Manipulator (The Forever Enemy): The consciousness that actually controls the vortex spacecraft. Think super AIs. They're a product of some very creepy alien tech.

Quantum Decoupler (1): A most excellent weapon that pulls the quarks apart in a proton. The energy released as they rejoin is amazing.

Yibitriander (Book 2, The Forever Series): Three-legged Deavoriath, past Form of Jon's borrowed vortex *Wrath*. A real tough cookie.

AND NOW A WORD FROM YOUR AUTHOR

Thank you so much for joining me, Jon, and the whole gang on this ongoing journey! The Ryanverse is terrific, and it even better with you along! The story really begins with *The Forever Life*. If you've not read that, and the rest of the series from the start, I suggest you do. You will not be disappointed.

The outstanding people at Podium Audio are working hard to get all the books of the Ryanverse into audiobooks. If you're having any trouble locating a book, look for it there.

Two favors. One, let me know your impressions, thoughts, or suggestions. You can do that by contacting me by email (contact@ craigarobertson.com) or on my Facebook Author's Page. Second, please post a review on Amazon/Audible. Those are more precious than you might imagine to us authors.

Finally, there will be more soon, so be happy, dudes! I know I will ...

craig

www.ingramcontent.com/pod-product-compliance
Lightning Source LLC
Chambersburg PA
CBHW070102030726
47506CB00002B/563